I0615545

REBEL SONG

REBEL SERIES BOOK 3

J.C. HANNIGAN

This book is a work of fiction. Names, characters, places, and incidents either are the product of the author's imagination or are used fictitiously, and any resemblance to actual persons, living or dead, business establishments, events, or locales is entirely coincidental.

All rights reserved.

No part of this book may be reproduced, scanned, or distributed in any printed or electronic form without permission. Please do not participate in or encourage piracy of copyrighted materials in violation of the author's rights. Purchase only authorized editions.

No AI was used in the creation of any part of this book. Editing, proofreading, and all other services rendered were done by human beings. No portion of this book may be fed into any AI program. This author firmly believes that stories should be told by humans, not AI.

Copyright © 2017 by J.C. Hannigan

Cover Design by Chelsea Barnes (CJPB Designs)
Edited by Shawna Gavas (Behind the Writer)
Formatted by Heritage Creek Formatting

ISBN 978-0-9951934-8-2(paperback)
ISBN 978-0-9951934-7-5 (ebook)

www.jchannigan.com

AUTHOR'S NOTE:

This novel contains the triggering subject matter of domestic abuse. There are possible upsetting situations within its pages that may be upsetting. Please proceed with caution.

CHAPTER ONE

 ecky

July 2013

I closed my eyes, drawing in huge gulps of air in rapid succession. My lungs felt like they were on fire, and my heart—it felt as if it was actually shattering. Fragments of pain pierced *everywhere*. I'd never experienced agony quite like it.

That was saying a lot. In my twenty-two years, I'd faced *plenty* of pain, both physical and emotional. My father had been an abusive drunk, my ex-boyfriend and the father of my child had nearly snuffed our lives out, and my brother had been locked in jail for my stupid mistake.

Yes, I'd felt a lot of pain. But losing Mom...it was a different kind of pain.

It was permanent. It was a void that I didn't think would ever be filled.

"Oh God, Mom," I sobbed into my hands, staring at the now-stripped bed where she had spent the better part of three months confined to. Her frail body was gone, the slight impression on the mattress the only remaining sign of her.

We weren't the perfect family, but we *were* a family. We were finally doing right by each other. I felt like I didn't get enough time with her, with my brothers. So much of our lives together was wasted, and it broke my heart that my son wasn't going to see his Grammy anymore.

My shoulders shook as I leaned forward and cried. I wrapped my arms around my stomach, trying to hold myself together because I felt as if I were unravelling.

The sound of a car door slamming had me freeze for a moment. I straightened, blinking back my tears. A moment later, another car door slammed and I heard voices.

I wiped at my face, trying to dry my eyes and cheeks. Of course, I would have picked the exact moment that Tessa Armstrong returned with my son to have my emotional break down. I had the worst timing for these things.

Tessa had picked Aiden up this morning so I could help my older brother, Brock, with the funeral arrangements. Afterwards, I'd gone to the florist to order the flowers, called the caterer and planned the reception. I'd even had time to come into Mom's bedroom to start stripping the bed.

And then I'd buckled.

It hit me. She was really, truly gone. She'd never sit at another Timbit soccer practice, or read another bedtime story to Aiden. She wouldn't be sitting in the audience when I finally graduated from nursing school after years of helping me balance parenting with school and work.

I had cried plenty of times since Mom's bleak diagnosis, but not like this. Not that god-awful, gut-wrenching wail of the mourning.

The front door opened and closed, and at the sound of feet thudding against the floor, I bolted out into the hallway, closing the door to Mom's room behind me. I didn't want Aiden to see

Grammy's empty bed and be reminded. "Hi buddy!" I said, pasting on a smile that I hoped conveyed happiness to my three-year-old.

The smile on Aiden's face was genuine, and his eyes shone with excitement. "I rode a horse, Mommy!"

"Really?" I looked up to where my older brother's girlfriend stood at the end of the hall, an anxious look on her face.

"I hope that's alright," she said, her brows creasing. "I had him wear the proper gear—helmets and pads and what not. I held the reins the whole time," she added anxiously.

"It's okay," I paused, drawing in air slowly. The pain in my chest was still there, as well as the desire to cry, but I had a bath to draw and a child to get to bed. There was a routine, and routines couldn't be broken.

I clung to the routine; thankful for it. The distraction and happiness my son provided helped me get through each minute. When he wasn't around, it was harder for me not to fall apart. I needed to do things, I needed to feel useful.

"Let's get the bath started and then you can tell me all about riding the horse, okay buddy?" I smiled. Aiden nodded and raced down the hallway to the bathroom. "Thanks again, Tessa," I told her, grateful.

Tessa was a saving grace. She had come to me at the recommendation of my friend, Katie Armstrong. Katie was married to Tessa's older brother, and had happened to toss my name out there when she found out Tessa was looking for a summer job and I was looking for a dependable babysitter.

She hadn't been working for me for very long, but she'd swooped in and helped with Aiden every moment she could. It hadn't even been twenty-four hours since my mother had passed, and yet she'd been with us practically the whole time.

It hadn't bothered me that my older brother, Brock, was seeing her. In fact, I'd secretly been thrilled. Brock had come back for the first time in years because our mother was dying, but I was terrified he'd leave again once the funeral was over.

I couldn't do this alone, and if there was a possibility that Brock would end up sticking around a little longer because of this girl, I was all for it. I didn't want to lose him too, and I had no idea how I was supposed to handle Braden if he left. I didn't even know *where* my younger brother was. He'd taken off shortly after the ambulance had left with Mom's body. He wasn't answering calls or texts.

As if I didn't have enough on my plate. Funeral arrangements, trying to cope with my own suffocating grief, not to mention my son's grief...and now I had to worry about my younger brother.

"It's no problem," Tessa assured me, drawing my attention back to our conversation. "If you need anything else, let me know. If you want, I can come over tomorrow morning and help with Aiden."

"It's alright," I smiled, exhausted with the collected act but unable to quit it. "I can manage tomorrow. I think my family and I will want to be alone. No offence," I added, wincing when I realized how that sounded. Tessa had only recently started dating Brock, and I hadn't meant to exclude her, but I still didn't know her all that well. This felt private.

"None taken." Tessa gave me a small smile to show me that she understood, her eyes lined with understanding. Family was important to her too. "I'll see you tomorrow. Call me if you need anything."

I nodded, watching her go. I stood in the hallway for a moment before turning and walking down the hall to Aiden's room. He was sitting cross-legged on the floor in his underwear, playing with his plastic dinosaurs.

"Alright, how about that bath?"

Aiden jumped up, racing away, his laughter echoing down the hallway. My heart swelled with love for him, for this precious boy that came out of a dark circumstance and made my world brighter.

***

I AWOKE with a start on the living room sofa. I'd fallen asleep while watching some cheesy movie on the Lifetime channel while the tears had silently slipped down my cheeks, coating them.

Bedtime had been a challenge. Before she got really sick, Mom had been the one to read Aiden his bedtime stories every night. Braden skipped parts of the story, just to get it over with because he hated reading, and I was always in a hurry. I had a heavy course load in my nursing program, and there was always an assignment to do or an exam to study for.

But Mom...she'd taken her time. Naturally, Aiden preferred her, and when it was time for bed, he'd quickly get ready before grabbing a book from his shelf and scurrying down the hallway, toward his Grammy's room.

My heart broke at the sight of him the moment he remembered. His blue eyes filled with tears, and he dropped the arm that had gripped the book tightly to his chest with excitement just moments before.

"Mommy," his jaw quivered, and I went to him, picking him up and cradling him to my chest.

When I finally calmed him down enough and started to read, I took my time and made all the characters have different voices. I did it as a way to remember her by, as a way to honour her and maybe ease the ache in Aiden's heart—and my own—a little.

But after that...I'd needed a good cry fest. Anxiety twisted in the pit of my belly as I waited for Brock to call me and tell me that he'd found our younger brother, who was *still* missing. I knew I wouldn't be able to relax until I heard Braden was okay.

Until that happened, all I could do was stared blindly at the television, not really seeing the movie I'd put on, my heart aching with each pulse.

At almost two in the morning, the front door flew open with a thud, smacking against the bench in the front hall. I pressed a hand to my racing heart as two men stumbled inside. One was leaning heavily against the other, wobbling on his feet.

The light from the glow of the television made it possible for me to see the outlines of the two stumbling men. My brothers, Brock and Braden.

"Oh my God, what happened?" I half whispered, half shouted as I raced over to them. The smell of liquor greeted my nostrils, and I wrinkled my nose in disgust. "He's drunk."

Brock said nothing as he dragged our brother to the sofa and dropped him down on it. He picked up Braden's legs and placed them on the couch, grabbing a blanket off the back and throwing it over him. Braden was snoring before his head even hit the cushion.

Brock looked down at our brother for several moments, a solemn set to his jaw, and sighed. "He'll be okay. He'll have one hell of a hangover, but he'll be at the wake. I'll make sure of it. If he doesn't go, he'll regret it for the rest of his life."

"Where was he? Flanigan's?" I hedged, worry pressing down on me. It wasn't uncommon for Braden to drink, but he was usually social about it. He drank to have a good time, not to forget. This was Braden drinking to forget, to numb the pain of Mom dying. This was bad, and my stomach felt heavy with dread.

Alcohol had ravaged our family once before, and I didn't think I could survive watching my younger brother walk down the path our father had.

"Mommy?" Aiden's tiny voice came from down the hallway, and I quickly went to him.

"I'm here," I told him, scooping him up in my arms. I pressed a kiss to the soft skin on his forehead.

"Will you lay with me?" he asked, resting his head against my shoulder as I carried him.

"Of course," I whispered, holding him a little closer the rest of the way.

I got us settled in his bed and he curled up beside me, facing me. His blue eyes bore into mine.

"I miss Grammy," he whispered, curling up in my arms. "I don't want her to be gone." His little voice broke, and it shattered my heart. I hated seeing my baby boy hurting.

"I know, sweetie," I told him, drawing him closer to me. I brought my hand up to brush his thick, dark hair out of his eyes. "Grammy didn't want to go either, but she'll always be in your heart. She'll always be your guardian angel."

"That's not the same as her being here," Aiden remarked sadly.

I said nothing—I had no response, he was right. It wasn't the same, and I was struggling with that too.

I rubbed his back in a small, circular motion, and it wasn't long until his breathing tapered off and he drifted back to sleep, his soft snores filling the darkened room.

Worry churned in my gut, a sorrow so deep I felt it in my bones. In a matter of months, my entire world had imploded in on itself—again.

Only this time, Mom was gone. She wouldn't be there to help me rise from the ashes. I had to do it on my own, and I had to find the strength to help my son and my younger brother.

Closing my eyes at the onslaught of fresh tears, I prayed with all of my heart that my family would survive this.

I WAS NUMB.

7

I knew it was only temporary, the numbness, but I welcomed it never-the-less. It was a quick, bittersweet respite before I endured more agony.

In less than fourteen hours, we would be laying our mother to rest. I'd cried on and off all day, pasted a smile on and powered through the wake. Hands grasping mine, apologizes and condolences passing lips, my responses automatic, each face a blur.

I wasn't sold on the idea of going out for drinks with Brock and Braden's friends after the wake, especially not with Braden's erratic behaviour lately, but Brock wanted me to get out of the house for a bit. We both knew Braden would go anyway, and Brock wanted to keep an eye on him.

Tessa had offered to stay with Aiden, along with Braden's girlfriend and Tessa's best friend, Elle. She was at a loss for how to help him too.

I couldn't remember the last time I let loose, and I had a feeling it wasn't going to happen on that particular night. After all, I was feeling raw, but I needed the change of scenery. Being at home right now *hurt*, it hurt because my mother was gone and I missed her more than anything. It hurt because I was fumbling through my own grief and blindly trying to hold everybody together.

"This is a bad idea," I muttered the moment I walked into Flanigan's with my brothers. I sent a wary glance to Braden as he immediately crossed over to the bar to order a drink. All day long he'd been sullen and angry, stealing sips of whiskey from a flask he'd kept in his pocket. My worry ran deep, unrelenting.

"I'll keep an eye on him," Brock promised.

"I'm worried about you too," I told him, frowning. I was worried about us all. I was worried about what would happen once this funeral was over. Would Brock go back to Alberta? Would he distance himself from us again? I couldn't stand the idea of losing another family member in any sense.

"Don't," he ordered with a frown before two of his friends, Gordon Armstrong and Travis Channing, approached us to say hello.

Gordon and Travis had always been around when I was growing up, along with Grady McDonnell and Steve Winters, both of whom were hanging out by the bar with a couple of other people I recognized from around town.

After the arrest, Brock stopped talking to everyone in town, except for Mom, Braden and me. Even for us, it was irregular to hear from him. He'd hung out with them a few times since his return, but his budding romance with Tessa had caused tension between him and Gordon. Mom's death seemed to have bridged that gap, and all seemed forgiven between them.

"Glad you could make it out," Gordon said to us. He was another one of Tessa's many brothers. Getting together for drinks had been his idea, his way of trying to infuse a little cheer into our dire situation.

"What's your poison?" Travis added, his hazel eyes drinking me in as he smiled. I felt my heart stutter in my chest, tripping over itself in his presence.

When I was in high school, I had the biggest crush on Travis Channing. His hazel eyes were always so warm and friendly, always sparkling with elation. His dirty blond hair was always slightly messy, like he'd run his hand through it a billion times, or the wind had mussed it. He was the kind of guy that lived for the thrill of adventure.

He came from a family like ours—poor and struggling, only he didn't have to grow up in a house shorn in darkness. Despite his circumstances—growing up in a trailer, fatherless, never having new clothes or the latest gadgets, Travis was inherently happy.

Sadness is drawn to happiness; sadness seeks out the light, hoping it will drive away the darkness, and so I was drawn to him, even then.

But Travis had always looked at me the same way the rest of Brock's friends looked at me: like I was their honourary little sister.

"Oh I don't know," I looked away, blushing. The way he was smiling at me made me feel like a teenager again, and not at all like his honourary little sister. "I haven't had anything to drink in a long time," I admitted, immediately regretting my confession. How pathetic was I?

"You look like a Sex on the Beach kind of girl," he responded with a charming smile. Brock slapped him on the back of the head, and Travis laughed. "I'm just saying, something fruity and tasty. I didn't name the damn drink."

I glared at Brock, annoyed at his interference. So what if Travis *was* flirting a little. It had been a long time since someone had flirted with me. It felt *good* and I didn't want Brock to scare him away.

I craved this.

"That sounds good actually. I'd love to have Sex on the Beach," I said to Travis, smiling as I accepted his outstretched arm and followed him to the bar. I shot Brock a warning glare, letting him know I wouldn't tolerate any further intrusion. Travis paused when we reached the bar, tapping his fingers against the glossy surface.

"Sex on the Beach for the lovely lady and an Old Fashioned for me," he said to the older man behind the bar before turning his attention to Grady and Steve, who nodded their heads at me and raised their beers in greeting.

"Evening, Becky. I'm sorry to hear about your mom passing. She was a sweet lady," Mick O'Riley, the bartender and owner, said as he mixed our drinks.

"Thank you," I murmured, unsurprised at the fondness in the old bartender's voice. Mick had always been kind and warm to me, not that I'd spent much time in his bar.

He'd also been kind enough to offer up his bar to Brock for

the reception, which saved me the trouble of hosting it at the house. Flanigan's was a short walk away from the church where the funeral would take place.

I had dreaded the idea of hosting it at the house. Our tiny, three bedroom bungalow was cramped, and it needed a lot of work. I didn't want people to focus on the old worn furniture or the roof that was in massive need of repair, or the water stains on the ceiling and walls from multiple leaks over the years.

I also sort of wanted to be able to leave if it got to be too much.

Maybe having the reception at the same bar our father had frequented when he was alive was in poor taste to some, but truthfully... a dark part of me was thankful for Flanigan's. This bar had kept my dad entertained and out of the house.

"I'm honoured," Mick said, flashing me a gentle smile as he slid the drink toward me. "Your mom was a sweet lady. She used to be friends with my daughter."

"Really? I didn't know you had a daughter," I said with surprise, my hand wrapping around the highball glass.

"She died when she was nineteen," Mick told me gruffly, and I could tell that the pain of losing her was still etched into every part of him. His eyes closed off, and he slid Travis his whiskey.

"Thanks, Mick," Travis said. He had watched our exchange quietly and with interest. He looked at me with care, his hand coming up to rest on the small of my back.

Once we had our drinks in hand, Travis led the way to a relatively private booth, his large palm still pressed to my back. I tried to ignore the fact that one of my brothers was basically acting like a self-proclaimed bodyguard and the other was already attempting to drink his weight in alcohol —*again*.

I wanted to ascend from my sadness, to lose myself in a moment that was only for me.

Travis regarded me from across the table. "How are you

holding up, Becs?" he asked. His eyes were gentle, and as always —I got the sense that I could really trust him.

"I've been better," I confessed, drawing in a shaky breath. I didn't want to talk about my grief, but he made me *want* to open up. I had to focus extra hard to keep my walls up around him.

My brothers had their girlfriends, and I had nobody. My closest friend was Katie and I hadn't made time for her in months.

I'd been so preoccupied with my mom's illness, school, and work, and she'd been busy settling in to married life and awaiting the arrival of her baby. The last thing I wanted to do was bother her with my grief, or discuss the heavy weight of my feelings over an impersonal message.

Katie and I hadn't always been friends. We'd gone to the same high school, but she had been one of the popular girls while I had fallen somewhere in the middle. We both worked at her parent's grocery store as part time cashiers, and we formed a quiet friendship, one where she'd smile at me in the halls and I'd smile back.

When I got pregnant and started to show, the rest of our classmates all stopped talking to me. All except Katie, she started going out of her way to talk to me. She fought even harder to be my friend, because she had sensed that I desperately needed one.

Over the years, we grew closer and closer, but when Mom got sick...I withdrew into myself, focusing only on my small world.

It was the only way I knew how to get through it.

Katie understood, but I still felt guilty for doing it...especially after I'd seen her round belly at the wake.

I'd heard she was pregnant, of course. She had told me herself six months ago when we met up for lunch. I'd happily congratulated her, but I wasn't there for her the way I should have been.

"I'll bet. Want to talk to about it?" Travis didn't ask questions that he wasn't interested in hearing the answers for, so I knew he was asking how I was because he truly cared, on some level. Maybe that would have been enough, but mentally, I slapped myself. Opening up to Travis Channing would be a mistake. He wasn't the same boy he once was—he was a country singer now, and a famous one at that. We were worlds apart, and I couldn't burden him with my sadness.

"I'd rather not, if you don't mind. I came here to forget about things for a little while."

"Alright," he smiled, the whites of his teeth bright against his thick lips. "And just how would you like to forget about them?"

His smile was easy, playful even, but his eyes smoldered and I couldn't help but question the meaning behind his words. The way he was looking at me evoked tingles of awareness across every inch of my skin.

"I don't know, tell me some stories about being a famous country singer," I replied, feeling light headed. "Your life is far more interesting than mine."

"I don't buy that." Travis shook his head, but he must have sensed my reluctance on the topic and obliged my request. I lost myself in his dazzling smile while he told me all about his adventures on the road, about the hilarious people he'd met. His stories intrigued me. His stories made me forget about things, for a little while.

With each sip of my beverage, I relaxed more and more. One drink turned into two, and two became three. My eyes traced his carelessly tousled dirty blond hair as we chatted. We drew closer and closer, our eyes never leaving each other's faces and a powerful desire overcame me. I longed to taste his thick, kiss-able lips.

After three drinks and nearly an hour of conversation with Travis, I started to get antsy. My carnal urges were consuming my thought process, helped along by the alcohol in my system. I wasn't kidding when I had told Travis I didn't drink—I really didn't, aside from a glass of wine during special occasions.

I wanted him. Desperately.

My first instinct was to run fast, but I knew that wasn't exactly healthy. Still, I knew I needed a moment to collect my thoughts and my composure.

"Excuse me, I need to visit the ladies room," I told him, instantly wishing I could retract that sentence. As if Travis needed—or wanted—to hear about my bathroom habits. But he smiled easily in response and nodded.

I darted quickly to the bathroom, relieved to see that it was empty. I used the restroom and washed my hands, studying my reflection in the mirror with uncertainty.

I had smooth skin, high cheek bones, a nose that wasn't too big or thick for my face, and my blue eyes were framed by naturally thick long lashes.

I wasn't ugly, and I knew that, but that knowledge didn't make looking in the mirror any easier. I wore my sadness and my scars like a cloak, even though I tried not to. I could see it in the worry line between my eyebrows, and in the depths of my eyes.

But for the first time in a long time, I saw something else. A spark; the urge to be reckless and selfish.

Taking a deep breath, I made my way back to the table. Travis was sitting there, alone. It was almost a rare sight...him alone. He usually had a bunch of women circling him like vultures, or he was hanging out with his friends.

I sat down, a peculiar look on my face as I studied him, allowing myself to drift away in the possibility of one night with him.

If I was ever going to have a one-night stand, it had to be with someone who made me feel safe, and it couldn't ever be serious. There was no way in *hell* I'd ever give my heart to another person again, not after Richie had destroyed it.

Plus, there was Aiden to think of. I didn't want to be the kind of mother who brought all sorts of men home. I didn't want him to get attached to anyone I saw. Again, a one-night stand made sense.

Travis seemed ideal because he was always on the road touring and had absolutely no desire to settle down any time soon. He seemed to enjoy casual sex, so I figured it was a no-brainer.

"What's up?" he asked, tilting his head and trying to figure out the meaning behind my strange expression.

I bit my lip and forced my eyes away from his. "I was wondering if you wanted to go somewhere with me?"

"Where?" he asked, his eyes sparking with interest as he watched me.

"A hotel room." The words were out of my mouth before I could stop them. My cheeks heated with embarrassment at the astonished look on his face.

To my surprise, the astonishment faded pretty quickly, and Travis's eyes smoldered as he stared at me. Tension crackled between us, making every fine hair on my arms stand up. That look melted all of the oxygen between us. It left me dizzy, a feeling akin to stepping off one of those twirl-a-whirl carnival rides.

"That's a very enticing idea, Becs," Travis drawled, pausing to take a heady sip of his whiskey, his eyes never leaving my face. I loved the way his lips shaped my nickname. He lowered his heady gaze to my lips, and my tongue darted out in response to the animalistic glint in his eyes. He shook his head, trying to snap out of whatever R-rated place his thoughts had taken him. I squirmed in my seat, squeezing my legs together to ease the ache between my thighs. "But you're grieving. You aren't thinking clearly."

I froze. His words doused me as if they were cold water.

I hadn't planned on him saying no. Travis was a known

womanizer, I figured he'd go for some no strings attached sex in a heartbeat. Immediately, embarrassment washed over me. "You're saying no?" I swallowed. I had no idea why I was asking for the clarification. I suppose I was shocked, and what he had said had taken a moment to sink in.

Travis leaned back against the booth and ran his hand across his stubble-free jaw. He studied me while he did this, like he was trying to figure out the easiest way to reject me without hurting my sensitive feelings. It got my hackles up, and I bristled.

"You know what? Forget about it," I said, standing up hastily. My eyes prickled, but I refused to let him see me cry. That would only make this situation more embarrassing for me.

I drew in a quick breath, trying not to let the rejection maim me. *What was I thinking*? Travis was a chart-topping country singer. He had been with models and actresses. What on earth had given me the audacity to assume he'd want to have a one-night stand with a broken, single mom?

This was exactly why I didn't drink, or give into reckless, spur of the moment whims.

Travis's hand shot out and grabbed mine before I could move away from our table. "Becky, you just lost your mom," his voice was gentle, and his eyes implored me to listen. "I don't want you to make rash decisions right now, especially decisions you're going to regret later."

"What makes you think I'll regret a one-night stand with you?" I deadpanned. "Unless you're confessing that you are terrible at sex, which whatever. I don't have much experience to go off here. Whether it's with you or not, I'm going to have sex. I have to."

I knew as soon as the words left my mouth that they were true.

"I'm not terrible at sex," Travis retorted, arching a brow and smirking. "I just want to know why? Why now? Why the rush?

Why *me?*" he added. The look that flitted across his face almost seemed…vulnerable.

"It's just time, and you were here," I answered, flushing a deeper shade of red. For a moment, he looked stricken. "I'm sorry I even said anything. Forget about it." I pulled away from his touch and scanned the crowd for an escape.

I spotted Braden over at the bar, his lips locked on a girl that definitely *wasn't* his girlfriend. Elle was back at my house helping Tessa watch Aiden. I stormed away from Travis without saying another word, intent on slapping the stupid off my younger brother. I needed to focus on his self-made problems so I didn't fall apart.

Brock was attempting to pull Braden away from the blonde girl. "Brock is right, we're going now," I told him, grabbing his arm and trying to tug him away. He shoved me, and I stumbled, the air leaving my lungs as I was propelled backwards.

Travis caught me, his strong arms enveloping me for a moment before he helped me find my footing. I hadn't even realized he'd followed me. I thought he was as eager as I had been to escape the awkwardness between us.

I tried to control my breathing. Seeing Braden like that scared me. In that moment, he seemed so much like our father.

"I'm not a kid! You can't fucking tell me what to do," he shouted angrily, acting every bit like a child.

Mick limped around the bar to confront Braden. "Hit the road, Miller. You're cut off," he said, his tired blue eyes flashing with anger. I'd never seen the quiet man respond to rowdy patrons like that. Then again, I didn't spend a lot of time at Flanigan's.

Braden still wasn't having it. He glowered at Mick. "Oh, you know how to cut people off, huh? Could've fooled me," he spat. "Maybe you should have tried cutting my old man off so he wouldn't come home and beat his family. But, then how would your shitty bar stay open without his wallet, eh?"

"Braden, you're making no sense. Let's just go," I pleaded, mortified. Every eye in the bar was on us, watching this altercation, hearing his words. The shame made me feel about two inches tall. I sent an apologetic look to Mick as Brock grabbed our little brother by his shirt collar and dragged him outside. "I really am sorry, Mick. If you've changed your mind about letting us have the reception here, I understand."

"It's okay," Mick said. "I've been called worse. We'll see you tomorrow."

"Thank you, Mick." Relieved, but still ashamed, I gave him a tiny smile and went to follow my brothers outside. Whispers followed me, and I did my best to keep my breathing under control.

I almost made it to the old oak door that lead to the street, but before I could reach it, Travis stepped in front of me, blocking my path. He stood there, his head titled down to look at me, his fingers brushing across the back of my hand. I looked down at where his fingers touched my skin, and tried my best to ignore the tingles they evoked.

"What?" I half hissed, half whispered at him.

"I just wanted to make sure you were okay," he said, pulling his hand away like touching me had burned him.

"I'll live," I responded, stepping around him and following my siblings outside.

I was livid at my little brother. I knew it wasn't any of my business, but I'd come to love Elle. She'd spent so much time with us and she had been a *major* help. Seeing her heartbroken expression when she noticed the lipstick on Braden's mouth infuriated me. Braden loved her, that was obvious, but he was hurting and he wasn't thinking clearly.

And he had shoved me. Braden hadn't pushed me since we were kids, and having someone push me like that triggered memories that were better left buried. I knew if he'd been sober, he would have never done it, but that didn't make it any easier to digest.

For a second night in a row, Braden was snoring loudly on the sofa, too intoxicated to get to his bed downstairs.

"He'll be okay, Becky." Brock sounded so sure.

"How do you know?" I asked, casting him a glance.

"He's not like *him*," Brock shook his head slightly. "He cares so much, almost too much. He just doesn't know how to process it."

"Well, I hope this isn't how he decides to process Mom's death. I can't have him around Aiden if he's going to be drunk and angry all the time. I can't go back there, Brock."

"I know." I felt the weight of Brock's heavy hand on my shoulder. He squeezed gently before releasing. "Get some sleep. I'll be by in the morning to deal with him."

Brock left and I got ready for bed. It took hours for me to fall asleep, between worrying about my little brother and beating myself up over the mortifying situation with Travis.

When I finally did sleep, the nightmares came.

My limbs were twisted up in my sheets as I thrashed about. Sweat coated my skin, and fear clenched around my heart like a vice.

I dreamt of him, of Richie. I dreamt of fingers around my neck, squeezing and cutting off my air supply. I woke up gasping for air, my hands scratching at my throat. My heart raced wildly, and the breaths I drew in didn't seem to be enough to fill my starved lungs.

I hadn't had a nightmare that intense in years.

"Mommy?" a little voice said. I turned my head, seeing Aiden's silhouette at the side of my bed.

"Yes, baby?" My voice shook from the adrenaline of my nightmare.

"Can I sleep with you? I had a nightmare."

"Of course," I untangled my legs from my sheet and opened

my arms. As soon as Aiden settled beside me, my heart started to return to its regular pace.

I LAID THERE with him for another five hours, but I couldn't sleep. My mind wouldn't shut off. As if I didn't have enough crap on my plate to deal with, but I couldn't stop beating myself up over my stupid decision to basically ask Travis for a one-night stand. His refusal was a fresh wound that wouldn't stop pulsing.

I mused that the nightmare could have come from my fear when Braden pushed me mixed with my attempt to force myself on Travis, and the rejection that followed.

Tears blurred my vision, and I blinked them away with frustration. I didn't have time to feel sorry for myself. The funeral was later that day, and I'd have to stand up and read my speech. I took comfort in the fact that our family wasn't very well-liked around here. At least that meant there wouldn't be a lot of people present.

Aiden was still snoring softly when I finally decided to give up on sleep. I slipped out of my bed and headed to the bathroom. The woman looking back at me had bags under her eyes and a sadness that seemed to seep out from every pore.

Sighing, I turned on the shower. I needed to wash away yesterday's mistakes. I dreaded seeing Travis later, but I knew he'd be at the funeral. Even if years had passed since they last saw each other, Brock was one of his best friends, and I knew Travis well enough to know that he would be there for him. Travis was *always* there for his friends.

I just hoped that he would have the decency to keep my blunder to himself.

Slipping into my robe, I snuck back into my bedroom to dress before I went to the kitchen to make coffee. I tossed on a t-shirt and a pair of shorts, knowing I'd have to give my son a bath before the funeral. I wouldn't be able to get ready until after he was dressed, not unless I wanted to accessorize with bath water and soap.

Braden was still snoring on the couch, and the sound of the coffee percolating barely stirred him. I poured two mugs—one for me, and one for him. Braden liked his coffee black, while I had to cut mine with an obscene amount of cream and sugar to even tolerate it. I took a quick sip and left my mug on the counter before I walked into the living room.

Sitting on the edge of the coffee table, I poked my little brother sharply. He grumbled, swatting blindly at me with his arm. I pulled the mug away from his reach instinctively, my reflexes quicker than his.

"You need to wake up now," I told him, my voice stern. "You need to shower and get ready."

"I don't want to. I'm not going," Braden grumbled, rolling over so that he was facing the back of the couch. I sighed, glancing at the digital clock on the cable box.

"We have less than three hours before the funeral starts. We need to get ready," I said, working to keep the patience in my voice. He ignored me, making no move to get up off the couch. He smelled like a liquor store, the scent reminding me of the night before. My brother had certainly made a giant mess for himself to clean up.

Elle had left our house shattered, after putting two and two together. His betrayal wouldn't be easily forgiven.

I stood up at the sound of a key in the lock, my heart pounding as the door swung open. I relaxed upon seeing my older brother. Of course it was him—burglars didn't unlock your front door with a key.

Brock walked in, already dressed in his suit for the funeral. His long hair was brushed and tucked behind his ears. His eyes landed on me, then dropped down to our sleeping brother.

He rolled his neck. "I'll take it from here."

I brought Braden's mug back to the kitchen and watched from the service hatch as Brock lifted the coffee table, moving it out of the way and walked behind the couch. He gripped it from the bottom and lifted, and Braden fell with a thud to the floor.

"What the fuck!" he shouted, jumping up to glare at Brock.

"Keep your voice down, your nephew is sleeping," Brock ordered, his expression hard. "Get your ass in the shower and get ready."

"I'm not fucking going," Braden scowled, anger coming off him in waves. His fists were clenched to his side. His blue eyes were bloodshot and crazed. I almost gasped—he looked so much like our father that it made me feel nauseous.

"We talked about this already Braden. I get that you're hurting—we're all hurting. But you're not missing this bloody funeral." Brock's tone was final. Braden glowered at him, sizing him up as if he actually planned to fight him.

"I miss Grammy too." Aiden's little voice took us all by surprise, and we turned to look at him. He was standing in the narrow hallway, his eyes wide and fixed on Braden. "Mommy says we can say goodbye today. Grammy would be sad if you didn't say bye, Uncle Braden."

The anger in my brother's expression broke, leaving undiluted grief. He drew in a shaky breath. He opened and closed his mouth several times, searching for a response that he didn't have. The fight left his shoulders, and he wouldn't meet any of our eyes as he passed us to head downstairs to his basement bedroom.

I pressed my fist against my heart, biting my lip to keep the tears from falling. Aiden's gentle, empathetic nature never ceased to amaze me.

"Alright, Aiden, how about we get a bath running for you while your mom starts breakfast?"

"I want scrambled eggs and Mommy always leaves the shells in," Aiden replied, rubbing at his eyes tiredly.

I flushed a deep shade of crimson. I didn't *intend* to leave pieces of shells in the scrambled eggs, I just wasn't a very good cook. Especially when it came to breakfast foods.

"Okay, I'll make you scrambled eggs," Brock grinned, his eyes sparkling with humour.

My embarrassment faded, and I allowed myself to feel this moment—to feel the hope in it. Our lives may have changed again, but my son was still smiling and cracking jokes. Sure, they were at my expense, but I'd take it.

CHAPTER TWO

ravis

I WAS SO SCREWED.

I probably would have stood more of a chance if I hadn't been lusting after her all these years, but she was the girl I could never have. Becky Miller, the younger sister of one of my best friends.

She was nothing like the other girls I knew. She didn't want me for my money, or my fame. She wanted me because she knew who I was beyond the fame. She wanted me because she trusted me enough not to screw it up.

But I didn't trust myself.

I knew very little about Becky's past. I knew that she was a single mom, and that the biological father of her son wasn't involved. She needed someone who could handle that, and I wasn't overly confident I could.

But that didn't change the fact that ever since she put the bug in my ear, I had a massive hard on for her. Maybe not liter-

24

ally the whole time, but any time I let myself truly imagine sinking into her, which was more often than I cared to admit.

More than anything, I wanted to ease the ache in her blue eyes. I wanted to bring a smile to her lips, like I'd done the night before. I wanted to comfort her.

Becky was drifting from group to group, trying to thank as many people as she could for being there. I waited until she was relatively alone to approach her.

"Can we talk for a moment?" I pleaded, nodding toward the hall that led to the bathrooms and the emergency exit. Becky eyed me warily and nodded. She led the way with her arms crossed over her chest, subconsciously shielding herself. She made sure to keep her distance from me until we'd stepped outside into the back alley behind Flanigan's and the hardware store.

"What do you want?" she asked, her voice guarded, a stark contrast to how open and trusting she'd been with me last night.

"I wanted to check in with you, make sure you were okay."

"I'm fine." Becky couldn't hold my gaze. Her shoulders slumped in defeat.

I stepped closer to her, pulling her toward me so that I could hug her. "It's okay to not be fine, you know that right? You don't have to keep it together all the time."

It didn't seem fair that Becky had nobody to hold her while she grieved. I could at least do that, even if I couldn't give her what she really needed.

But she felt so good in my arms. Her scent was intoxicating, like peaches and honey. She smelled good enough to eat, and I couldn't help but wonder what she tasted like.

"I know that," she replied, her voice muffled against my chest. Her hands hung limply at her sides for a moment, and then she brought them up to wrap them around my waist, hugging me back. I rested my chin on the top of her head and inhaled.

Becky lifted her face, studying me while I tilted my head so that I could look down at her. Her blue eyes were full of hurt. She swallowed hard. "Why are you being so nice to me?"

"Haven't I always been nice to you?" I asked her, surprised.

"Not like this," she pointed out. It was true—we'd never touched like this before, and we probably wouldn't be touching today if she hadn't asked me for a one-night stand the night before. She needed physical comfort, she'd all but said as much. I couldn't deny how amazing it felt to have her in my arms, and the appealing thought of spreading her legs had consumed me since the moment she asked me.

I had to back away before she felt the effect she had on me. I ran my hands through my hair, tugging at the roots, and dragged in a ragged breath. I started to pace, restless with just standing there.

"I feel like this is a big thing, you coming to me like you did last night, and I'm sorry if I made you feel like I didn't want you, because honestly... that's not it. You're gorgeous, Becs, and I want you...badly. But you're my best friend's little sister, and you can play things off as much as you like, but you've been hurt...badly. I can't promise you the commitment you deserve. I travel a lot, and I like to have fun," I winced, realizing how crass that sounded, but it was true...and Becky deserved my honesty.

With my grand speech over, I stopped pacing and looked at her, trying to gauge her reaction to my words. I couldn't bear the idea of hurting her, but I had to make her understand. She didn't seem put off by my honesty, she looked at me earnestly.

"I'm not looking for commitment. I don't need those things. We've been fine on our own and we'll continue to be fine. I just...I need..." Becky broke off, her eyes misting. She inhaled sharply, her eyes finally landing on mine again. "I need to feel desired, Travis. That's all."

I stepped up to her, unable to stop myself. Her broken confession sliced into my resolve. Becky was too gorgeous to feel undesirable, and I knew I could make her feel that at least. I looked around, making sure the coast was clear before my hands gently went to her hips and I pulled her against me.

"Do you feel that?" I murmured, my eyes never leaving hers. She drew in a sharp breath, swallowing hard and nodding as I pressed my hard length against her. Even just talking about this in an abstract way with her had me throbbing. "You are desired. Don't ever doubt that. Any guy would be lucky to have you."

"Just one night, Travis," she pleaded, her eyes wide. "Then we can go back to just being acquaintances, almost friends."

"What if you want more afterwards?" I suggested, waggling my eyebrows at her. I may have been playing it off with humour, but I wasn't exactly willing to face the consequences.

Like Brock's fist against my jaw, for example.

I had only just reconnected with him, and I didn't want to screw things up now that he was back. He'd been gone for four years, and we'd barely spoken. After his arrest, he stopped talking to everyone. It stung, but I was beginning to understand his reasons.

"Let's not get ahead of ourselves. Maybe we won't even like each other afterwards," she countered, her lips twitching to repress a bemused smile.

"Oh, I doubt that very much," I murmured, arousal making my throat feel thick. Her chest rose and fell with each frantic breath she dragged in. Her nipples pressed against the thin material of her dress. Almost like my hand had a mind of its own, it moved to cup her breast over her dress. My thumb brushed across her nipple, and she let out a tiny gasp.

She looked so responsive, I couldn't help but lower my mouth to hers. Her lips were soft and seemed to fit mine perfectly. I kissed her slowly at first, then deepened it when she moaned and parted her lips. My tongue darted out, finding hers and beginning an erotic dance.

My hips pressed her against the brick wall, and I felt like I could spend hours just kissing her. Her hands came up to my chest, her fingers gripping the material of my shirt. Then she pushed on me, breaking our contact.

"Not here," she whispered, flushed. Her eyes lingered on my lips for a moment before she rose them to meet my eyes. "I can meet you tomorrow night."

"Where?"

She bit down on her lip. "The motel off of Bowes Street?"

I stepped back, rubbing my chin while I studied her. It seemed cheap, and Becky didn't deserve cheap. I understood why she didn't want to meet up at her place, and I couldn't very well invite her back to mine. My mom lived there, and that didn't exactly set the mood either.

I got the impression Becky *needed* to be in control of this, so I'd let her set the pace.

"Okay," I told her, swallowing hard.

"You don't have my number," she reminded me.

"So give it to me," I grinned. I pulled my phone out of the pocket of my jeans and added her number in. I typed out a text and hit send so she'd know my number too. I wasn't worried at all about her leaking it, and that was refreshing. Usually, I avoided giving women my number. I'd unfortunately had to change it monthly for the past couple of years due to security issues.

"I need to get back," Becky said, stepping even further away from me and heading inside. I adjusted myself, shaking my head. As soon as she disappeared, the doubt set in.

What in the hell did I just agree to?

THE NEXT DAY, just after ten o'clock at night, I walked up the concrete steps of the motel. I wore a baseball cap low on my forehead and a brown leather jacket to protect my identity. The less people saw of my face and the full sleeve tattoo on my left arm, the more successful I was at going undetected. It didn't always work, but it was my best shot at anonymity.

My eyes scanned the door numbers, and I moved toward *202* with my heart pounding in my chest.

When we had made the plan to meet up, I was all for it; I couldn't wait to sink into her. But then I had spent the last twenty-four hours torturing myself with all of the reasons why it was a bad idea, and it really didn't take much.

A few memories from high school had done the trick. Becky shared those hallways with me—with *us*—for two years. Brock, Gordon, Grady, Steve, and I used to intimidate any guy stupid enough to look in her direction. Brock wanted to make sure that whoever asked Becky out *knew* they had to go through us if they hurt her. Nobody was up for the challenge.

I didn't want anybody to touch her, but it hadn't started out like that. At first, it was just fun. I didn't have any siblings, and watching my best friends with theirs made me feel envious of that fact. I told myself I was protecting her on Brock's behalf.

I had to acknowledge the fact that maybe I had ended up using my status as Brock's best friend to stake a claim, in a quiet way.

I guess I thought of her as mine, even though I kept my distance from her. She'd always been beautiful, and I didn't think I could hide my attraction to her. Brock would have kicked my ass if he caught on. We had a bro code—sisters were off limits. That meant both Tessa Armstrong and Becky Miller were no touch zones.

It was easier to abide by those rules with Tessa, obviously. She was six years younger than us and when I knew her, she was a lanky freckle faced kid. Becky fell under my radar because of those two short years we attended the same high school.

When I was in grade twelve, I went to semi-formal with one of the hot, popular girls at school. Her name was Kristen Base, and I used to joke about how I was gonna hit *all* her bases, if you know what I mean.

I drew in a breath, letting the memory wash over me.

I'd basically spent the first half of the dance making out with Kristen and trying to cop a feel through her satin dress. I didn't even clue in that Becky had gone to semi-formal until I saw her taking shots with Greg Brimstone. It wasn't really an activity I had ever thought I'd catch her doing, lest of all in the gymnasium of our high school.

I'd known Greg for years, and he always came across as a self-entitled asswipe. He came from money and loved to wave that fact around in everybody's face—especially mine. Ever since grade school, he'd show up with some crazy expensive device and drone on and on about it before making comments about how it must suck being trailer trash.

It didn't sit well with me that he'd chosen to take Becky as his date, so I watched them.

Losing all interest in my date entirely, I debated on what I should do. I didn't want to ruin her night, but I also didn't trust the way Greg and his friends were openly leering at her. The shots kept coming, and Becky started dancing with him.

I hated him, and I hated the fact that his hands were on her. I hated that he was basically pouring hard liquor down Becky's throat, high fiving his friend whenever she wasn't looking. I knew Becky hadn't had much experience drinking—Brock made damn sure of it, but he avoided functions like this and she knew that.

I dragged Kristen out onto the dance floor so I could keep a closer eye on things and not have to talk to her anymore. We were a few feet away from Greg and Becky as they danced. His hands gripped her ass as he pulled her against him.

Rage like I'd never seen before made my vision waver as he whispered something in Becky's ear. She blushed and nodded slowly, and they started to make their way toward the doors that led outside. She was stumbling, and his arm was around her as he guided her through the bodies on the floor.

I pulled away from Kristen and stepped in front of them, blocking their path. Becky swayed against Greg, her eyes diluted and unfocused. "Where you going, Brimsnot?" I demanded, my tone ice.

"It's Brimstone," Greg scowled. "And none of your business."

"See, that's where you're wrong," I said, stepping toward him with a playful grin on my face that did little to hide my rage toward him. "It's definitely my business, because you're with my buddy's little sister. I know that if he were here, he wouldn't let you leave with her."

"Well he isn't here," Greg retorted, standing tall. He was still a little pipsqueak. The top of his head barely came up to my chin.

"No," I responded, rolling my neck and cracking my knuckles. "But I am. You've fed her so much alcohol that she can barely fucking stand. She's not going anywhere with you."

Gordon was there too, with his girlfriend at the time Melanie Clayton. He ditched her the same way I'd ditched Kristen when he noticed the altercation happening on the dance floor. Steve and Grady, also in attendance, joined us as well, the four of us standing as a united front.

"Whatever, she's not worth it," Greg the coward muttered, releasing Becky and pushing through us.

Becky's eyes filled with unshed tears and she swayed, off balance without him there for support. The broken, hollow look in her blue eyes called to me. Gordon stepped forward and caught her before she could fall. Her face was red with shame and hurt. "Get her home," I said to Gordon before taking off after him.

Greg Brimstone deserved more than the black eye I had given him when I caught up with him in the school parking lot. Even now, my fists clenched in repressed anger. It still pissed me off that he'd said those things, that he had made her feel worthless.

I slowed when I passed room *200*, knowing hers was next. I swallowed, my heart pounding in anticipation. A moment of hesitation had me stopping between the two red doors as I seriously contemplated what I was about to do.

My hesitation came from a place of not wanting her to feel worthless. I knew that no matter what I said, Becky would find someone to do this with. I knew that she needed it, and I even understood why. That fact alone had me moving again, and two large steps later, I raised my hand and knocked twice.

Becky opened the door in a white silk robe that ended just above her knees and did little to conceal how very naked she was beneath it. Her dark hair hung heavy and wet over her shoulder, and I could see beads of water on her collarbone from her recent shower.

The air around us seemed to dissipate, or maybe I was having a heart attack. Something was seizing within me.

Enchanted, I walked into the room, my feet moving on their own accord, my eyes unwilling to part from the sight of her in that robe. My hands twitched as my eyes dropped down to her creamy legs. I was hard in two seconds, if that.

"I already had this robe," she blurted out, and a bemused smile broke out on my face. She flushed, clearly flustered, and I chuckled at her nervousness. "I just meant I wasn't trying to impress you. I worked tonight and I wanted to shower, I just didn't want to use the hotel robes. Who knows how often they wash them?" She shrugged, closing the door when I had cleared it.

"That's both deeply disturbing and amusing." I arched a brow, the corner of my lips twitching up.

"I watched a documentary on hotels once," she said, giving me a small smile.

The hotel room wasn't very large, there was enough space for a queen sized bed, two bedside tables, and a dresser with a television on it. "Guess that explains the comforter on the floor?"

She nodded in response, chewing on her bottom lip nervously.

I stepped toward her, stopping so that her breasts were just inches away from me. I brought my thumb up and tenderly brushed it across her bottom lip. "You don't need to be nervous," I told her. "It's not too late to put the brakes on this."

"I don't want to put the brakes on this," she murmured. I had to swallow back my own wave of nervousness, and it unsettled me. Random hook ups, no strings attached—that was my deal. She knew it, I knew it, but this felt different and I didn't want to think about why.

A shiver rolled through Becky's shoulders as she peered up at me, her eyes were locked on mine. I knew there was no turning back.

I kissed her, my lips tasting hers tentatively, like I was afraid she would bolt. I was almost expecting it, but she surprised me by returning with fervid kisses of her own. I picked her up and pressed her against the door, grinding my pelvis into her.

The silk tie of her robe came undone. I paused, my cock throbbing at the sight of her supple breast. I lowered my head to catch her nipple in my mouth and she arched her back, letting out a sound caught between a whimper and a moan.

And I was a goner.

CHAPTER THREE

 *ecky*

I DIDN'T DO things like this. I hadn't been with anybody since Aiden's sperm donor. He had been my first, and so far, my only. Between parenting, going to school, working and taking care of Mom, there wasn't time for extracurricular activities.

The ache of missing Mom was profound, I couldn't breathe without feeling it, and I couldn't escape my thoughts, or at least...I hadn't been able to until Travis flashed his killer smile at me.

Kissing Travis awoke something primal in me, a hunger that I hadn't known existed, and it ignited when my robe fell open on its own accord. Or maybe his expert hands had untied it, and I just hadn't noticed because I was too busy nearly coming undone from just his lips and the way he kissed me.

Never, in all of my life, had I been kissed like that. Like I was wanted, cherished.

I moaned, and he swallowed it. He tugged my bottom lip

gently with his teeth and my hands raked through his hair. His hands squeezed my ass as he lifted me against him and pressed me against the hotel door.

"Bed?" he suggested, and I moved against his hardness in response. He carried me to the mattress, practically falling on top of me.

Travis's hand cupped my cheek. He brushed my hair out of my face, his eyes smoldering and my heart pounding. For several beats, he looked at me like that, like he could see into the very depths of my soul, and as if what he saw there didn't frighten him.

Our lips collided again, tongues stroking and teeth nipping at tender flesh. I pulled on the buckle of his belt, releasing it, and used my hands to free him from his jeans. I loved the way that he felt in my hand—velvety smooth, thick and long and so very hard. He let out a low hiss when my fingers brushed across his tip. His tortured expression made me feel more powerful than I'd ever felt before.

He made me feel *desired*.

I watched as his finger gently brushed against my core. His eyes widened at my body's response to him, and I flushed. He tugged his wallet out of his back pocket and grabbed a condom before discarding his jeans somewhere on the floor.

Once he had the condom on, I crawled over top of him, moving my wetness against his tip. "Fuck, you're gorgeous, Becs," he murmured reverently. He slipped his hands through my open robe and held me, almost guiding me, as I slowly dropped down on him, taking him to the hilt. I paused, my eyes locking on his as I rocked my hips.

I thought it would hurt, but I was too turned on. I thought he'd be selfish—I only had one lover to compare him to, and he was as selfish as they came—but Travis wasn't. Everything about this moment felt ethereal.

Travis gave me the control, he let me set the pace. He was

gentle and thorough, even as we moved frantically against each other.

With Richie, I never had an orgasm. Often times, he was too lazy for foreplay. I was never ready for him like I'd been ready for Travis, and that was just with one look. The kissing...that had been foreplay in itself.

My orgasm came hard and fast, and I'll never forget the look on Travis's face when I trembled around him. His brows furrowed and his eyes drank in the sight of my pleasure, the feel of it. He kept moving my hips, driving into me several more times before he found his release. He shuddered, pulsing inside of me.

His eyes were wide with wonderment, and he was looking at me in a way he never had before. He tenderly brought his hand up to cup my cheek. As his thumb brushed across my swollen lips, I drew in a heavy breath.

Everything about that moment scared me. The look in his eyes, the tenderness of his touch, the *feelings* being with him that way had brought up...it was all too much.

I moved off him and laid against the mattress, tugging my robe together. I tried not to look at his heavy cock as he removed the condom and tossed it into the waste basket beside the bed.

Travis let out a sigh of contentment and rolled over to face me. His peaceful expression changed when he looked at me. "Hey, what's wrong?" he asked, his brow creasing with concern. His hand came up to cup my face once again and his green eyes peered intently into mine.

"Nothing's wrong," I told him. "I'm just...that was..." I trailed off, unable to complete my train of thought. My body was still tremoring with little shocks of pleasure. I never knew that sex could be like that. Had I known, I wouldn't have ever gone down this path with him.

It would only lead to my self-destruction.

For some stupid reason, this revelation depressed me. I could feel the tears brimming, but I held them back. I'd wanted this, and Travis had delivered. I tried to control my breathing the way my therapist had instructed. *Breathe in, breathe out. Breathe in, breathe out.* I'd had many therapists over the year to help me deal with my varying levels of trauma, and they all had similar methods of coping with the crippling panic that would hit me at odd moments.

"I know," he grinned, buying my excuse. He pulled me to him so that my head rested against his shoulder and my breasts settled against his rib cage. I could feel his heart pounding beneath the palm of my hand. "That was incredible, Becs. You're so stunning."

Then he kissed me. His lips were slow and gentle on mine, igniting more embers of desire but working to soothe me at the same time.

His actions confused me. *None* of this felt like a one-night stand. I'd seen enough movies and read enough books to know that they were supposed to be quick and dirty. Once the deed was done, they'd part ways. No emotion, no conversations. That's what I'd expected from tonight, and the fact that I wasn't getting it made me feel completely out of control.

I broke away from the kiss, tugging my robe back on as I practically jumped out of the bed.

"Whoa, where's the fire?" he chuckled, still gloriously naked.

"Thank you for tonight," I said, my mind made up. "I'd appreciate it if you could keep this between the two of us," I added as I started to walk toward the bathroom. I wanted to get dressed and go home, where I could fall apart in peace.

"Wait just a minute," Travis demanded. He was tugging on his jeans as I froze, my hand on the handle of the bathroom door. "Can't we just talk about this?"

"It was a one-night stand, Travis," I said tiredly.

"I know that," he argued, his brow furrowed. I couldn't tell if he was confused or hurt, or both. "But our night's not over yet, is it?"

"I have to get home," I told him, crossing my arms as he walked over to me.

"Neither one of us is leaving until we talk about this," he insisted. Although he was close, he was careful to not invade my space or corner me. He gently took my hands, holding them in his as he looked into my eyes. "I can tell you're freaked out, and I get it—I *expected* it Becky. I wasn't going to come in here, fuck you and leave you, and honestly I'm insulted you thought I was that kind of person."

I gaped at him. I had no response. "I wasn't counting on you caring."

I hadn't meant to speak the words out loud, but they tumbled from my lips without consent, coaxed out by the devout look in his eyes.

"Of course I care," he told me, shaking his head like he couldn't believe I thought otherwise. "I told you that the other night. I care about you, I always have. Brock is the brother I never had, and you are—"

"Don't you dare say like a sister," I scowled, pushing away from him as my eyes narrowed. His lips twitched with a repressed smile.

"I can honestly say I've never looked at you like that," he confessed.

"Because you never looked at me?" I challenged. I don't know why I was standing there, talking to him like this when I should have been dressing and getting the hell out of Dodge, but this conversation intrigued me.

Maybe because I'd always been aware of him. How could I not be? Even before the fame, Travis was irresistible. His charisma, his dimpled smile, and those hazel eyes that sparkled with mischief were known to entice every woman he encountered. In high school, he'd had washboard abs and a dimpled smile that made every girl in a forty-mile radius swoon. He was in even better shape now, and that fact didn't go unnoticed by me.

"Oh trust me, I've always looked at you," he told me, smirking. "But the point is; I care, you are my friend. So talk to me. What are you feeling?"

I hesitated, biting my lip. "Overwhelmed," I finally answered, almost sagging in exhaustion. I was tired of fighting my impulse to trust him. "I've never...it's never been like that for me."

"You've never got off?" Travis arched a brow, surprised.

I blushed, embarrassed. "Well, if I did...it wasn't like that."

He nodded, unable to hide his smug grin. "I won't lie, hearing that makes me feel good."

"I'll bet," I replied dryly. He stepped toward me again, his hands tugging my hips against him.

"That's not the only thing bothering you," he hedged, his eyes reading every raw emotion in mine. "We're friends, right?"

"...Yes..." I breathed.

"Do you trust me, Becky?" he asked thickly.

"I do," I replied, my answer easy and honest.

"Then tell me about it. Don't just repress it. Lean on someone else for a change," he said.

I pulled away from his embrace, walking back to the mattress. I sat down, drawing my robe closer to my body. "This is the first time I've been...intimate with someone since... Aiden's father."

Hearing this, Travis frowned as he sank down beside me. "You're not feeling guilty, are you?"

"No," I shook my head animatedly. "It's not that...it's just, I haven't let anyone touch me since then and you...well, you were so gentle and...I just. I didn't know it could be like that. It scared me."

"Why?" he questioned, his voice soft. He brushed a strand of hair out of my face, tucking it behind my ear.

"I don't want to get hurt again," I whispered, closing my eyes. I couldn't bear to see the pity in his.

When I finally did open my eyes, there was no pity; only tenderness and empathy. My heart wavered, along with my certainty and control.

"I will never hurt you. You don't have to worry about that, Becs," Travis assured me. "If you just want tonight, I understand, but I personally wouldn't mind doing that again," he continued, his eyes caressing me with sincerity. The charismatic, devil-may-care attitude was gone; he was open and sincere. It was a side to him I'd never seen, a startling opposite to his carefree nature.

"So, what...like a friends with benefits thing?" I asked dubiously.

"We don't have to define it, we can just hang out when I'm back and you're free. But yeah, basically friends with benefits," he shrugged, grinning. "I can't treat you like a one-night stand, Becs. You're a friend first, and I want to see you again. It could be fun, what do you say?"

The lump of emotion in my throat made it impossible to speak. My heart was pounding in my chest, *maybes* and *what ifs* cascading down on me like heavy raindrops.

"I don't know," I finally said when I found my voice. I stood up on trembling limbs, my heart thundering in my chest as I stared at him with confounded astonishment. I truly hadn't expected him to want more from me, which was why I'd approached him about this in the first place. I figured he'd be down for one night and content to go on his way, back to his life of concerts and tours and models. "What's in it for you?"

"I get to help you face your fear of intimacy, without the pressures of an actual relationship, *and* I get to have sex. Lots of it. With you," Travis winked playfully at me. "I'd say we both get something positive out of this arrangement."

"But you could have sex with any woman, why me?"

"You're real," he shrugged. "I don't have to worry about you selling what happens between us to the highest bidder, and you don't expect me to be any more than I am." His words were vulnerable and he seemed uncomfortable with his honesty.

I sank back down beside him, facing him, and chewed on my lower lip as I contemplated his words.

"Sex is a great stress reliever," he pointed out, waggling his eyebrows.

I stared at him for a few seconds, weighing the pros and cons as I fought off a smile. He was right; sex *was* a great stress reliever. While my mind was still whirling, my body was as relaxed as if I'd spent the day at the spa. The knots in my neck weren't bothering me for the first time in days. "If we do this, we're going to need ground rules."

"Like what kind of ground rules?" he asked cautiously, his lips twitching with amusement.

"Like..." I trailed off, contemplating. "Nobody can know, and you can't do boyfriend things."

"I'm going to need clarification on 'boyfriend things'. Technically speaking, *this* would be a thing that a boyfriend does..." Travis pointed out, moving closer to me. He kissed the side of my neck while his left hand drifted down my collarbone, parting my robe. His calloused fingers teased and taunted the peak of my nipple.

As good as it felt to have his fingers toying with my breast, I needed to regain control of the situation. In one fluid movement, I'd straddled him, my eyes locking on his.

"We meet up, we have sex, we go our separate ways and we don't tell anybody about it. You don't text me when you're gone, and aside from providing me with orgasms, you don't do nice things for me," I said urgently. Nice was bad, nice meant succumbing to feelings, and the next step after that was a place I definitely didn't want to go.

His cock had grown harder and harder with each demand I

made and he held my gaze with serious, unblinking eyes. "I think I can handle that," he murmured, kissing his way to my breast.

I PULLED into the driveway at just after two in the morning, feeling exhausted and satisfied. I was relaxed, and felt as if I could finally sleep for the first time in days.

As I turned off my engine, headlights pulled up behind me. I stepped out of the car, looking over in time to see Ezra Johnson jump from the cab of his truck.

"Hey, Becky," he said somberly, walking around to the passenger side. The calm, sated mood I'd been in evaporated when he opened the door and my brother practically fell out from the cab. Ezra caught him before his face hit the ground. I rushed over to help him carry Braden into the house.

Tessa was sleeping on the couch, her head nestled into Brock's lap. They both startled awake when Ezra, Braden, and I stumbled inside. I smashed my elbow off the corner of the wall, and swore under my breath.

Brock hurried over to help, and Tessa watched with wide eyes full of concern, her brow furrowed. With Brock on one side of Braden and Ezra on the other, they were able to get him downstairs to his bedroom. When they returned, the four of us stood wordlessly in the kitchen, the silence thick with thoughts we couldn't voice.

Braden was rushing down a dangerous, destructive path, and none of us knew how to stop him.

CHAPTER FOUR

 *ecky*

TWO WEEKS HAD PASSED, and I reflected upon that passage of time as I sat on the plush white sofa and gazed out of the office window. It overlooked the choppy waters of Georgian Bay, and the view was actually quite spectacular. My fingers ran against the threads, listening to the soothing sound of the aquarium behind me.

I'd already spent the last two sessions recounting Mom's passing, the wake, and the funeral. Today, I'd mentioned Travis. I didn't go into detail about what happened between us—I couldn't, I was still processing—but I'd had to tell someone and my paid therapist seemed like the safest bet.

"Why do you think the intimacy upset you so much?" she

asked, urging me to open the door to the past. She felt that we needed to get to the root of my intimacy issues.

"I met Richie when I was sixteen. He was the first boy to ever pay me a lick of attention. I'm not counting the way my brother's friends would treat me—like I was their little sister, an annoyance under foot. He was the first one to see me as more than Brock Miller's little sister, and to me—that was a huge deal."

"Why was it a huge deal?"

I pushed my hair out of my eyes as I considered the psychologist's question. "I guess I was desperate to feel loved, you know? My dad never—he never showed us affection or love. He was just angry all the time...angry and drunk. I think any girl who doesn't get positive attention from her father will seek it elsewhere eventually."

"That's a wise assessment," Dr. Rootham nodded in agreement, her copper bob bouncing along with her. "So, your brother kept you from making this mistake for a while. Then what happened?"

Dr. Rootham had been my psychologist for the last two years. I started seeing her weekly to help deal with the trauma I'd been through. Although I still wasn't completely comfortable speaking about my experiences, I knew that in order to heal I had to revisit these wounds.

This wasn't the first time that I had discussed this story, but each time I recounted it—I revealed more details and dealt with more realizations.

"Yeah, he kept the guys away I guess," I said, almost chuckling at the memory of my over-protective brother. "Brock wouldn't let me put myself in those situations, and any guy I was interested in...he managed to scare off simply by being my brother. When he wasn't around, his friends were. Richie was different because he wasn't a part of that circle, he didn't grow up with us, didn't go to our school and by the time we got together, my brother had already left to work in Alberta." I paused, reaching over to the coffee table to grab the bottle of water Dr. Rootham always supplied for me.

She gave me a gentle smile. Dr. Rootham moved to Parry Sound from Mississauga. She was very much a city dweller, and always seemed somewhat mystified by the strange customs in Northern Ontario, even after living here herself for the last several years. "What made Brock want to work in Alberta?"

"The distance?" I answered, lifting my right shoulder in a small shrug. "The money was good and I bet the distance felt great..." I trailed off, imagining what it must have felt like for Brock to break free of this town. "We'd always been that family, you know? The family everyone talks about. Brock dealt with a lot of discrimination from everybody in town—we all did, but he bared the brunt of it. Plus, he had to take care of Braden and me when Mom was working. He was our buffer; he would make sure that Dad would take his frustrations out on him instead of us."

Every time I confessed this, my heart squeezed painfully in my chest and my eyes welled up with tears. I couldn't imagine Aiden having the role that Brock had in our house growing up, although I understood why Brock did it. He was bigger than us, and in his eyes, that made him able to withstand it a little more.

Dr. Rootham nodded solemnly, looking to the pad of paper in front of her. She scrawled some notes, and I tried not to let that get to me. I hated that about psychologists, but I knew it was necessary. They couldn't possibly remember every anecdote a patient tells them without jotting notes down. I took a shaky breath, drawing bravo I didn't have.

"How did you and Richie meet?" she questioned.

"He moved to town the summer before I started grade eleven. He was a year older than me and I thought he was mysterious, with his dark hair and eyes, and I liked the fact that he wore a leather jacket, rode a motorcycle and lived in an apartment by himself. He would come to the grocery store where I worked and even if I had a huge line up, he'd wait in it. One of those times, he asked me out and I said yes. I liked the attention this stranger was lavishing on me, and I wanted to get to know him...I thought I found my happily ever after."

I didn't realize that I was crying until Dr. Rootham grabbed a tissue and held it out to me. The tears were the silent type, they trailed down my cheeks on their own accord. She encouraged me to go on with a gentle smile.

"He wooed me with fancy words and rides on the back of his bike. I fell hard and fast for him. I didn't question how he made his money, how he was able to stay home all the time and still afford his apartment and his bike, and when I finally did ask him—I believed him when he told me he lived off the inheritance his dad had left him."

"Why do you think you so readily believed him?"

"I should have known better, but at the time...it hadn't seemed that farfetched to me because I had an inheritance. I had a slice of land on the lake that had belonged to my paternal grandfather that I was set to inherit on my 21st birthday," I shrugged.

My paternal family had owned the majority of land around a small lake in the outskirts of Parry Sound for centuries, since they'd immigrated from Scotland in the early 1800s. Apart from giving us life, the land was the only other good thing to have come from our father, and technically—it'd come from our grandfather.

I closed my eyes for a moment, knowing that the hard part was coming up soon. I just had to get through it, and then I could press it all back, deep down inside where it belonged.

"Things with Richie were great at first, exciting even. He took me on all kinds of adventures on the back of his bike. The honeymoon stage of our relationship was short lived. I got pregnant a few weeks after we started seeing each other," I said, looking past Dr. Rootham and out the large window behind her desk. Her view overlooked the eastern shore of the sound. I tried to detach from the story I was telling.

"The pregnancy came as a shock to me. I'd thought we were being safe, we used condoms every single time, but condoms are effective 98% of the time. We must have landed in the 2%. I was too ashamed to tell my family, and I tried to keep it a secret. I had a falling out with my mom a week after I found out, and I used that as an excuse to move in with Richie. I figured it would be easier to hide the pregnancy until we had a solid game plan. I knew that then, I wouldn't feel so ashamed of myself."

"Why were you ashamed of yourself?" Dr. Rootham inquired gently, stirring me back to the present.

"Because I made the same mistake my mother did, I got pregnant young," I shrugged, smiling without humour. "Richie didn't want the baby, he wanted me to 'take care of it', but I couldn't do that. I dropped out of high school and took a correspondence course to get my GED while I worked at the grocery store. I thought that Richie just needed time to adjust to the idea of fatherhood, that he'd love the baby as much as I did when he held it in his arms."

I drew in air slowly, trying to strengthen my resolve. Revisiting these memories was hard, so I usually tried to avoid thinking about the past. It was too painful, too jagged. That wasn't to say that I had completely gotten over it—far from it. The scars of my past affected me even now, four years later. It seeped into my mornings, my afternoons, and any time I tried to get close to someone romantically.

Granted, I hadn't really *tried* to get close to anyone romantically. At least, not until Travis Channing.

Memories of the night that I'd spent with him two weeks ago washed over me, and I swallowed hard. I hadn't been prepared for the heady rush of emotions being with Travis would pull out of me. His gentle touches had been a stark contrast to the type of touch I was used to.

In that moment, he had made me want more, and that was dangerous.

The fear I'd felt that fateful night in that hotel room propelled me to dive deeper into my personal bank of horrors. I had to sift through the complicated mess of emotions somehow, had to make sense of my feelings, and that's what Dr. Rootham was there for.

I couldn't talk about this stuff to anyone else; my brothers definitely didn't want to hear about my intimacy issues, and with Mom gone, I'd never felt so alone. This loneliness prompted me to talk more than I ever had in any session before, and I know my therapist was pleased with this change.

"Richie lost his temper on occasion, but he'd mostly just rant and rave and break things. He'd always apologize afterwards, telling me that he didn't know how to handle his anger and he didn't mean it. I told myself he was just worried and stressed about the baby coming. Deep down, I knew that I should leave."

An ominous cloud had lingered over my head, but I was afraid. I was too stubborn to return home.

"Word had gotten back to my mom that I was pregnant, and I told her haughtily that we had everything sorted out and to not worry about us. I told her that Richie was ecstatic about the baby. I didn't want to admit that we didn't have anything figured out, that Richie hadn't even started looking for a real job, or that he resented the baby and me..." I swallowed, trailing off as I lost all my confidence.

"Why did you lie to your mother?"

"I was angry with her," I admitted, tears falling freely down my face now. "I didn't want to admit that I was just like her—too much of a coward to leave someone who was hurting me." I felt guilty for those feelings now that she was gone for good.

Dr. Rootham leaned forward, catching my eyes with her

warm brown ones. "You were not a coward, Becky. You were sixteen and scared."

I drew in a shaky breath, nodding. I didn't believe her, not really. Fear and age weren't good enough excuses for me. I couldn't look at her while I spoke, so I stared back out at the sound, watching the waves and the boats in the lake her office overlooked.

"The abuse didn't start until I was in my third trimester. There were signs before then, the resentment and the anger, but I ignored them because I was afraid to admit what they meant. Then he started calling me fat, telling me I was going to be a horrible mother. That's also when I noticed the drugs—streaks of cocaine on the coffee table, the shady people I would find hanging out with him in the apartment when I returned home from my shift at the grocery store. I discovered that Richie *didn't* have an inheritance at all; he scammed the welfare system and sold drugs."

"We started fighting more, with me trying to tell him to stop doing and selling drugs and stop inviting those kinds of people into our home. He'd tell me *"this is my home, not yours. You're lucky I even let you stay here, you nagging bitch."* The words were out of my mouth before I could stop them. "Sorry, doctor," I sighed, flushing. I hated swearing, but sometimes I got caught up in the memories; locked within them.

"It's alright," Dr. Rootham smiled with understanding, still pleased as punch about all I was revealing. "Did you ever try to leave, Becky?"

"Yes. I tried to leave a few times. I'd pack my bags and go to leave and he'd grab my arm, tears streaking down his face, and beg me to stay. He told me he wanted to stop doing drugs. He told me that it wasn't him when he was screaming and yelling, it was the cocaine. He said he needed my help, and that he wanted to be a part of the baby's life. He promised to do better. I bought those lies two times. The third time, I told him nothing he could say would change my mind."

"What happened then?"

"I went to leave, for good this time," I answered, forcing myself to pull my eyes away from the picturesque window and the breathtaking autumn colours. This story was far too bleak for such beauty. I'd finally reached the point where crawling back to my mom was preferable to staying with him.

I'd finally opened my eyes and realized that I had it *good* with her and Braden, and I'd been punishing her for years for a situation that I'd found myself in; I was tethered to an abusive user.

The thing I remembered most about that day was the rage in his eyes before his fist came down and shattered my cheekbone. I'd crumpled like a rag doll, but he didn't stop his quest to break me. He kicked me in the back and in the ribs over and over again, as he told me I was worthless and the worst mistake of his life. His heavy boots with the steal toe drove each point home. I cried, pleading with him to stop, my arms wrapped around my pregnant belly. I tried to pull myself up, shaking and crying and begging him. He stomped on my wrist, the sickening crunch and the blinding pain had made me black out.

I didn't speak as the memories washed over me, stealing my breath and filling my lungs with pain—almost like drowning, but without the water.

I still heard his voice in my head, and relived it in my nightmares.

Rubbing at my right wrist—the same wrist that Richie had broken, I looked down at the faint scars from where the doctors had drilled pins to set it. Sometimes, it would ache and throb, reminding me about the past I couldn't seem to escape.

"I thought we would die that night. Miraculously, we didn't. He left after breaking my wrist, likely to go to the bar or one of his druggie friend's houses."

"The pain was so severe that I faded in and out of

consciousness. I hurt *everywhere*, my eye was swollen shut and my wrist was dangling at an odd angle, throbbing every time I tried to move. I knew it was broken, but the worst part was my stomach. It felt like the muscles were ripping. I knew something was wrong with the baby." My voice didn't sound like my own. It sounded foreign and far away, like I really was drowning.

"Sobbing, I'd dragged myself across the floor, to my phone on the coffee table. I dialed home, trying to fight the darkness. My relationship with my mother was still wrought with tension, and I never made social calls—but she was who I called in that moment. I begged her to come to me before passing out again."

After the phone call, my mother showed up at the apartment with my little brother. I came to, seeing their tear streaked faces as they crouched before me. Between the two of them, they were able to get me into the car and drive me to the hospital. From there, they had to transfer me by helicopter to Mount Sinai in Toronto, as the Parry Sound hospital wasn't equipped to handle babies born before 35 weeks. There wasn't time to talk to the police or to press charges; not when my body felt like it was going to snap in half, and not when the hospital staff was more concerned with saving my son's life and getting me treated."

I stopped talking again, letting the memory of my son's birth envelop me. Aiden Miller was born at 31 weeks. He weighed 3 ½ pounds, less than a bag of sugar, and was only sixteen inches long. He was hooked up to heart rate monitors and a CPAP machine that helped him breathe. He had been born with fluid on the lungs, likely due to swallowing so much amniotic fluid when I was in labor.

"The doctors did their best to patch me up; I'd escaped with a broken wrist and cheekbone, and three of my ribs were badly bruised. I hurt everywhere, but the worst pain I felt came from my heart. I'd nearly lost my son, and he was still in critical condition. He was so tiny, so helpless."

"Where was your family during all of this?"

"They were watching over me, keeping a vigil in the waiting room. Any time I left the NICU—which wasn't very often and only to use the washroom—they'd be there, ready to force me to eat and take a break. Braden had even called Brock. He'd been at work, but he flew back immediately."

When he came in to meet his nephew, he had vibrated with anger at the sight of us both.

"My family didn't know exactly what happened to me, but they had a sneaking suspicion that it was Richie's fault. After all, we'd grown up with an abusive father. We knew what it looked like, what it felt like."

"You sound ashamed," Dr. Rootham assessed, the corners of her lips drawn downward in a slight frown.

I nodded. I remember being unable to meet any of their eyes. I was so ashamed that I'd ended up with someone *so much* like the devil we'd grown up with, so ashamed that I had put my own child in danger because I'd been too afraid to leave when I should have. I felt weak and stupid.

"I felt like my mother, and while I loved my mother...I also hated her for staying with him, for keeping that monster in our home for so long. If he hadn't died, there was no way of telling if she ever would have left. Then I did the unspeakable...I'd let the monster remain in my child's life too, until it was almost too late...until he had almost died. I failed to protect my baby."

There was no greater shame than that, and the guilt of it nearly consumed me to this very day.

"I remember laying my head against his incubator, my shoulders shaking as I cried. The movement was excruciating for my ribs, but I didn't care. I deserved the pain. Then I met Christina."

"Christina?" Dr. Rootham asked, her pen gliding across the page as she jotted the name down.

"Over the eight weeks that Aiden was in the NICU, Christina was our primary day nurse. She was the nurse to first place Aiden in my arms, a few days after his birth. She was forever patient and gentle, and she didn't let me stew in grief or guilt. That woman is the reason why I went into nursing," I explained, smiling at the thought of the friendly nurse who saw me through one of the darkest times of my life.

"It sounds like she helped you," Dr. Rootham noted, her eyes fixated on me.

"She did," I nodded. "She wanted me to talk to the hospital psychiatrist. My patient file had been referred to Dr. Kennedy as the nurse on the maternity ward thought I was at risk because of the trauma, my age, and the fact that my son was born nine weeks early. She was also the one to set me up with a room in the Ronald McDonald House for five weeks, since I lived over two hours away and wouldn't be able to drive myself to the hospital once they discharged me."

"You've spoken before about your hesitance to seek psychiatric help," Dr. Rootham pointed out. "Why were you so against it?"

"I was a mess," I added, shaking my head. "Given the emotional traumas I'd been through, the fact that I'd just given birth and my hormones were completely messed up, *and* the fact that my older brother was sitting in jail—I was a complete mess. But I hadn't been able to talk to Dr. Kennedy about it. I was afraid that more people would get hurt with my words."

Dr. Rootham furrowed her brow in confusion. I knew I was shoving a lot at her, and I gave her an apologetic smile. In our previous sessions, I hadn't mentioned Brock's stint in jail. I mostly discussed my grief over Mom dying, and how my anti-depressants were making me feel.

"After seeing me and Aiden, Brock went straight to the apartment. Richie was there, and he beat the ever living hell out of him. He inflicted as much pain on Richie, as Richie had on me—broke a few of his ribs, his wrist, and went one further by breaking his jaw. It was a crime of passion, I guess. Brock was sick of watching people hurt me, hurt *us*. He'd always been tough, but he was never violent. He went to jail because of me. He spent two years locked behind bars, and when he came out… he was different."

"How so?" Dr. Rootham asked gently.

"He stayed away," I replied, my heart aching. I still felt like it was my fault, and I worried that he blamed me. "For years, he kept his distance. He took a job far away from home, and he'd send us money and occasionally talk to us on the phone…but he didn't come back to Parry Sound until Mom was dying."

"But, you said he was planning on staying now," Dr. Rootham pointed out with a small smile.

"I guess he is," I replied. "He built a cabin, he's seeing someone in town. He's happy—and I'm happy for him. She's a really great girl."

"I sense a but…" Dr. Rootham ventured.

"There's no but," I replied honestly. "I just…I guess I sometimes wish it could be that easy for me. I wish I could fall in love." The revelation escaped my lips before I could stop it, and I inhaled deeply. The problem wasn't that I couldn't fall in love, the problem was that I *wouldn't* let myself.

"Why can't you?" My psychologist actually sounded surprised.

"I vowed that I would never put myself—or Aiden—in that position again," I answered, somber. "That kind of love breaks you."

I purposely avoided thinking about hazel eyes and blond hair. I wouldn't allow myself to get sucked into another realm of *maybes* and *what ifs*. Even if my thoughts had no trouble circling back to Travis on their own.

"I don't think that's necessarily true, Becky," she said, her eyes gently assessing me. "It's normal, and understandable, to feel hesitant, but I wouldn't close yourself off to the possibility of something real just because of your past experiences. Not every man will hurt you."

I said nothing. I didn't believe Travis would ever physically harm me, but I didn't expect to feel what I felt in that hotel room. It unnerved me, it wasn't simple like I'd hoped, and I resolved that it was done between us. It had to be. There could be no more Travis and me, not in any sense. He had to be my brother's best friend again, and I had to be his best friend's sister.

Dr. Rootham's timer buzzed on her desk, and she sent me an apologetic look. "We've made a lot of progress today, Becky, but I'm afraid we're out of time."

"I understand," I stood up, bringing my purse with me. "Same time next week?"

"Absolutely. Take care of yourself Becky—and please remember, you are not a coward. You've been through so much and you're still standing. Try to be a little more forgiving and be kinder to yourself."

"I'll try," I replied, knowing that she was right.

Four years ago, I picked up the shattered pieces of my heart and spirit and vowed to get better by any means necessary. In the early stages of my recovery, that meant telling Dr. Kennedy about my childhood and my time with Richie and taking the anti-depressants she prescribed to help me cope with my post-traumatic stress disorder. Now, it meant therapy sessions with Dr. Rootham, just to keep my issues at bay, and it meant keeping romantic love the hell away from me.

I was too fragile for love.

I would only break.

CHAPTER FIVE

ravis

OCTOBER 2013

I WAS ALMOST FINISHED RECORDING the final track for my upcoming album I'd been working on for the past three months. My last visit to Parry Sound had been incredible for my creative flow. I'd had a lot of good times with my old friends which got my creative juices flowing. There was nothing like being back home, especially when the entire gang was there, including Brock.

It was the first time I'd seen him in years. Brock had avoided Parry Sound since his release. We were both infamous in this town; we couldn't go anywhere without people noticing us. Our stories were known by everyone, but the community's perception of me was pride and awe, while their perception of Brock was judgement and contempt.

When he left, things didn't feel the same. With him back, it almost felt like the good old days. It brought back a lot of memories, memories that definitely helped craft the fun in the final three songs I'd written for the album.

Then there was the inspiration Becky Miller had left in me. It lingered, this creative high that I felt whenever I thought about her.

That night had surpassed my expectations. I hadn't anticipated things to feel so intense with her. I hadn't counted on feeling a connection as strong as the one I felt with her. I'd had sex with plenty of women before, only I could honestly say that with Becky, it was different.

Her scars ran deeper than I could have even imagined. The ache and vulnerability in her sky-coloured eyes had told me everything, even though she said little.

She shared a few morsels of information with me before ultimately deciding that serious conversations were off the table for us. I followed her lead, because I wanted to keep the smile on her face...and I was captivated by the way she looked when she felt free.

After that night together, my mind refused to quit, inspiration was running through my veins. I grabbed my notebook and my acoustic guitar and took a walk down to the docks, where I sat with my legs dangling off the end of the dock and played for hours, pausing only to write down lyrics and musical notes. I worked until the sun rose high over the lake and the blisters on my fingers bled.

I hadn't composed like that in months, and it birthed one hell of a single to complete the album.

In the studio, I played my last guitar riff and crooned the final vocals on one of my favourite new songs, *Back Forty*.

My producer, Rick O'Malley, gave me a standing ovation. "That's a wrap!" he announced excitedly, tossing a look at my personal assistant. "We'll put the finishing touches on it, and in the meantime...get some rest! Tour starts in a couple of weeks!"

"Great!" I said, forcing a smile and ignoring the strange feeling pressing down in my chest. The usual excitement that typically came with a tour was vacant. Instead, I felt a little homesick.

The tour was kicking off in November. If I was lucky, I'd get to fly home for Christmas, then it'd be straight back to the tour bus. My next real break wouldn't come again until the summer, which I'd always insisted were mine.

The next two weeks were also mine for the taking, and I knew I wanted to spend them at home. It had been a grueling three months with long hours spent in the studio recording, but I was proud of the album. I was excited for it, but in all that time...I hadn't forgotten Becky.

Images of her bathed in the hotel light constantly played in my mind's eye. I couldn't wait to get home.

I didn't know what would come of this visit, but I knew I had to see her again.

Placing my trusted guitar back in its case, I prepared to leave. My personal assistant, Barbara, was waiting for me in the hallway.

Barbara was a pure southern belle with strawberry blonde hair, brown eyes and her debutant beauty. There was a time when I lusted over her double Ds, but now...the only woman I thought about was back home, constantly on my mind.

"Your flight leaves in an hour," Barbara told me before relaying a few messages and going over the upcoming week's schedule. "Your return flight leaves two weeks from today, and you'll hit Nashville just in time to board the bus. I've emailed you the itinerary."

"Thanks," I said, flashing her a flirty grin. Even if I wasn't feeling like my usual self, it was still easy to flirt. I wore my charm like a mask.

"Your bags are in the trunk of the car and Rob is waiting for you out front," Barbara added, her eyes raking over my chest and arms. She drew in her bottom lip, gently biting down on it. A couple months ago, I'd be having a hard time keeping my dick from jumping at the sight of her looking at me like that, but no lust stirred within me. It was all reserved for that dark haired, blue eyed beauty.

Besides, I'd learned a very hard lesson after sleeping with my last personal assistant. Don't mix work with pleasure.

"Thanks," I said before walking around her.

I SLEPT for most of the two hour flight, pulling my baseball cap down over my eyes. There weren't many people on the plane, but the airport was jammed with travelers. I made it through customs and was waiting for my baggage when an eager fan spotted me.

"Oh my God, it's Travis Channing!" she squealed, practically diving at me. My bodyguard, Rob, stepped in front of her before she could make contact with me.

"That's close enough, Miss," he warned, keeping his voice respectful yet assertive. Rob looked like a guy even I wouldn't want to fuck with, but the girl was young—maybe sixteen.

She flushed a deep shade of crimson, stuttering her apology out with wide eyes. I stepped around Rob and held my hand out, flashing her a smile that I knew would dazzle her. "What's your name?"

"Natalie," she practically whispered, her eyes widening. "I didn't mean to run at you like a maniac, but my sister is your number one fan and she would be so happy if she got to meet you."

"Take me to her," I said, grinning. Rob frowned and made a

move to follow us. I held my hand up to stop him. "Grab my bag when it comes around, eh man?"

The girl, Natalie, lead me over to where the rest of her family was waiting. "This is my mom, my dad, and that's Alexis. She's your biggest fan, her entire room is like a Travis Channing shrine. She has a 6 foot cardboard cut-out of you!"

Alexis grinned up at me from her purple wheelchair with an ecstatic smile and reached out to me with shaky hands. She looked to be about fourteen or fifteen years old. "Travis Channing!" she said, working hard to pronounce each syllable in my name through her excitement.

"Hello darling," I grinned at her, reaching out to grasp her hand in a gentle shake. "It's a pleasure to meet my biggest fan!"

Alexis screeched with excitement, putting her hands to her cheeks in awe.

"Maybe we could get a picture of you two together?" Natalie asked timidly, holding her cellphone up.

"Sure!" I crouched so that I was level with Alexis and smiled like an idiot while Natalie took a few pictures. Alexis's happiness was contagious, and I couldn't help but feel humbled that I had brought so much joy to this girl's day, simply by being at the same airport as her at the same time.

"It was really great meeting you Alexis," I told her, smiling warmly.

"Nice to meet you too!" Alexis responded slowly, her eyes sparkling. I stood up and fished a card from my wallet, turning to offer it to the girls' parents. Their father was holding their mother in his arms, and both of them were looking on with expressions full of love for their daughters and this moment. "Call this number and I'll hook you up with free backstage passes for any concert on my upcoming tour."

"Thank you," the mother said, a tear escaping down her cheek. "You have no idea how much this means to Alexis. She's been a fan of your music for years now, it's helped her through some hard times."

"My pleasure! Your daughters are wonderful," I replied honestly, watching as Natalie showed the photos she'd taken to Alexis with an indulgent, loving smile on her face. Giving this family VIP passes was the least I could do.

I said goodbye to Alexis and Natalie and started walking toward the parking lot, pausing only to send a quick text message to Barbara about the family and the backstage passes. "You know, you don't have to follow me everywhere all the time," I pointed out to Rob, catching him in my peripheral intimidating folks left right and centre. "Isn't there somewhere else you'd rather be?"

"I love coming out to rural Northern Ontario," Rob replied dryly, arching his bushy brow at me. Born and raised in Arizona, Rob found weather in Canada to be too humid. The man's dry sense of humour about it always made me chuckle. He was close to twenty years older than me, but he didn't look a day over thirty.

He'd been on my security team for five years, but Rob still wasn't forthcoming about himself. It wouldn't have surprised me if he had been a Navy SEAL at one point. He was intimidating as all hell and he could cut a man down with one steely look. Even the paparazzi would give him a wide berth when he was by my side.

"Well you don't have to come to Parry Sound with me," I reminded him. "You could rent a hotel room and spend your days in the strip club. Or borrow a boat and go fishing on the lake. Do you know how to drive a boat? You probably do. Necessary knowledge for a SEAL, right?" I quipped.

"I know how to drive a boat," Rob grumbled darkly.

An autumn blanket had fallen over Lake Rosseau. The trees that lined the water's edge were bathed in rustic paint, and the air had a crisp bite to it. Winter always came quickly up North, and I knew it was only a matter of weeks before it started to snow.

I made a mental note to remind Grady to tend to the driveway and road. During the winter months, my buddy relied on his snow removal company to earn an income, and I hired him every year to make sure that the cottage was accessible for my mom.

Walking through the front door, I was greeted to the scent of Mom's homemade spaghetti. My mouth watered, and my stomach growled.

"Travis!" Mom gave me a quick hug, standing on her tippy toes to kiss my cheek. She barely came up past my sternum. My charming smile wasn't the only thing I inherited from my sperm donor. "I'm so glad you could make it home before the tour started!"

"Me too," I told her, giving her a tight squeeze before releasing her. "Is there enough spaghetti for Rob? I told him he could stay in the guest house this time. Makes sense, if he intends on following me everywhere."

"I'll be staying at a hotel," Rob corrected, shaking his head with exasperation.

"Well, join us for dinner at least," Mom decided, gesturing to the kitchen. "Come on in, make yourself at home."

My mom and Rob were around the same age, and I figured if I kept tossing them together, they'd hit it off, and maybe he'd be distracted enough to leave me alone for a bit. So far, both of them remained impervious to my feeble match-making attempts.

I pulled my phone out of my pocket before I sat down at the kitchen table. Unlocking it, I pulled up Grady's number and sent him a text, asking if the guys were still planning on meeting up for wings and beers. It had felt like ages since I'd seen every-one, and I needed the distraction—otherwise, I'd show up on Becky's doorstep, and I knew that wasn't a well thought out plan. I needed to give it a day or so, just so I didn't seem too eager.

"Put your phone away," Mom scolded, setting a heaping plate of spaghetti down in front of me. "You know I don't like them at the table."

"Sorry Ma," I apologized, slipping it back into my jeans. "Just following up on some work stuff," I added, not wanting Rob to know and tag along.

I wouldn't have been able to get away with a stunt like this in Nashville, but Rob was a little less intense about me going places alone when we were in Parry Sound when it wasn't tourist season. I still didn't want to take the chance that he'd shadow me.

My mom's nose twitched, a small indicator that she knew I wasn't being honest. Luckily for me, she wouldn't call me out on it in front of guests. To her, Rob was still a guest—probably because he was stiff and formal, and had never once taken us up on the offer to stay in the guest house. He'd drive fifteen minutes to the nearest dive motel and sleep there—which I was counting on tonight.

I made it through dinner, and waited until Rob left before kissing my mom on the cheek. "Leaving so soon?" she asked.

"I'll be back later tonight, Ma," I answered, shoving my arms through my coat sleeves. "I need to blow off some steam." Whether I was in Nashville or on tour, I rarely had a moment to myself. I was always shadowed by someone from the label, be it Rob or Barbara. It was nice to shake everybody off for a little while, to get back to my roots and remember who I was before the fame.

Humble beginnings and what not.

"Alright. Have fun and be safe."

I headed out to the garage and jumped into my truck. As I drove into town, my hands tapped against the steering wheel in time to the music pumping out of my speakers.

Gordon, Grady, and Brock's trucks were all parked in the small lot in between Flanigan's and the hardware store. I parked and hopped out, tugging up the collar of my brown leather jacket to ward off October's chill.

The heavy wood door swung shut behind me as my eyes scanned the old bar. The hardwood floors had seen better days, and the lighting sucked—but it was still the best place to go for brews in town. The wings were good too, and it was blissfully quiet. During the summer months, it was packed with locals and tourists alike, but aside from the six people sitting at the bar, a few people shooting pool, and a couple of occupied tables —Flanigan's was almost empty.

I spotted the guys sitting at a booth to the left of the bar, near the pool tables. Surprise shot across Brock's face when he looked up and saw me making my way over. "Speak of the devil!" he said with a grin that didn't quite reach his eyes.

Dread rendered me frozen for a moment, and I had a panicked thought that somehow, Brock had found out about me and Becky. I didn't relax until Gordon spoke up to clarify.

"Heard you were spotted in Toronto earlier. I figured you'd be bringing your ugly mug back around soon," Gordon ribbed, moving over to make room for me.

"How long are you back for?" Grady asked as I slid into the booth across from him.

"Just two weeks, then I'm on tour until July," I answered tiredly. Jet lag was hitting me, but I knew I'd get my second wind in due time.

"Lifestyles of the rich and the famous," Gordon smirked.

"Whatever, Gordon," I snorted, glancing around for the old bartender, Mick. I was thirsty, and a beer would wake me up a little. I grinned when I saw that he was already on his way over with a tray of beers in his hand.

"If it isn't our resident celebrity," Mick exclaimed, setting a beer down in front of me.

"How's my favourite barmaid doing?" I shot back with a smile. "Still as gorgeous as ever."

"It's the red meat diet I've been on for the last seventy years," Mick responded with a humorous grin. "Let me know if I can get you fellows anything else."

"We're good," Brock said. Something in his voice had me turning my head to look at him. He appeared exhausted and tense, but he wasn't looking at me. I followed his gaze as it went over to the bar. Braden sat at one of the stools, hunched over an amber glass, not paying attention to anything happening around him. The tension left my shoulders when I realized that Brock's mood had little to do with me and everything to do with his younger brother.

"How's he doing?" I asked as Mick walked off, gesturing to Braden with a slight tilt of my head.

"Still drinking his face off every night, causing a shit ton of trouble for Mick," Brock sighed, scratching at his jaw. "I don't know what to do with him."

"I told you, kick his fucking ass," Gordon chirped from beside me. "That's what I'd do if Tommy ever pulled that shit."

"Not every problem can be solved by your fists," Grady supplied with a frown. He clapped Brock on the shoulder in a show of solidarity. "I think it's gotta be up to him."

My thoughts circled round to Becky, and I wondered how she was doing with all this. I'd known that Braden hadn't handled the death of their mother very well, I'd seen as much the last time I was down, but I figured he would have come out of it by now.

"How's Becky handling things?" I asked, hoping my voice sounded causal enough not to draw attention to my interest in his answer. Luckily, Brock was distracted with watching his brother.

"She's doing alright for the most part. She's still in school full-time, and she graduates from her nursing program in April. She misses Mom and it's hard for her to see Braden this way, but she's not giving up...which is good."

We all watched as Braden tossed back his drink and brought the empty glass down heavily against the bar. "Another round," he barked at Mick. The old bartender watched him while he continued drying the glass in his hands.

"I think you've had enough, son," he finally responded with an air of authority and quiet disappointment.

"The fuck I have, I'm a paying customer and I want more fucking whiskey," Braden retorted angrily.

Mick arched his white wispy brows. He set the clean glass he'd been drying down on the shelf beneath the bar and tossed the towel over his shoulder. "Paying customers still get cut off when they've had too much."

"You're not the judge of that, I am!" Braden said, as he shoved the glass toward Mick a little too roughly, and it fell off the edge of the bar top, shattering against the ground.

Brock stood up warily, cracking his neck. He said nothing as he made his way over to the bar where Braden was still belligerently arguing with Mick.

Gordon, Grady and I all exchanged a look. I got the impression from the lack of surprise on their faces that this was a regular occurrence. We stood up and crossed over to the bar, ready to assist Brock if need be.

"What the fuck do you want?" Braden slurred, scowling at Brock from where he stood beside him.

"Time to go home," Brock said warily, grabbing Braden's arm to try and guide him out of the stool.

"Fuck off," Braden shot back loudly. He yanked his arm free and lost his balance, falling sideways off of the stool to the ground by my feet. He didn't get up, and a second later he began to snore loudly.

"For fucks sakes, Braden," Brock huffed, irritation and concern lining his features as he crouched to check the damage. Braden had a small cut on the bottom of his chin from when he'd hit it on the bar stool coming down, but seemed to be okay otherwise.

I helped hoist Braden up, tossing his arm across my shoulders while Brock took his other arm. Braden was like a dead weight between us. He came too, his head rolling as his eyes searched through the spins to lock on his brother.

"Sorry," he said, shuddering as he closed his eyes.

Every person in the bar was watching as we moved toward the door, and I could feel their judgement. It wasn't directed at me, but at the Millers.

Anybody else in this town could get piss drunk and fall off a bar stool and not get judged for it. They'd probably get a pat on the back and a few chuckles. If a Miller did it...the whispers and the stares were full of contempt.

The townsfolk had always seen the Millers as hellions. It went back to their old man, Brett. He'd been the town drunk, and in his younger days had gotten into a hell of a lot of trouble. It wasn't fair that they couldn't get out from under his shadow, that their every action in this town was watched and scrutinized.

"Oh, like none of you fuckers have gotten too shitfaced before?" Gordon barked at the patrons staring at the show, just as pissed off with the stares and pointed hushed conversations as I was, only more adept to show it. "You drank so much that you pissed your pants last week, Carl!" he added to one of the middle aged men sitting at the bar casting looks of contempt toward Braden. Carl Hanson flushed and looked away, and I grinned with pride.

I used to run my mouth like that; I used to speak whatever

was on my mind, but too many times before, something I'd said would get taken out of context and then blasted all over the Internet. Gordon could poke fun all he wanted at my profession of choice, but at least he could give someone shit without it blowing back in his face.

Gordon tossed some bills down to cover our tab as Grady held the door open for Brock and me. We practically had to drag Braden through, and out to Brock's truck.

Between the three of us, we managed to get Braden in, although he immediately laid down in the back seat and started to snore.

"Mick said he can't leave his truck here again or it'll get towed," Gordon reported, running a hand through his dirty blond hair. "Maybe you should let it get towed. Might teach him a lesson."

"That truck belonged to our grandpa, I'm not letting it get towed," Brock sighed, sounding torn.

"I can drive it back to the house," I suggested. The situation wasn't the greatest, and I knew it wouldn't result in me getting lucky...but even still, the prospect of seeing Becky again had me perking up.

Brock looked at me for a moment, weighing his options. I knew if he could drive both his truck and Braden's truck home at the same time, he would. Brock hated getting help, he liked to be the one to handle everything himself. Sighing heavily, he patted down Braden's pockets to find the keys to his truck. He tossed them at me, and I caught them one-handed.

"Well, that was a fun night," Gordon said dryly. "I've gotta be at a client's house early tomorrow, so I'm going to have to take off. Are you guys good from here?"

"Yeah, we'll be fine."

CHAPTER SIX

IT WAS NEARLY MIDNIGHT, and I had classes in the morning. I should have been sleeping. Instead, I was pacing the length of the living room, glancing out the window every so often. Brock had called ten minutes ago to let me know that he was on his way home with Braden.

Brock was the one who Mick called when Braden caused trouble at the bar, and those calls had been happening more and more lately, especially with Elle in Barrie for school. She hadn't tried to talk to him after the night of the funeral, when he snapped at her at the reception, and I know it hurt him. I think he thought she'd keep coming around, keep fighting for him.

When Mom died, I'd been so worried about losing my brothers too. I thought Brock would surely go back to Alberta, if even just to escape for a while. I wouldn't have blamed him if he did, but he hadn't. He remained here, unwilling to leave with Braden the way he was, and I couldn't even be happy about it because our little brother was sinking quickly to rock bottom, if he wasn't there already.

I didn't know what was worse—the many nights I spent like this, waiting to open the door and get my alcoholic brother to his room without waking up Aiden, or the nights when he didn't come home at all.

The weight of this new reality was crushing me. I was exhausted, overwhelmed, and stressed out. It was hard seeing Braden like this, and it was hard not seeing him but knowing that he was still drowning his sorrows in a bottle every night.

Mom died three months ago now, but some days it felt as raw and painful as the day we'd lost her. Sometimes, I'd forget. I would come through the front door and go to call out to her, only to remember that she was gone.

Two sets of headlights shone brightly through the living room window as two trucks pulled up. I rushed to open the door, pulling the sweater I'd been wearing tighter around my body as I stepped out onto the porch.

Brock shut the door of his truck just as the door to Braden's Ranger opened. Travis stepped out, his eyes locking with mine for a moment as he stood between the open door and the truck, his muscular arm draped across the top of the door.

It was the first time I'd seen him since our night together in the hotel room, and the onslaught of memories made it hard to breathe.

"I'll take him inside, then give you a lift to your truck," Brock said over his shoulder, addressing Travis. Braden was standing, but barely, secured by Brock's iron grip.

I went to close the door, but Travis called out quietly. "Hey!"

Pausing, I looked over my shoulder. My brothers were just clearing the basement door, entering the stairwell that lead down to Braden's room. When I looked back, Travis was walking toward me.

His eyes didn't leave mine, a thousand unspoken words passing between us as he paused at the bottom of the stairs.

"You look really good, Becs," he said, a bemused smile on his face. The unspoken innuendo lingered heavily between us.

"So do you." I couldn't stop looking at him. My body remembered exactly what it was like to be with him, and those memories made me surge with desire for him again. An awareness grew between us, the energy changing.

It didn't help that he looked irresistible, and it had been a difficult, isolating few months.

I could use an escape, and I knew the one that Travis provided would be more than sufficient.

"I'm in town," he told me. "For two weeks."

"And?" I asked, folding my arms across my chest and watching as his hazel eyes tracked the movement. I tried to feign indifference, but my heart leapt at his suggestion. He wanted me, and it was exhilarating.

I was dressed in ratty pajama bottoms and a loose fitting sweatshirt, my dark hair piled up on top of my head in a messy bun, but Travis looked at me like I was standing naked before him, his for the taking.

That particular thought made me involuntarily clench my thighs together. His lips twitched up in a devilish smile, like he could sense my arousal from six feet away.

"And I hope I'll see you around," he clarified, running a hand through his dark blond curls.

I studied him, my eyes roaming from his Lucchese boots to his tapered waist. I drew in a shaky breath before continuing upward, pausing on his lips. I wanted so badly to feel them pressed against mine, if only for a little while.

"Maybe," I said, bringing my shoulder up in a delicate shrug. He moved toward me, but paused when he saw Brock approaching from over my shoulder.

"Braden's out cold," he announced, pausing beside me. "Thanks for helping out, man."

"No problem," Travis smiled, his eyes flicking back to mine when Brock turned to address me.

"I'll see you in the morning. Mind if I take Aiden back to my place? I need to get some things done around the cabin." I had classes and Brock had taken over helping me with daycare now that Tessa was in Barrie.

"Sure," I murmured, conscious of Travis's eyes still on me.

When they were gone, I locked up the front door and started turning lights out. Pausing by Aiden's bedroom door, I slowly opened it. Moonlight filtered in through his window, illuminating his skin in its pale glow. His lashes were dark against his cheeks, and his tiny chest rose and fell with each breath he took.

I counted every one of those breaths as personal blessings.

My socked feet were quiet against the floor as I crept over to kiss his cheek and adjust his blankets. I left the room wordlessly, crossing the hallway to mine.

I'd left my phone on the night stand, and I grabbed it before crawling under my blankets. I pulled Travis's contact information up, my finger hoovering near the little message icon. The last time I'd texted him had been to plan our last tryst.

Sighing, I put my phone back and rolled over.

AFTER CLASS THE NEXT DAY, I texted Brock to see how Aiden was doing. When he replied telling me that they were going out on the ATV, I stopped in to visit Katie Armstrong.

I tried to go over as often as I could, to hold the baby while she showered or just talk to her. I remember how isolating it had been having a newborn and no social life, and I didn't want Katie to feel that way, and I wanted to make amends for bailing out on her in the friend department when my mom was sick.

Plus, baby therapy was even better than psychological therapy for me. Before Alyssa, it had been three years since I'd held a newborn baby in my arms, and I loved all the little coos and gassy smiles.

I'd stopped off at the deli for sandwiches and coffee, and Katie nearly wept when she opened the door and spotted the paper bags with the deli logo. "I'm starving! How did you know?" she asked, standing aside to let me in. She had Alyssa cradled in her right arm as she nursed.

"Because I remember what breastfeeding was like," I laughed, walking into the living room and dropping my purse down on the plaid arm chair. I handed the turkey sandwich to Katie, who masterfully unwrapped it and started eating it with one hand. "Where's Ben?"

"At the farm," Katie answered in between bites. Her husband, Ben, helped run his family's farm, alongside his father, Bill. "Sometimes I think we should just move there."

"You knew what you were getting into when you married a farmer's eldest son," I pointed out.

"I know," she sighed. "Oh crap, she fell asleep again," she added, looking down at her daughter.

"Let me take her while you finish eating," I offered, holding my arms out. Katie gently passed her to me. She handed me the burp cloth and I threw it over my shoulder, bringing Alyssa up to gently pat her back. After she burped, I cradled her in my arms the way she liked and sat down on the sofa beside Katie. I got comfortable, knowing I'd be there for a while.

"You're a life saver," Katie moaned gratefully, pausing to take another bite. She chewed it and swallowed, and dabbed at the corner of her lips with a napkin. "I honestly don't know what I would do if I didn't have you around. You're a baby guru, and you bring food. I think I might love you more than Ben."

I laughed lightly, careful not to jostle the sleeping three-month-old in my arms. While Katie finished her sandwich, I gazed down at Alyssa, my mind still fixated on seeing Travis again last night.

The temptation to text him and meet up with him again was so strong, the only thing preventing me from actually going through with it was the baby in my arms and my exhausted friend sitting on the other side of the couch.

But all day long, I'd been consumed with the thought that maybe…Travis was *exactly* what I needed. I wasn't looking for a relationship, and I honestly didn't know if I'd ever be in the place for one. But I didn't want to be afraid of the act of intimacy any more.

Travis had offered to help rectify that issue, and I knew that if anybody could do it…it was him.

"I don't know whether to grab a shower, because I *definitely* need one, or break out the wine and have a serious girl chat—because I definitely need one of those too," Katie sighed, leaning back.

"Go shower, then we'll have girl time—minus the wine."

"Seriously, I really *do* love you more than Ben," Katie told me, skipping off to have her shower.

Alyssa snored peacefully in my arms, and the house was quiet except for the distant sound of running water and the ticking of a clock. With each second that passed, I grew more and more restless, more and more aware of the fact that my phone sat less than an arm's length away.

Just as I finally worked up the nerve to reach for it, the water shut off and I knew that Katie was finished with her shower. She didn't take long to dress, and within five minutes she was back in the living room, dressed in a new pair of sweat pants, her hair wrapped up in a bath towel.

"You have *no idea* how badly I needed that shower. God I hate the smell of sour milk," she shivered.

"How are you?" I asked, smiling warmly at my friend.

"Good, exhausted…but good. We've finally gotten the

hang of nursing, and she's sleeping five hour stretches through the night now," Katie answered. As if she understood that she was the topic of discussion, Alyssa stirred and started to whimper. "What about you? Did you give my suggestion any thought?"

"I'm not joining Tinder," I responded, my brow pinching together.

"You've just got to get back on the saddle. This time, we'll choose a good one," she remarked, nodding decisively.

Katie had been on a mission to get me to date again, especially lately. A lot of it probably had to do with how bored she was.

"What about a friends with benefits arrangement?" I remarked, trying to sound as nonchalant as I could.

"Wow, that came straight out of the left field," Katie said, her eyes widening as she stared at me. "Do you have one?" she added, her brows lifting in surprise.

"No," I shook my head. "I was just wondering what you thought about it."

"Friends with benefits can be a good thing..." she added, her tone considerate and cautious.

"I sense a 'but'."

"But it depends on the people involved, I guess," she shrugged. She looked at me again, this time with suspicion. "Do *you* want a friend with benefits?"

"Well...I'm thinking about it, anyway. The last thing in the world I want right now is a relationship. I don't have time, nor do I want that. But before I can even do that...I should practice being intimate with someone, right?"

"I guess that makes sense," she responded thoughtfully. "What does your therapist say?"

"My therapist is big on the whole 'open communication' thing," I said, making air quotations with my fingers as I spoke. "She's been telling me for years to start doing things for myself, and I don't know...I feel like this could be good for me? It'd definitely be for me, at least."

"Then give a go," Katie said, her hand reaching out to grasp mine. She gave me an encouraging smile, but the crease between her eyebrows told me that she was worried. "Just... listen to your intuition. I don't want to see you get hurt again."

"Me either," I confessed.

CHAPTER SEVEN

 *ecky*

JUNE 2017

WHEN MOM DIED, it felt as if the chapter had ended before a resolution could be reached. Unfinished, untethered.

For all of the years of hurt we each harbored, we'd only just begun to sift through the baggage and find peace with one another. I'd spent so much of my life angry at her for not leaving my dad. After what happened to me, I understood why she stayed a little better. But so many things had been left incomplete, and so much of our time together had been wasted.

It wasn't fair, and for months I carried that ugly feeling around with me like an anchor.

It didn't help that I had to watch as my little brother descended into his own personal hell, and I tried with feeble, fumbling hands to help him. So did Brock, but we couldn't face

Braden's demons on his behalf. He had to do it himself, and for a while there...I worried that nothing would bring him out of it.

Six months after Mom's death, six horrible months of watching my brother drink and rage, and I'd had enough. I told him that I couldn't have him around Aiden anymore. I told him that he was too much like our father, that unless he went to rehab and got sober...he wasn't welcome in my house.

It was one of the hardest things I've ever had to do, but it woke Braden up, and he was getting his life back on track. He'd been accepted into the mechanical engineering program at Algonquin College, and graduated top of his class.

He came back home last September, and was working at Chuck's Garage. He was doing well, although I still worried about him from time to time.

After graduating top of my nursing program three years ago in April, I'd landed a full-time position at the hospital, which was a godsend. It had been a challenge and a half to find sitters willing to put up with the odd hours of my school schedule and my old job as a cashier. With my new job, I was able to put Aiden in daycare during the summer months.

Brock had gone back to work once I'd graduated from college and once Braden seemed to be doing better. He couldn't live off his savings forever, so he went back to working one-month on and one-month off.

On this particular sticky late June evening, Aiden was camping with his uncles and Tessa, and I had needed to get out of the house. The walls were closing in on me so I texted Katie and asked her to meet me at Flanigan's.

We arrived early enough to snag one of the best booths, closest to the already occupied pool tables. Mick brought us a pitcher of beer and a plate of nachos to share while we waited for a pool table to free up.

"How's everything going?" I asked.

"Not good," Katie sighed, her shoulders slumping with

disappointment. "Still not pregnant. I don't get it…it was so easy to get pregnant with Alyssa. What am I doing wrong?"

"Maybe you're just stressing too much?" I shrugged helplessly. My heart went out to Katie. She and Ben had been trying to conceive for the last two years. They wanted to have a bunch of kids all close together in age, like the families they'd both come from.

"Maybe," Katie said, grabbing a nacho and popping it in her mouth. "What about you?"

"I'm fine," I shrugged. My thoughts went back to Travis. Soon, he'd be back for the summer, and our arrangement had to end. This summer wasn't like the previous summers. My older brother was getting married, and both Travis and I were in the wedding party. We'd be spending a lot of time together, and I was worried it would be just a matter of time before we were caught.

I didn't want Brock to find out about Travis and me. He wouldn't understand it, and he'd likely be livid at Travis. He'd assume that Travis was taking advantage of me and likely wouldn't believe that I'd been the one making the rules and drawing the lines.

"Are you bringing anybody special to the wedding? FWB perhaps?" Katie leaned forward, snagging another chip.

"No, I'm not bringing anybody to the wedding," I answered with a shrug.

"Will FWB be there anyway?" Katie pressed hopefully. I gave her a look, and she pouted. "I can't believe you won't tell me who it is. I'll figure it out, you know."

I laughed to cover my unease, hoping that she wouldn't figure it out. Katie had been relentlessly pushing me to move on and actually *date*. If not FWB, then someone else. Every year, she got more intense in her quest to convince me. Having a friend with benefits had only appeased her for a short while.

"It doesn't matter, I'm going to break things off with him anyway," I responded with a shrug.

"Why? Did you catch the feels?" Katie asked, her eyes sparkling with mirth.

For the last four years, she'd been my cover story.

"No, I didn't catch the feels," I responded, rolling my eyes. But even as I said it, I knew it wasn't exactly true. "We're both too busy, now."

Feelings—especially feelings of the romantic kind—unnerved me, so I wouldn't allow myself to think about them. But I'd be lying if I said my desire to call off the arrangement with Travis was *only* because of the wedding and not wanting to get caught.

Memories of that fateful night when I'd blatantly asked him to sleep with me rushed over me. Maybe my decision making skills, marred by grief, were questionable when I made the offer.

In truth, I hadn't believed he'd show up at the hotel room I'd booked us. I wasn't naïve enough to assume that Travis hadn't heard rumors of my broken life. He was a part of Brock's circle, he had to have known. He could have any girl he wanted, why would he want me, as broken and lost as I was?

But despite that, he did...and when I was with him, I didn't *feel* broken. I didn't hear the ghosts of my past. I just enjoyed being in the now with him, because ultimately I knew we'd both return to our separate lives. There was a security in that, and I clung to it. I knew what to expect.

I enjoyed the escape he offered.

And yet...I cared about him. I considered him a friend, which wasn't necessarily a bad thing. What was bad was just how much I looked forward to our summers together, to being with him. Not only was he skilled at reading my body and figuring out my needs before I could even voice them, but he was fun. He encouraged me to let my hair down a little, something my life of structure and routine was sorely lacking.

His life was such a stark contrast from mine; and I was drawn to it. It was like he was the sun and I was the earth, always striving to have his rays of warmth on me, never truly satisfied in its absence, in the darkness.

Those were feelings, and they were not a good sign. And recently, I'd started having dreams. I blamed the wedding—weddings were notorious for stirring up emotions better left sleeping.

I liked my life the way it was. I liked that it was just me, Aiden, my brothers—and Tessa, of course. I had a family that loved me, and a son that was my entire world.

Sometimes it got isolating and lonely, but not letting people in was preferable to accidentally opening the door for a monster.

Travis wasn't a monster; I knew that. He would never purposely harm a hair on my head, but he did carry the ability to wreck me in far more devastating ways than that. The dreams I'd been having as of late proved it.

"Well, *I* don't think it'd be a bad thing if you felt something for the dude you've been casually screwing for the last several years," Katie shrugged. She grabbed the last nacho off the plate and ate it.

I sent her a withering look much like the one I'd use on Aiden if he was getting smart with me.

"Don't do that, I recognize that look. I give it to Alyssa at least six times a day," Katie laughed. "I just want to see you happy, is that so wrong?"

"I am happy," I told her. "I like my job, I have an incredible kid, my brothers, Tessa, *you*. What more could I want?"

Katie said nothing, watching me with a sad smile. "Someone to share that with?" she finally said, shrugging.

I chose not to respond.

Her cell phone vibrated in her back pocket, and she pulled it out with a frown. "Hello? Seriously Ben? Alright. I'll be right home." She ended the call and sent me an apologetic look. "I'm sorry, I have to go...Alyssa is throwing up. Ben can handle a cow giving birth but he can't handle a little bit of kid puke." Katie rolled her eyes dramatically.

"That's alright, I'm tired anyway. I think I'm going to call it a night."

"God, I feel terrible," Katie exclaimed, her brows drawn together in regret. "You barely ever get out for a night on the town, and here I am leaving before nine."

"It's not like you're intentionally ditching me. Your daughter's sick," I said, standing. I gave her a reassuring smile.

She hugged me tightly before releasing me. "Keep an eye on my girl, Mick!" she instructed the old bartender.

"Will do," Mick nodded, drying out a beer glass behind the bar. Katie squeezed my hand again before leaving.

I wasn't quite ready to go home yet. I still hated going home to an empty house. It was too quiet, and I found the silence suffocating. Aiden wouldn't be home until tomorrow, and I'd officially run out of prospects to keep me entertained.

"Plenty of patrons here that wouldn't mind keeping you company," Mick said with a wink as he paused by the table with a tray full of empty glasses. He grabbed Katie's glass, his translucent eyes sparkling with mirth. I tried not to laugh as I looked around at the near-empty bar. The majority of customers were baby boomers, and a lot of them were fathers of old classmates.

"That's alright, I'm gonna play a quick game of pool and call it a night," I told him, noticing one of the pool tables had freed up. He nodded and made his way into the kitchen.

Reaching the pool table, I started to set up. I stroked the cue before driving it toward the ball with a steady hand. The tip hit it off the side, as I intended, and it ricocheted off the side of the pool table before it took another one of my balls right into the middle pocket.

My dad had taught me how to play—it was one of the only

things he'd taught me. He thought it would be funny to hustle people using his eight year old daughter. He earned a lot of his drinking money that way, for a while. Until I learned to make myself scarce.

After sinking the eight ball, I set the game up again. I lined up my shot, but before I could take it, the door swung open and Travis walked in. He paused, his eyes scanning the patrons until they landed on me. A dimpled smile broke out on his face, and he strode toward me purposely.

"Want some company?" he asked, grabbing a free cue.

For a moment, all I could do was stare at him and wonder if I'd conjured him up by wishful thinking. Shaking my head, I fought a smile. It was ridiculous how *light* he made me feel, simply by showing up.

"What are you doing here?" I asked.

"I called Brock to see if he wanted to meet for some brews, but he's camping with Aiden, Tessa, and Braden."

"Really?" I feigned shock, my lips twitching slightly at the giddy lightness in my chest. "So that's where they went."

"Funny girl," Travis said, his lips curling up in half a smile. His jawline was scruffy, and I wanted to reach out and touch it —to know what it felt like when it brushed against my inner thighs. The last time we'd seen each other, he'd been clean shaven.

My teeth sank into my bottom lip in an attempt to snap out of the carnal thoughts. His eyes were fixated on them, and he licked his own lips in response, as if he could read my mind and the dirty thoughts it contained.

"Sure, you take the first shot," I told him, stepping away from the table.

He sunk two stipes and with the second, one of mine. Then it was my turn. I grabbed my cue and lined up my shot. I sunk the rest of the solids, then went for the eight ball.

"Are you hustling me?" he asked lowly, his eyes twinkling

mischievously from across the pool table. He had no idea that I spent a lot of my childhood hustling people over a game of pool.

"I can't help it if I'm better than you," I shrugged, setting up for the next game. We played again, but he was more focused on watching me than actually playing. The more he watched me, the more mistakes I made.

Casting a nervous glance over my shoulder, I relaxed when I realized nobody was paying any attention to us. The other patrons didn't care what the younger ones were up to, so long as they still had their dart board and their spots at the bar in front of the TV.

"Let's go somewhere," Travis said.

I brought my eyes back to him, arching a brow. "Where?"

"Anywhere you want. We could drive down to the lake and skinny dip or get a hotel room and spend the night getting reacquainted with each other's bodies."

"Both of those suggestions end up with me naked," I pointed out, fighting back a smile.

"Which is why I'm fond of them both," Travis said, leaning against his cue and sending another dimpled smile my way. "What do you say?"

I knew I should say no, especially given the fact that I was hell-bent on calling off our arrangement.

But tonight? I wanted his company.

What we were doing got riskier every time we did it, especially with the upcoming wedding. Ending our little arrangement made sense...but at the same time, I didn't want it to end. Travis was familiar and simple; we kept it strictly sex and fun. No heavy topics, no conversations that could change the delicate balance in which we existed.

I had two choices: I could either go with him, or spend the evening alone.

I chose to go with him. I wanted to exist in that world, if

only for one more night. Then I'd tell him the arrangement was over.

I left before him, like I had so many times before. I drove home, knowing that he'd follow me, thinking about all the stolen moment's we'd shared over the years. The prospect of ending the arrangement sat heavily on my chest, but I pushed it away.

I stepped out of my car as Travis pulled up to the curb in his monstrous Chevy Silverado.

"Your chariot awaits you," he called out of the open window. Shaking my head and biting my lip, I opened the door and climbed in, hoping none of my neighbours had chosen that moment to peer out of their windows. "Did you decide between the hotel and the lake?"

"Let's go to the lake," I answered. It had been a long time since I'd done anything reckless—almost a year, actually.

"Mine or yours?" Travis asked, referring to his place on Lake Rosseau and the Miller heritage property on Miller Lake.

"Mine," I replied without hesitation. With my brothers out of town, there'd be no chance of getting caught.

I buckled up and we took off, my hair whipping around my face.

WE PARKED on the grass just before the sandy beach, with the cab facing the lake. Travis turned the engine off, and our eyes took a moment to adjust to the plunge in darkness. The moon was high in the sky and the night was silent save for the chirping of crickets and the occasional bullfrog. Fireflies glowed, spelling out their secret messages to one another.

"Well?" he asked, looking at me expectantly.

"Well what?"

"I believe you promised me skinny dipping," he said, his kissable lips twitching.

"The lake is cold," I retorted, arching a brow at him.

"I'll keep you warm," he challenged with a grin. He'd moved closer to me, his lips pressing against the side of my neck.

"I thought you just wanted sex and were trying to be creative about it."

Travis pulled away to look at me. "Nope, I wanted sex and a swim—maybe at the same time," he waggled his eyebrows playfully and nipped at my earlobe.

"You're a fiend," I laughed, rolling my eyes as I pushed him away. I pulled my hair back from my face, studying him through narrowed eyes. The man was actually pouting at me, putting on the puppy dog eye effect and everything. "Fine, I'll swim."

"Naked," Travis clarified with a grin as he tugged at my shirt.

I opened the door, stepped outside, and shaking my head, I began to strip. I pushed my shorts down my thighs and stepped out of them, tossing them into the back seat. Travis opened his door and stepped out, his eyes never leaving me as I continued to peel off my layers.

He swallowed hard, his lips curving up in a smile that made my centre ache.

It had been almost a year of celibacy for me. It was a mixture of a self-imposed and circumstantial sentence. I didn't need sex to survive, and I hadn't met anybody I'd wanted to sleep with. It seemed an awful like I was waiting for him, but I wasn't...or at least, I wasn't pining for him. Travis understood my body and he was careful to toe the line I'd drawn. He didn't push me for more than I was willing to give, so he was safe.

But, the way he was looking at me in that moment was anything but safe. I bit my lip, watching as he kicked off his jeans and boxers. His cock was hard, and he stroked it a few times, watching me with a smirk dancing across his lips. "I want to spread you out in the cab of my truck and lick you until you cum so hard you forget your name and beg for me to be inside of you."

I pressed my thighs together, his words threatening to undo me. "You'll have to catch me first," I said decisively before sprinting toward the lake.

It was the end of June; the air was warm and sticky, and I ran as fast as I could, hoping to reach the water before Travis caught up to me. I had no such luck, and in three long strides he'd caught up. He threw me over his shoulder and ran straight into the lake.

Cold water splashed over my legs as he waded out until the water hit his collarbone. I let out a gasp before he dunked us both under the water and shot back up immediately. He held my ass as I slid down his body. I slapped his hard chest playfully, and he chuckled.

With the moonlight reflecting off the lake, it was easy to see his face—and the look of reverence in his hazel eyes.

I pushed my dripping locks out of my face, my breath catching in my lungs. Needing to break away from the heaviness in the air, I turned and dove back into the water. Kicking my legs out, I swam hard and fast toward the floating dock.

I grabbed the ladder at the same time Travis did. He grinned at me, barely out of breath, and moved closer. "Are you ready for the sex part yet?"

"More than ready," I admitted, grinning. His arms gripped the sides of the ladder, caging me in.

He kissed me, his lips fitting against mine as if he'd done this on a daily basis, even though it'd be months since we last touched each other.

I wrapped my hands around the back of his neck, kissing him back with greed that bubbled over from the cracks in my heart.

A moment later, I pulled away, drawing in a much needed

breath. He let me go, moving his lips to pepper kisses along the side of my jaw.

"I'm cold," I said, my teeth chattering less from the temperature, and more from anticipation. I needed him, I craved him. I could think of nothing else but him in that moment. Not tomorrow, not next month.

It was a poignant, all-consuming, and very confusing feeling.

Shivering and wet, we raced across the sandy beach to his truck. I threw open the passenger door and jumped in, rubbing my hands over my arms to try and warm up. He turned on the heat and then reached into the back seat to grab two towels. I took the one he offered me and dried off, using it to clean the sand off my feet last. I sat up, tucking my wet hair behind my ear, still shivering.

"Come here," he said, his gruff voice breaking the silence that filled the cab. I moved closer to him, my heart pounding ceaselessly in my chest as he lifted me almost effortlessly onto his lap. His legs were so long that his seat had to be pushed back all the way, which meant I had no trouble fitting in the spot between him and the steering wheel.

I rolled my hips, my core brushing against the length of his hardness. Travis let out a deep groan. He caught my bottom lip with his teeth and tugged gently as his hands gripped my hips, bringing me against him again. His skin was hot, despite how cold the water had been just moments before.

He kept kissing me while he reached forward and popped open the glove box, searching through it blindly. He found what he was looking for and drew back, flashing the square foil packet at me with a wicked grin. "Always come prepared," he remarked, rolling the condom over his thick, hard length. My heart clenched in momentary crushing disappointment, and before I could mull over the reason *why* I felt that way, his hands went to my hips again and he held me while he slowly eased inside.

I forgot who we were. I forgot where we were. I forgot every single thing except how he felt inside of me.

He pumped into me, hard and sure. I met him thrust for thrust, eager to take every last drip of pleasure he gave me. My orgasm hit hard, and I bit a little too hard on his bottom lip. He didn't seem to care, he continued to drive into me a few more times before he found his release.

"Jesus, Becs," he panted afterward, his eyes fixed on mine. The grin on his face eased the panic I felt in the moments after our joining, when the gentle touches and the long gazes would spark thoughts better left unspoken. "I've missed being in you."

"That sounds dangerously like something a boyfriend would say," I warned him, climbing off his lap. I twisted around, trying to reach my clothes in the back seat. I'd said it to remind him of my rules, but it also served as a reminder to myself.

"Or it sounds dangerously like something a dude would say right after sex," Travis shot back, slapping my ass.

I turned my head to look at him, letting out an aggravated huff as my fist closed around my pile of clothes. Each beat of my heart hurt, and I couldn't look at him while I dressed. Once finished, I turned to face him. He was standing outside, slipping back into his jeans. "We're going to have to stop this, you know," I finally said.

Travis paused for a second. He didn't meet my gaze as he straightened and buttoned his jeans. "Stop what?" he asked. He sounded casual, but the slight tick in his jaw suggested my words had upset him.

"Sleeping together," I clarified.

"Why do we have to do that?" he asked, grinning at me as he leaned into the cab, his chest still gloriously bare. He reached for his t-shirt, pulling it on and obscuring my view of his six-pack.

"Because Brock's getting married next month, and when you come back we'll have to be around each other *and* everyone else.

I don't want anybody suspecting anything. We had our fun, but I think it's time this arrangement ended." Each word burned like acid on the way out, but it was necessary. In that moment, I knew I'd gotten more invested than I ever intended on getting.

"This arrangement," Travis repeated, still smiling...only without the amusement. He nodded his head once, pursing his lips as he absorbed what I was saying.

"Yes." I don't know why, but it felt an awful lot like I was hurting him, and I didn't like how knotted my stomach was over it.

"So you're saying that you no longer want to have incredible sex with me, because your brother's getting married and you don't want anybody to find out that we're having incredible sex?" he paraphrased, his brow raising in question. I nodded. "Would it really be all that bad if they found out?"

His question threw me completely off guard. My heart stuttered in my chest and I felt a rush of adrenaline, a desire to take flight from this situation that I couldn't seem to stay in control of anymore.

"Yes!" I finally replied after overcoming my shock. I looked at him like he'd lost his ever loving marbles. "You really don't think Brock would be pissed if he found out what we've been doing behind his back for the last four years?"

It wasn't like our sleeping together had been a one-time thing, like I'd planned for in the beginning. That could have been easily forgiven, but we had met up many times. Every summer, and whenever else he came home and sought me out.

I worried about what that betrayal would do to Brock and Travis's friendship. I couldn't stand the idea of causing another rift between them.

Travis hesitated. He opened and closed his mouth a few times, searching for something to say. He looked like he wanted to argue with me, but he knew that I was probably right about Brock.

"If that's what you want," he finally said. He climbed in, closed the door, and started the engine. He said nothing as he backed away from the beach and pulled out onto the private road.

We didn't talk for the entire drive back to town. He pulled into my driveway, finally lifting his chin to look at me. "See you around, Becs," he said, his eyes focusing straight ahead again. Dismissing me.

Even though it was for the best, watching him drive away burned.

CHAPTER EIGHT

ravis

July 2017

RECENTLY, I had come to realize that the women I hooked up with only wanted me because I was rich and famous. Every single person in my life wanted something from me. More platinum albums, more chart topping hits, extravagant gifts and attention in magazine spreads.

But there were a few exceptions to this rule: my mom and my friends, the people I grew up with, the people who knew me and loved me before I was famous.

Her. Becky Miller.

She'd always been a part of my life for as long as I could remember. I'd always thought she was gorgeous, with her dark hair and the prettiest blue eyes that I'd ever seen. But Becky was off-limits. You weren't supposed to screw your best friend's little sister, especially not Becky. Becky was special, she'd been through hell and back.

She didn't deserve to be someone's secret, and I hated that she was mine for the last several years. I was determined to do it right this time, because Becky wasn't the kind of girl you got over.

Before I got a taste of her, it used to be easy to forget about loneliness and isolation with the chaos of a tour and the high of performing on stage for thousands of people. It was easy to lose myself in the company of attractive, willing women, but then she sort of fell in my arms and messed me up.

Now, I felt disquieted.

I started feeling this way more and more over the last few years, and that feeling got worse when I was back in the Musko-ka's, back around the people I'd known forever...back around Becky. Nothing beat coming home, even if it was a painful reminder that my life was lacking substance: that it was lacking *her*.

I found myself heading to Parry Sound whenever I got the chance; even if it was just for a few days between shows. If I got to meet up with her at least once, it was worth the extra time spent traveling.

During our off time, I'd done my best to throw myself back into the casual fling pool. Truthfully? It hadn't really worked out for me.

In fact, it was damn near pathetic. I hadn't hooked up with anybody but her in three years. I kept that from her, because I'd worried if she found out she would flip. It was supposed to be just sex between us, and I was supposed to live my life the way I had before.

But one-night stands had lost their allure, and no other woman had since captured my attention the way that Becky had. Early on into our arrangement, I'd had a few one-night stands. After each of those hookups, I'd felt terrible, like I'd betrayed someone. Like I had betrayed *her*.

She wasn't the kind of girl you played games with; she was the kind of girl you committed too. But she'd been hurt before…badly.

The irony was not lost on me that she was a lot like my mom. My mother had relationships—plenty of them, I'm sure. She was a gorgeous woman and she was only forty-four years old. But, like Becky, Mom had never let anybody get close enough. She'd never moved in with anyone, had never gotten engaged, and hadn't even had a serious relationship.

Becky had opened my eyes to what was real and what was an illusion. The women who easily fell into my bed did so because I was famous and had money. None of them saw past that to the man I was beneath it all, and none of them cared to know him.

I played her game and followed her rules because I'd wanted to fill up on her wordless love, but there was no doubt about it; I *was* committed to her. She'd inspired every piece of music I'd written in the last four years, and I wanted to tell the world who my muse was. But Becky was cautious and I had to tread carefully, or I risked losing her completely.

I stopped the one-night stands, and every time we were together, what I felt for her grew. I thought it was the same for her, and I was working up the courage to tell her. But a few weeks ago, she told me she wanted the arrangement to end.

I met Tasha and Sandra on the plane, and they were "big fans of mine". They were best friends that looked almost identical, and they certainly played off their similarities.

They had a one-night layover in Toronto, and kept talking about how awesome it would be to see the town I grew up in. So I thought, *why the hell not?*

If I could get a rise out of Becky, if I could make her jealous, then maybe I could make her see that we could have so much more than our arrangement. And if she didn't care, at least I had two very willing women as a fallback.

But the unsettled, anxious feeling in the pit of my stomach hadn't let up since the moment I walked in with Tasha, Sandra, and my bodyguards and saw the devastated look on her face.

I wanted to make Becky jealous, not hurt her, and I didn't feel any better knowing that she cared, not with the wounded look in her eyes. In fact, I had a sneaking suspicion I'd fucked things up even more.

The jealousy trick might work on most women, but not her. I should have known better.

Still, I couldn't take back what I'd done. I did my best to disentangle myself from them, sending them off to the bar for drinks the first chance I got. They seemed content enough being the focal point of every male in the bar.

Every male but me. I was busy, surveying the bar, looking for the dark hair and blue eyes that tormented me in my dreams, the ones where I'd be moving toward her and she would just get further and further away with each step I took.

I didn't see her at the table she'd been sitting at when I walked in, nor was she around the pool tables or bar. My shoulders relaxed. I hadn't seen her leave, so she was probably hiding out in the bathroom.

Becky retreated when things got complicated. It was something she'd always done. Eventually, she'd have to come out, and I'd be waiting.

"And who are the Playboy bunnies?" the soon-to-be wife of my best friend asked, calling my attention back to her as she arched her pale eyebrow and frowned at me with disappointment. "If I recall, the invitations said plus guest, as in singular, not plus double penetration twins."

I threw back my head and howled with laughter until tears formed in my eyes. Tossing my heavy arm around Tessa's slender shoulders, I pulled her close to me. "This is why I love

Tessa, because she's hilarious and witty," I said, grinning at Brock.

I really did love his fiancé; Tessa was a sweet girl with a whole lot of brains. She was heading to vet school in the fall. But probably the best part about Tessa was the fact that she made my best friend extremely happy, and kept him coming home on the regular.

"Unlike the two high-class call girls you brought home?" Tessa's best friend, Elle, rolled her eyes. "What Travis, you can't find girls with IQs in Hollywood? As if you had to bring more trash into this town."

They weren't wrong, the girls I'd walked in with where every bit as shallow and sultry as they looked. I hadn't chosen their company for their great conversational skills, I'd brought them back to Parry Sound with me on a whim.

And I was already deeply, *deeply* regretting that whim.

"Easy, Elle," Tessa said, interrupting before I could think of a single thing to say in response. "Play nice. We don't know what their IQs are."

"Where's Becky tonight?" I asked. I was done with the conversation of my guests, and impatient as all hell. My eyes roamed the room again, seeking out her silky hair. I studiously ignored Tasha and Sandra, who gazed at me with star-struck longing.

"She just left," Elle said through narrowed eyes. "Unlike some people around here, she has responsibilities."

She was pissed, and I couldn't figure out if she was mad at me or mad at her ex-boyfriend sitting at the table beside me, but usually Elle's greetings were a little warmer.

"Ouch," I drawled, easily hiding my disappointment and regret. I couldn't believe I hadn't noticed Becky slipping past me. "She's feisty tonight," I added, sending a knowing look to Brock's younger brother, Braden. He had dated her for the longest time when they were both still in high school. Four years ago—around the time of the first legendary hook-up with Becky—they broke up. I hadn't seen them together since then, but damn, the sexual tension rolled off them both in waves.

"That she is," Braden said, his eyes fixated on her. I left them to it, trying to press down on the uneasy swirl of disgust I felt over my own actions. I was laying it on thick, but really—it was a defensive mechanism.

My public persona was an easy going flirt, and I'd gotten used to the mask.

"Let's go, I think we've done enough planning tonight," Elle said to Tessa, nodding to the door. The two friends looked at each other, seeming to communicate without speaking. I used to call them the terror twins when they were kids.

"Alright, later everyone," Tessa said, wrapping her arms around Brock's waist when he stood up. They kissed, molding into one. "Brock, get your groomsman in line," she warned.

"Yes ma'am," Brock grinned, kissing her again before they separated. The girls left, and I slid into the booth beside Braden.

"Anybody need another beer?" Grady asked, standing up.

"I need one," I nodded. "Tell O'Riley to put it on my tab."

"The whole night's on your tab," Gordon joked.

"So be it," I shrugged, unaffected. I didn't mind sharing my wealth, but he was just kidding. None of these guys would let me pay for their beers without a scrap. Pride ran deep in this town.

"Alright, let's plan this shit. What are we doing for the bachelor party?" Grady asked once he had returned to the table with several bottles of Budweiser. He slid one across the table for me, and I grabbed it gratefully, drinking it back.

"We could go to Vegas," I suggested a moment later, deadly serious. I loved Vegas. Even though I'd just come from there, I'd be willing to go back tomorrow.

"Or we could go to the strip club," Gordon countered, grinning widely and waggling his eyebrows.

"There's strip clubs in Vegas, dumbass," I pointed out with a smirk.

"I don't want a bachelor party," Brock cut in, shrugging. "And I definitely don't want to go to Vegas." He stole a quick glance at his younger brother. Braden was still watching after Elle like a lovesick puppy, but I caught his reference. I knew Brock didn't want to make it difficult for him.

"Travis, are you ready to go yet?" Tasha's singsong voice rang out just as her hand landed on my shoulder, and I fought the urge to wince. I'd forgotten they were still there. "Sandra and I are super tired," she hinted, biting down on her lower lip and giving me fuck-me eyes. The old me would have found it sexy as hell.

Now, I just found their routine tiring. Tiring and *fake*.

"Paul will take you back to the hotel," I told them, flashing them a cheeky grin to lessen the blow a little. I gestured to the burly man lingering near the door. "I'll join you later."

I had no desire to go back to the hotel to meet them later, and I wouldn't. I'd still make sure they got to the airport to catch their flight, and I'd cover everything because I felt like a fucking jackass for inviting two girls I didn't even want around in the first place, but I definitely wasn't feeling the hookup vibe.

My thoughts were firmly rooted on someone else.

"If you insist," Tasha pouted, linking arms with Sandra. Paul stepped toward them and they allowed him to lead them away, and I turned my attention back to my friends.

"You're fucking crazy," Gordon remarked, shaking his head ruefully. "You've got two gorgeous girls practically begging you to screw them and you're hanging out with us? What the fuck?"

"I haven't seen you guys in months," I shrugged, taking a swig of the beer. I ignored Gordon's imploring eyes and looked at Brock. "Why don't you want a bachelor party? It's a rite of passage."

"It's unnecessary," he responded. "I'd much rather go ATVing or fishing."

"We can do both," I told him. "We could go ATVing this weekend, then still throw a wicked bachelor party that will rival all other bachelor parties before it."

"I'm down for ATVing this weekend," Grady grinned. "Feels like we haven't been in forever."

"That's because we haven't," Gordon pointed out. "Jesus, when did we all get so goddamn boring?"

"Speak for yourselves, Travis is living the life still," Braden smirked, glancing toward the door where my guests had just left.

"Well he's a fucking millionaire, so no shit. Some of us have to work real jobs with shit pay," Gordon retorted, grinning at me to show he was just kidding.

His dig pissed me off a little. I worked damn hard for my money, sacrificed sleep and time with my loved ones to bring albums to life. I spent hours on the road travelling and had paparazzi all up in my business every time I turned around.

When you're in the public eye all the time, it was *very hard* to make mistakes, and the rumors that float around are vicious.

Some days, I wish I had a normal job like my friends.

"So Sunday, after the chili cook-off?" Grady suggested.

"Sounds good," I nodded.

"Let's make it a group thing. Unless you're all cool with Tessa kicking our asses for leaving her out," Braden suggested.

"Smooth, little Miller," I called out, reaching over to give him a noogie. I was impressed with his nonchalant, smooth deliverance. It was obvious that he was looking for an excuse to spend more time with Elle. I admired his tenacity.

"Shut the fuck up, Travis," he scowled, hitting my arm away.

I LOVED the Parry Sound Stampede, I'd been going since I was a little kid. I used to participate in the talent shows, and when I got older they'd set up a small stage and I'd play by the beer tent. When my first album went platinum, I continued playing every summer out of nostalgia and tradition.

The little stage by the beer tent turned into a massive stage that drew in crowds by the hundreds.

The week before the stampede was full of radio interviews and other promotional gigs that would bring in waves of fans from all over Ontario.

I was full of pent up energy. I could barely go anywhere without one of my bodyguards present, which kind of put a damper on enjoying my time back home. It was necessary, though, as a lot of the tourists were fans of mine here to watch me perform at the stampede. I couldn't walk a foot into town without being spotted.

A few weeks after the stampede, having both Paul and Rob in the Muskoka's wouldn't be necessary. But during the height of tourism season, with people coming from all over to attend the renowned Parry Sound Stampede, the label didn't give me much of a choice.

All of the bridled energy was put to good use during my show; I owned the stage, the crowd, the night.

I would never tire of performing music live. There was something about it—an energy in the air, a magic in the moment. I was in my element on stage.

After the show, I had little time to gather my wits before I headed to the Clayton's barn for the after party. I didn't know for certain that Becky would be there, but I hoped she was.

My eyes immediately spotted her the moment I walked in. She was standing up in the loft, leaning against the railing beside Braden, watching the dance floor. It reminded me of the past three summers, how we'd escape this party separately the first chance we got, only to meet up in a hotel.

Our eyes locked, and she stiffened, squaring her shoulders. I made a move toward the stairs that would take me up to the loft, take me up to her, but a hand on my arm stopped me. I turned my head to look, seeing Elle Thompson and a tall guy with dark blond hair I'd never seen before.

"Hey Travis! Great show!" Elle said, giving me a huge hug that I knew was her way of apologizing for the harshness she displayed the other night. "This is my boyfriend, Alex Hastings."

"It's so nice to meet you," Alex grinned, shaking my hand. "I'm a big fan of your music."

"Thanks man," I said, pumping my arm a little harder than necessary. I was tweaking out being so close to her yet unable to see her. We made small talk for a few minutes about the concert turn out and the weather.

Alex wasn't a bad guy, by any means, but it was obvious that Elle wasn't digging him as much as she was pretending to. The chemistry between her and Braden the other night had been off the charts. She held Alex's hand, but she might as well have been on the other side of the room. Her eyes kept going up to the loft where Braden stood.

"Well, we should head on up to see everyone. Catch you later, Travis," Elle said, leading Alex toward the loft. I watched them go, my eyes raising to the railing. Becky was no longer leaning against it. She'd taken several steps back and was resting against one of the wooden beams that supported the roof, engaged in a conversation with Tessa.

I did my best to keep moving through the crowd quickly, but several more people stopped to talk to me. They were buzzing from the concert still, amped up and excited to talk to me and snap pictures with me. These were the people who got me where I was, and I couldn't blow them off...even if I wanted to.

Finally, after what seemed like hours later, I was able to break away from the adoring townsfolk. I passed Brock and Tessa on the dance floor, completely enthralled with each other.

It didn't look like they'd be staying for much longer. Chuckling, I made it up to the loft.

Becky was still leaning against the wooden support beam, a drink in her hand that she occasionally sipped from while watching the people dancing below.

She wore brown cowgirl boots, a denim jacket and a sundress, the white lace falling just above her kneecaps. Her dark hair was pulled up in a high ponytail, with soft curls falling just above her shoulder blades. Her outfit was cute and classy, and it made the lust stir acutely in my veins.

"Do you want to dance?" I asked, startling her from her thoughts.

"Travis," she sighed, her tone one of warning.

"Come on Becs, one little dance won't hurt. Bet it'd be a lot more fun than just leaning against that beam. We're friends, aren't we?" Her eyes darted back to the dance floor. I followed her gaze, watching as Brock led Tessa through the throngs of dancers and out the door. I had a feeling they wouldn't be coming back.

She looked back at me and bit her lip, debating as her blue eyes searched mine. She could tell that I wasn't going to so easily give up—especially with both of her brothers gone. Sighing, she tossed back her drink and set it on the bar. "Alright, fine. Just one dance."

I took her hand and she allowed me to walk her down the loft stairs to the dance floor just as The Zac Brown Band came on with *Whatever It Is*.

Gently, I placed my hands on her hips and pulled her toward me. She reached up, encircling my neck, her hands resting between my shoulder blades. She kept her back straight and a respectable distance between the two of us. Her eyes skirted across the crowded dance floor nervously.

"What's wrong?" I asked.

"Nothing," she said, biting her lip, the white of her tooth

sinking in to the natural pink flesh. I brought my thumb up, freeing it. "People are staring."

"People always stare, there's nothing else to do in this town," I pointed out. She laughed reluctantly, her eyes softening as she looked at me.

I could very well lose myself for hours in her eyes, but she looked away. For the rest of the song, her head rested against my chest. I didn't ever want to let her go, but when the song ended…I had no choice.

"Thanks for the dance, Travis. I'll see you around," she told me, pulling out of my embrace. I reached out, my fingers brushing against the back of her hand. She paused, looking down at our hands before glancing back at me.

I wanted to tell her that I missed her; that I wanted a chance to prove to her that what we had between us was real and deserved a chance, but I choked.

"It was good seeing you again, Becs," I said instead. She bit her lip, nodding at me before disappearing into the crowd.

CHAPTER NINE

 *ecky*

"OH GOOD! Braden and Elle just pulled up," Tessa called out the next afternoon.

"Braden and Elle? As in... together?" I asked, raising my head to glance at her. She was staring out the open screen door, but she turned to look at me over her shoulder. Her honey coloured hair was pulled into a long, somewhat messy braid that hung thickly down her back.

"Yes, together. I may have sent him to fetch her," she answered, a mischievous glint in her eyes and a wicked little smile on her face.

I opened my mouth, but before I could ask what her motives were, the screen door was already slamming behind her. It didn't really matter, I sort of *knew* what her motives were.

Although she didn't say as much, Tessa kept throwing Braden and Elle together, as if she hoped they'd work out their differences. I adored Elle, having gotten to know her when she was dating Braden and almost a permanent fixture in our house. She used to be great for Braden, but that was then.

Now she was seeing another guy, and the last thing I wanted was for my brother to get hurt again. Braden didn't handle hurt well.

Neither one of us did.

Pushing the overbearing, protective big sister thoughts aside, I continued laying out the bread for sandwiches on Brock's wooden cutting board.

Nervous anticipation danced in the pit of my belly as sounds from out front drifted into the kitchen. It was the calm before the storm; Travis would be joining us at any moment.

Aiden was the only child within the group, as Katie and Ben had a birthday party to attend for Katie's niece, and it looked like I would be the only single person, unless Travis came without his groupies. I almost hoped he would bring someone, ridding me of the temptation I felt when around him. After the dance we shared the night before, I was having an even harder time sticking to my resolve to end our arrangement.

His touch had evoked strong desires within me, and I knew if I had stayed any longer...I'd let those desires take the wheel and end up right back in his arms again. So I'd left, returning home to send the babysitter on her way and bask in the silence and my thoughts.

My head wasn't any clearer after all that thinking.

Tessa walked back into the kitchen, followed closely by Elle. They came to stand in front of the island, where I'd set out three coolers and spread out all the condiments I'd need to make sandwiches.

"You're such a mom," Elle grinned at me, affectionately shaking her head.

I froze. Even though she meant no harm with her statement, her words had struck a nerve within me. I *was* such a mom.

There wasn't anything wrong with that, either. I smiled and lifted my shoulder in a shrug. "You can't turn it off."

We worked in compatible silence for the next ten minutes, quickly putting together the sandwiches and packing the coolers.

"That should be enough." I closed the lid on the food cooler with an inward sigh. No more hiding out in the house.

Grabbing the first cooler, I carried it outside while Elle and Tessa grabbed the remaining two. I tied my cooler to the storage racks on the back of my ATV while Tessa tied the one she was carrying to hers and Elle secured the final cooler to Brock's ATV.

I glanced around at the people gathered by the garage. Brock, Braden, Grady, Gordon, Tommy, Peter, and Ezra were busy talking about all the work Brock had done with Gordon's crew. They'd built the cabin a few years ago, and had just completed the detached garage that housed our ATVs and the two snowmobiles Brock bought.

Aiden was beside Braden, trying to stand as tall as his uncles and be included in their manly conversation. Hunter lumbered over, nudging Aiden's hand with his large head, looking for attention. I smiled at the way my son's eyes lit up as he kneeled to pet the dog.

When Brock first brought Hunter home, I'd been hesitant to let a wolf mix hang around my son. But he had never so much as growled at a child, and he was the most well behaved dog I'd ever been around.

He was happiest when Brock was around, but Aiden was a close second. Hunter watched out for him ever since meeting him four years ago. Any time they were together, the old dog would place his body between Aiden's and any potential threats —be it the road or a stranger.

"He's really shot up," Elle remarked, smiling in his direction.

"He did," I agreed, nodding as I gazed at my son. At seven

years old, Aiden was fiercely independent. His attempts at sneaking into my bed at night were less frequent. Now, he only crawled in with me if he'd watched a scary movie and couldn't fall asleep.

"I bet he doesn't even remember me," she sighed. "Four years is a long time..."

"He remembers you," I said, unintentionally sounding gloomy. Aiden had a remarkable memory. When Elle arched a brow in question, I shrugged. "There's pictures of you in Braden's room. He never packed anything away before he left, and I wasn't about to do it."

Tessa chose that moment to drag Elle away to meet the girls that her brothers had brought along. I remained near my ATV, watching the scene carry out before me, as I had already introduced myself when they first arrived. Paige and Samantha had seemed very friendly, and to her credit—Annaka did too. She was just intimidating with her artfully made up face, beautiful tattoos and ash-purple hair.

Next to her, I felt desolate in my high-waist denim jean shorts and boring white tank top over my modest one-piece swimsuit, my hair tossed up in a ponytail with no makeup on my face.

"This is Paige, Grady's girlfriend. Annaka is foolishly with Gordon, although hopefully she wises up soon—" Tessa said, her voice carrying over clearly.

"Hey! I heard that!" Gordon yelled out, scowling at Tessa. She flipped him off and he grinned.

I tuned out, gazing over to where my son stood. I felt awkward, leaning against my ATV between the two groups of people, but Aiden was enjoying hanging out with the guys without my involvement, and I wasn't comfortable or assertive enough to march over to the girls and interject myself into their conversation. It almost was a perfect analogy for my life.

It was hard to relate to women in and around my age who

weren't moms, and it was hard to relate to the women older than me that were.

We ended up waiting another fifteen minutes for Travis to finally show up, solo without so much as a bodyguard. Hope bloomed once again in my chest, and I dropped my gaze to my worn rubber boots.

Once his ATV was unloaded off his massive truck, we got ready to hit the trails.

"Come on bud, it's got to be tighter than that," I told Aiden, tightening the strap on his helmet so it sat more securely.

"Mom, stop. I can do it myself," he pleaded, his cheeks flushing with embarrassment.

"You're only seven, you can't be embarrassed by me already," I frowned, a little hurt.

"I'm not," he assured me, looking up at me with his bright blue eyes. "I can just do it myself now." Aiden hated the idea of hurting someone's feelings. He hugged me before racing over to the Trailrover ATV that Brock and Braden had bought him for his birthday the year before.

Brock led the way with Hunter running alongside him. Tessa followed, with Elle as her passenger. I waited until everyone else had followed before I motioned for Aiden to go. His youth size ATV was slower than the others, and I didn't want him getting accidentally run over.

Travis waited until everyone else had gone too. He sent me a long look full of promise before following after Gordon and Annaka.

"Go slowly, Aiden," I cautioned, my heart in my throat as I watched him zip along the trails.

I'd started driving regular sized ATVs at his age at my grandpa's, but it was different when it was your child. The amount of anxiety that accompanied fun adventures like this was suffocating. But to their credit, everyone was cautious of my seven-year old, not riding as hard or as fast as I knew they usually did.

It took ten minutes to get to our regular mudding spot in the clearing. We rode through the swampy area, so everyone's legs were covered in mud by the time we made it to the clearing. Aiden was grinning widely, his face caked in mud. He was the kind of child who could have a blast with kids or adults.

Near the end of Brock's section of property was a clearing, and Brock and his friends had created a large track there with miniature jumps for their dirt bikes and ATVs. When I was fourteen, I'd tagged along a few times, but it was my first time going in years.

The clearing had a couple of springs underneath running through it, but the ground wasn't as muddy due to the lack of rain. I relaxed a little, trying to lessen the ferocious hold on my mom reins.

We took turns running the track and eating sandwiches. Aiden hooted and hollered when the guys called for a race. I let Elle borrow my ATV, knowing she could handle it. She beat Braden, a wave of mud splashing him directly in the face.

After winning, she paused to gloat before pressing hard on the gas and shooting forward, driving back to where I was waiting with Aiden. I'd made him take another break to drink more water, and he was pestering me to race.

"Come on Mom! Just one race? PLEASE!?" he pleaded, his blue eyes wide with hope.

"I don't know, Aiden," I said, uncertainty ringing in my voice. Aiden had only been riding ATVs for a year, and his youth sized one likely wouldn't hold up against the other, more powerful machines. I didn't want him to be disappointed, or get hurt trying to keep up with the adults.

"But Mom!" he whined, pouting. "Even the girls got to race!"

"Hey now, that's not fair," Elle frowned, a hand on her hip. "Why are you using us girls as an example here, kid? Girls have every right to race. Hell, we're better than your uncle!"

"I know," Aiden replied sheepishly, his pout growing as he

kicked at the dirt. "But I'm seven now! I can race too! I bet I'd beat Uncle Braden. It doesn't look hard at all!"

I couldn't help but laugh at his response.

"You can race me, little man," Travis offered, grinning at Aiden. He ran a hand through his wavy, dark blond locks. My eyes shot to his, and I frowned.

"Now I really don't know," I scowled, angry at the frantic beating of my heart, and at his intervention. It was unwanted... and yet, it felt right.

"I promise, it'll be fine," Travis assured me, his eyes lingering on my face. A look of longing passed across his features. I sighed heavily, my lips lifting in a reluctant, tight smile.

"Fine, just one loop," I told Aiden, trying to maintain my authority. It was challenging; the look Travis had sent me had all but melted me.

As much as I liked to pretend I was impervious to his charm, I really wasn't.

"Three! Two! One!" Tessa called out, playing flag girl with a delighted grin on her face.

I watched with my heart in my throat as Travis and Aiden raced around the track. Aiden was going as fast as his little ATV would allow him. I chewed on my nails, anxiety swirling around in my gut as I watched. I couldn't relax until Aiden had finished the loop first and was tossing his fists up in victory.

My eyes found Travis's from across the field, and my heart paused in its frantic rhythm at the esteemed smile he flashed at me.

EVERYONE WAS COVERED in mud and sweat when we finally got back to the lake. I helped Aiden peel out of his sodden kinetic trifecta pants while everyone else dismounted.

Tessa jumped off her Grizzly, watching the trail where we'd come from with a satisfied smile on her face.

"Where'd you leave Elle?" I asked. She nodded as Braden's ATV came into view, speeding onto the beach. Elle clung tightly to Braden, and jumped off as soon as he came to a stop.

She stalked over to Tessa, a scowl on her lips. "How could you do that? Leave me with him like that?" she hissed.

Tessa seemed to wince apologetically. "I'm sorry, he paid me off."

"How much?"

"A hundred bucks, actually. I figured we could split it," Tessa laughed.

"No, I'll be taking it all," Elle informed her. Before either girl could say another word, Braden had scooped Elle up in his arms and was sprinting to the dock.

"Don't you dare!" she screeched, trying to fight her way out of his arms. But Braden was strong, and we laughed as he jumped into the cold lake with Elle in his arms. I smiled at the scene, shaking my head at my brother's playful antics. I hadn't seen him this happy and carefree for a long time.

But while the playful moment had brought a smile to my face, it also worried me. From the little time I'd managed to spend with Elle since she returned home, I'd picked up on her quiet depression, and I hoped fiercely that my little brother knew what he was doing with her.

"Do you want to go swimming, Aiden?" Tessa asked, and I watched as he nodded eagerly. They ran into the lake together, screeching when the cold water splashed against their legs.

I watched them for a bit, a small smile on my face. Aiden *loved* his Aunt Tessa. She would take him horseback riding in the summer and tobogganing down the huge hill on her father's farm during the winter.

When we celebrated our first Christmas without Mom, Tessa had gone out of her way to make the holiday meaningful and special. She included us in all of her family's traditions, and when I tucked Aiden into bed after a day spent with the Armstrong's, he told me that he felt like Tessa was a guardian angel sent by his Grammy, to make sure we'd be okay.

I had to agree with him.

"Whatcha thinking so hard about?" a familiar voice asked, prompting my skin to erupt in goose bumps. I turned my head, watching as Travis lifted a beer to his lips and took a deep sip, his hazel eyes warm as they appraised me.

I tugged at my mud-splattered tank top, uncomfortable with how the heat in his gaze made me ache.

This seemingly invisible pull between the two of us was driving me crazy. The air between us seemed to hum with anticipation and electricity. His gaze skimmed the lake once before he focused on me, desire burning in his irises. His thoughts had likely taken the same route mine had with recollections of the last time we'd been on my family's beach together, the night I'd ended our arrangement.

Recalling the two girls he'd brought to Flanigan's in my mind's eye, I looked away. The wave of jealousy and disappointment that had washed over me that night made my feelings undeniably clear. All the more reason to try to avoid the whole thing.

"Just so you know...I brought those girls to Flanigan's the other night to purposely make you jealous," Travis said, breaking the cozy silence with his soft-spoken admission. I tensed, sensing him move closer to me. "I'm not really all that sorry for doing it, either."

The second confession was spoken near my ear, and the warmth of his breath tickled against the sensitive skin on my earlobe, igniting the slow burn of desire in the pit of my belly. His words evoked a fluttering in my chest that I refused to analyze.

"And why's that?" I demanded lowly, my voice shaking as I

folded my arms across my chest. The reaction his words had coaxed out of me was bewildering.

"Because, it made you jealous." He arched a brow at me, like I should have guessed his reasoning. "Because it makes me think that maybe, you didn't end the arrangement because of the wedding and the possibility of getting caught. You still want me."

My shoulders trembled and my chest rose and fell with each quick breath I took. I glanced around at everyone else, they were too occupied in their own conversations to pay ours any attention.

"I do want you," I finally said, my voice thick with emotion. I was tired of denying it. I was tired of holding my feelings—and myself—back out of fear. I was tired of being afraid, and I couldn't carry it anymore. "That's not the problem."

"What's the problem, then?" Travis asked, his lips twitching with humour.

I arched my brow, intentionally mimicking his earlier move. I cast a worried glance around us, just to ensure nobody else was watching. "I've got enough to deal with. I don't have time to be your occasional play toy anymore, and to be honest...I'm not sure I want to be."

Maybe it wasn't fair of me; I'd been the one to insist upon keeping it strictly about sex between us, so to throw the fact that he'd given me exactly what I wanted back into his face was low.

But somewhere down the line, my wants and needs had changed, and my flight response had kicked in.

Travis took a hesitant step toward me, catching himself when he realized that we weren't *completely* alone. He stopped so that he was standing directly beside me, his head turned toward the lake as if he was watching the others swim.

"You aren't and would never be just my plaything, Becky. I want you, I want you in more ways than you can possibly imagine. When you told me you wanted to end the arrangement, I agreed because that's what I thought you wanted. But you don't want that, do you Becs?"

His eyes slid over to mine, watching me, reading me. *Seeing* me.

"I—" I trailed off, staring at him with astonishment. "I don't know what I want anymore," I admitted. I felt woozy, and a little disoriented. Maybe I had heat stroke, or maybe watching Travis interact with my son all day had done strange things to my head and my heart.

I'd melted at the way Travis spoke to my son. He treated him like an equal, like he was extremely interested in hearing every little thing that my seven-year-old had to say.

If I allowed myself to think about it, that's exactly what I would want my partner to do: treat my son with respect and interest, take the time to get to know him, because any man I chose would need to accept Aiden into his life.

"That's okay, we don't have to put a label on it Becs. I feel it, you feel it...so let's just see where it takes us?" he suggested. His hazel eyes burned with desire and promise, and my heart stuttered in response to the heady way he looked at me.

"Can we talk about this later?" I pleaded, clearing my throat. My eyes itched, a sign that tears would surely follow. Now wasn't the time or the place for this conversation, although I agreed we needed to have it.

"Yeah, of course," Travis nodded, crestfallen. He brought the bottle of beer to his lips and took several long sips, his eyes never leaving my face. He lowered the bottle a fraction, running his tongue along the seam of his lips. "But, we will have this conversation, Becky...and we will have it soon."

I nodded, watching with pursed lips as he strolled over to Gordon, Grady and Brock. I turned on my heel and walked up to the cabin, grabbing the cooler off the back of my ATV as I went.

Setting it down on the island, I took a deep breath. Travis's words confused my already twisted heart. They scared me at the same time that they gave me hope. Wiping away a lone tear that had the audacity to escape, I squared my shoulders and set to unpacking the cooler.

A moment later, the bathroom door opened. Turning, I watched as Tommy's friend, Samantha, walked out. She startled when she saw me, bringing her hand up to her heart. Her eyes— so blue they were hauntingly violet—were red rimmed and swollen.

"Is everything okay, Samantha?" I asked her, walking around the corner.

"Yes, I'm—" she paused, her voice scratchy and weak. She cleared her throat and tried again. "I'm good. Just...allergies. And please, call me Sam."

"Brock has some allergy medication if you need it," I offered, turning to open the cabinet over the sink where I knew my brother kept it.

"Actually, I'm good," Sam said awkwardly. "I..." She hesitated again, her eyes going to the screen door and the voices from outside. Tommy had the kind of voice easily picked out from the crowd; it was the most boisterous of them all. We could hear him razzing Braden from inside the cabin. Hearing it, her shoulders dropped in disappointment. "I should head home."

"Why?" I asked, surprised.

"To be honest? I feel very out of place," she shrugged, a small yet sad smile on her face.

"I feel out of place sometimes too," I told her, giving her a comforting smile. "There's a certain energy about this group, isn't there?"

"Yeah," Sam nodded in agreement, biting down on her lip. She glanced back outside wistfully, like she longed to be a part of the group but didn't know how.

I could relate.

I took a closer look at her, my nursing instincts in high drive. Sam's skin was pale and clammy, and she seemed to be in pain. "Are you sure you're alright, Sam?"

"Ah, you're a medical professional, aren't you?" Sam asked, a dismal smile on her lips.

I nodded, my brow furrowing slightly with confusion as I tried to figure her out. "I'm a nurse."

"Thought so. I can always tell the nurses, they pick up on the stuff us chronic warriors try to hide," Sam sighed lightly.

"Chronic warriors?" I arched a brow, unfamiliar with the term—and assuming she was referring to the cannabis she'd left the bathroom smelling faintly of.

"It's what me and a few other chronic pain warriors call ourselves," she shrugged, seeming a little embarrassed. "Since we're constantly fighting pain...I don't know."

"Oh, makes sense I guess," I laughed lightly. "Do you mind if I ask what your chronic pain disorder is?"

"One is called Multiple Hereditary Exostoses," she said. "I have bone growths—or exostoses—growing off the limbs and clustering around the joints of my regular bones. The exostoses cause a lot of pain because they can, and often *do*, impede mobility and interfere with nerves and tendons. I've had about ten surgeries to remove exostoses—and I've had about forty-five benign tumors removed."

"Wow! That's a lot of surgeries...it sounds painful."

"It is," Sam nodded solemnly, though a slight smile tempered her lips. "I experience joint pain, muscle weakness and tenderness—plus a lot of fatigue. Sometimes, my legs don't work the way I need them to, and I drop things constantly because my wrists give out. I also have an 'unknown' bleeding disorder."

"And you came ATVing?" I asked, raising my eyebrows. I was impressed. ATVing—even when you're riding on the back of one—is rather hard on the body. I could see the toll it had taken on her.

Sam nodded. "I like it, it's fun. Tommy started making me go a few years ago, but it's been a while. I forgot how hard it can be."

"Understandable. Does Tommy know you're sore?" I asked, my heart going out to her.

"No, I don't think he'd understand, anyway. I should probably just go home, call it a day." She cleared her throat again. "It's not really like Tommy will notice either way."

"I'm sure he will," I tried. Sam gave me a somber, knowing smile. It was clear that she didn't believe me.

"Well, it was nice meeting you, Becky. Maybe I'll see you around," she said, making her way to the door. She moved gingerly, as if she was trying to hide a limp.

Before she could reach it, Travis burst in, the screen door slamming behind him, startling the both of us. He paused when he realized I wasn't alone.

"Everybody's getting ready to go to the bonfire," he finally said before he turned, letting the screen door fall shut behind him.

"I still can't believe you guys are friends with *Travis Channing*," Sam sighed dreamily, watching as he walked back to the garage. "He's really nice, but super intimidating. How do you stand it?"

"We knew him before he was famous," I shrugged. For the most part, Travis's fame was just an extension of him. He was still the same guy he always was—girls had fawned over him even before the albums and the tours. He was friendly, social, and loved attention. But he would give the shirt off his back to help a friend in need, then and now.

"You guys seem super close. Like...romantically close," Sam remarked, her eyes sparkling with mirth. "Are you together?"

"No," I responded, perhaps a little too quickly. I looked out the screen door, catching him throw back his head in laughter at something Gordon had said. "It's not like that."

"What's it like then? Clearly he's into you. I don't think he's stopped watching you once today," Sam commented. "Are you not into him?" she added, as if the idea was so farfetched she couldn't comprehend it.

"We're into each other, I guess," I responded, surprising myself by answering her rather intrusive question. For whatever reason, I felt relaxed around Sam. I knew she wasn't asking maliciously, she was just curious. "But there are a lot of things at play...he's, well. A celebrity. I'm a private person, and a single mom. I don't know...it's complicated."

"Minor details," Sam said dismissively, waving her hand. "All couples have their issues, things that make it hard for them to just be together. That doesn't mean they shouldn't. Look at Jack and Rose from the Titanic, I mean, she was a wealthy engaged woman and he was a penniless artist."

"Didn't he die at the end?"

"We all die at the end," Sam responded, shrugging. She gave me another one of her half smiles. "That doesn't mean we shouldn't live in the meantime."

CHAPTER TEN

BECKY LEANED AGAINST HER CAR, waiting for Aiden to finish changing from his damp clothes. She still kept to herself at social functions, like she'd done in high school. She preferred to think of herself as the wallflower, someone that faded easily into the background.

She didn't know that she was the focal piece.

With Becky, what you got was what you saw...and I loved what I saw. She didn't need to wear makeup, her dark lashes framed azure eyes that made me think of summer skies. Her body had me going for days—slender hips, and supple breasts that spilled over my palms when I'd held them.

She wore form fitting clothes, but didn't skank it up. She wore things that were comfortable and functional. She was a breath of fresh air.

Becky had changed into a pair of denim jeans that clung to her in all the right places. She held a sweater in her arms, anticipating the temperature drop. Catching movement in my peripheral, I watched as Aiden raced down to his mom.

She opened the rear passenger door for him, and he hopped in without complaint.

"Let's try and take as few vehicles as we can since parking will be ridiculous as always," Tessa suggested. Sensing an opportunity, I took it.

I strolled over to Becky's car, opened the passenger door and leaned in. "Mind if I bum a ride off you?" I asked, grinning. "I don't want to unhook the trailer."

"I guess so…" Becky frowned, looking over her shoulder at Aiden, who was pulling the seatbelt strap over his chest and buckling it in.

"I'll be on my best behaviour, Scouts honour," I assured her, sliding in.

"You were never a Scout," she pointed out, her lips twitching with amusement. "Do you even know the oath?"

"Sure I do!" I laughed. I had no fucking clue what the oath was.

Still laughing, my eyes locked on Becky's. The smile on her face made my heart jump.

She turned on the stereo and *Autumn Fields* pumped through the speakers. I arched a brow, a little surprised. "I didn't know you liked *Autumn Fields*."

"Yeah," she flushed, changing it to a country station on the radio. "I like a lot of different genres."

I turned it back to the *Autumn Fields* CD, flashing a playful grin at her. "You don't *have* to listen to country just because I'm in the car. I like *Autumn Fields* too. They are a talented group of people."

She smiled, still a little uncomfortable. My fingers tapped along to the beat, and when I started singing—she laughed and relaxed some more.

When we pulled into the parking lot twenty minutes later,

Becky's easy smile faded as she searched for a spot amid all the cars and trucks. She finally found one at the edge of the fairgrounds.

We barely made it onto the midway when a group of women in their early twenties swarmed us, asking me to sign tits and other various body parts that shouldn't be on display with a seven-year-old present.

I used to love every aspect of being a celebrity. I loved that people recognized me, I loved that they loved my songs. I loved that they were interested in the things I had to say.

Hell, I loved signing tits.

But then, the rose coloured glasses came off and I realized how intrusive it is, having paparazzi snap pictures of you and people swarm you when you're doing regular things like grocery shopping or going to a county fair, and the appeal of signing boobs wore off pretty quick too.

"Whoa!" Aiden exclaimed, his eyes widening at the attention I was receiving.

"Come on Aiden," Becky said, grabbing his hand and tugging him away from the small crowd.

"I'll just be a minute," I called out, feeling helpless. I shouldn't have told Rob to take the night off.

"Take your time," she frowned, making her way over to our group.

I pasted a smile on for the photos, all the while thinking about the situation with Becky. Her words and mine rang around in my head like a bell in a cathedral all afternoon long.

"Thanks so much, Travis!"

"Here's my number, call me if you wanna hook up," one of the girls said, handing me a slip of paper with a sultry flourish.

"Thanks," I said, breaking free finally and heading toward my friends. I threw the piece of paper into a nearby garbage can.

My friends had set up and spread out on blankets, sitting in clusters. Brock, Tessa, Braden and Elle sat on one blanket, while Tommy, Gordon, and their dates sat on another. Braden's friends, Ezra and Peter, sat with Krista, Grady and Paige.

I dropped down beside Aiden and Becky. I felt her eyes on me, could practically hear the wheels turning in her head. There was plenty of space for me to insert myself wherever, and I knew she was worrying about what her brothers would think, but I didn't see an issue.

Nobody seemed to be paying us any mind, coupled off as they were. Elle and Braden were busy with their own tug-of-war. If anyone asked, I'd tell them the truth; I was hanging out with a friend and her son.

While I desperately wanted to finish the conversation we'd started earlier, I knew it wasn't a good time. Instead, I focused my attention on Aiden.

He was a pretty fantastic kid—quick wit, great sense of humour, smarter than me for sure. I'd had a lot of fun hanging out with him and getting to know him. It was really the first time I'd had the opportunity to do so. He loved soccer and Pokemon, two things I'd been nuts about as a kid.

"You have over a thousand cards?" Aiden repeated, his eyes wide with wonder. "I only have two hundred!"

"Yeah man, I collected them for years," I answered.

"We should have a battle some time, I'm really good at it. Undefeated, right Mom?" he boasted, looking toward his mom for reassurance.

She smiled lightly at him. "Number one," she said.

Aiden fell silent when the fireworks started. He watched the colours exploding in the sky, completely enchanted, and I was struck with possibility.

For the last four years we'd been sneaking around, fulfilling our arrangement, Becky had never allowed me to hang around her son like this.

This felt real, being here with the two of them. Now that I

knew she wanted me, I just had to find out exactly what was holding her back and help her through it.

No big deal, I was up for the challenge.

AIDEN FELL asleep with his head resting in Becky's lap and his legs curled beside mine twenty-minutes before the grand finale of the firework show. Her expression was full of unmeasurable love as she gazed down at her son, gently brushing the dark hair from his eyes.

"He's a great kid, Becs," I told her, my voice thick. "And you're a great mom."

"Thanks," she said, her cheeks flushing slightly. "I should probably get him home."

"Let him sleep, I'll carry him for you," I offered, standing up. I squatted, picking up the sleeping boy like he weighed less than a sack of potatoes. His head lulled against my chest, but he didn't wake up.

"Are you sure?" she asked, hesitating. I knew she was thinking about how I'd gotten swarmed earlier.

"It'll be alright. I usually don't get bugged like that when I'm home. I think they were out-of-towners. Besides, I doubt people would ask me for an autograph if I'm holding a kid," I replied, winking.

Becky nodded reluctantly and stood up, grabbing the blanket we'd been sitting on and folding it. She carried it under her arm as we weaved our way through the crowds.

Thankfully, people saw the sleeping child in my arms and kept the squealing to a minimal, although I could hear tongues wagging already.

Becky frowned, catching her name among the whispers. She tugged the sweater she was wearing closer to her body and moved quicker. Unlocking the rear passenger door, she held it open. I set Aiden down, looking to Becky for help. I had no younger siblings, no cousins, no nieces or nephews to speak of.

My experience with kids was limited to being one, and that was a long time ago.

I watched while she pulled the seat belt across Aiden's lap, holding his head in place. "Once he's out, he would sleep through the apocalypse," Becky commented, laughing lightly as she gently pressed the door closed.

"That's a bonus," I joked, waggling my eyebrows.

She smiled faintly, looking around. People were climbing into their cars, getting ready to leave the fairgrounds. She had parked far enough away from any lamp posts, and the dark provided a shelter from prying eyes.

I took a step closer, leaving less than three inches between the two of us. I brought my hand up to tuck a strand of her thick hair behind her ear. I traced the shell of her ear, and she drew in a shuddering breath. "Let me take you out some time."

"Travis…" she started.

"I don't want our arrangement to end, Becs," I told her. I had so much more to say, but I feared that unloading all of my feelings on to her in that particular moment would just scare her. I worried that she wasn't ready for those confessions, that she wasn't ready to hear that I wanted her in every, real sense of the word.

"What's the point, Travis?" Becky demanded, biting down on her lip and stepping away from my hand. "The bachelorette party is next weekend, and I work every day this week. Between Aiden's soccer practices and work, there's no way I'd even be able to get away any time soon."

"Let's just do what we've always done, make time for each other when we can. If we're too busy before the wedding, then we're too busy and we'll hook up after. Directly after," I answered, my lips curving up in an enticing smile. I knew when she was close to bending, and Becky was definitely close to bending.

"Okay," she inhaled. She walked around the length of her car, pausing after opening the door. She hesitated before climbing in, her eyes darting over to me once more before she climbed in her car and drove away.

CHAPTER ELEVEN

ecky

Six days after the community bonfire, I was dropping Aiden off at my brother's so I could go to Toronto for Tessa's bachelorette party.

"Please call if you need me. I'll come straight home."

"We've got it handled," Brock assured me, practically shoving me out of his cabin. I waved at Aiden through the screen door, my heart tightening painfully in my chest with anxiety's grip.

"Come on, Becs, you've already subjected the poor kid to enough of your goodbye kisses," Braden pointed out from the other side of the screen door with a smirk. "We'll be fine!"

"I know," I sighed, shooting him a dirty look. I didn't expect either of them to understand. Sure, I'd had nights out since having Aiden, but I'd never gone far, and Toronto was *far*. Or at least…farther than I was used to going.

"It will be fine," Brock said again, nodding to my car where Katie was patiently waiting for me.

"I'm so ready for this weekend," Katie sighed when I opened the door and climbed behind the wheel a moment later. "I haven't had a weekend with the girls since...well, before Alyssa was born," she laughed, brushing back a strand of dark cooper coloured hair from her face.

"Yeah," I said absently, pulling away from the cabin. My eyes watched it in the rearview mirror, and I drew in a stabilizing breath.

"Everything okay?" she asked softly, drawing my attention away from the rearview mirror.

A soft sigh escaped my lips, and I turned my head to give my friend a small smile. "I guess I still get a little nervous about leaving Aiden."

Katie sent me a sympathetic look that told me she understood, and I knew she did. "Tell me about it. I've left Alyssa at my parents' and with my sisters' a few times for a day or so, and that wasn't easy. But it's definitely not easy staying at home every day, either!"

"I would have loved staying home with Aiden," I commented wistfully. I took a year and a half off of work after he was born, just to recover and settle in, but I studied the whole time. I took some online courses to improve my grades in biology and chemistry so that I could apply to college for the nursing program.

My family helped me get back on my feet, but I had to miss a lot of Aiden's firsts due to school or work. My top priority was ensuring that I could provide for my son, that he had a roof over his head, food in his belly, and clothes on his back.

That he didn't have the same childhood I had growing up.

"Maybe you'll get to stay home the next time around," Katie said, giving me a hopeful smile.

"Ha," I laughed dryly, looking at her over the top of my sunglasses.

"I'm serious," she frowned, shifting so that she was looking directly at me. "I know things with FWB didn't work out, but you should meet my cousin. I'm telling you I think you guys would hit it off." As far as Katie knew, I hadn't seen FWB since I'd called things off.

"No, thank you," I responded, shaking my head animatedly. "I'm sure he's a nice guy, but I have no interest in blind dates. Besides…I'm already thinking about dating someone."

I hadn't meant to say the last bit out loud, but the secret had been festering and bubbling. The last several times we'd talked, he'd said things and done things that confused my already conflicted heart.

Katie was one of my best friends, and I knew she wouldn't betray my trust by telling anybody—lest of all my brothers. Now that Travis had animatedly expressed his interest in having *more* than just the arrangement with me, I needed her to be my sounding board.

For as long as I'd known him, Travis been commitment free. He loved having fun and coming and going as he pleased. I couldn't help but worry that he would change his mind once he realized he didn't enjoy being tied down with a girl and a kid who wasn't even his.

I really wasn't the kind of person who believed that love healed all. I wanted to be, but in my experience…love—especially romantic love—broke you more than it healed you.

At one point, I truly thought that my love for Richie would save him, that he'd stop doing drugs and get help. But it didn't, and I almost lost Aiden because of my own inability to walk away.

And here I was, considering doing the same thing again, knowing the chance of it ending and destroying me were higher than the chance we could make it work. The thought was a sobering one that made my blood run cold in my veins.

"Who?" her eyebrows shot up as she appraised me deliberately. "Spill, Becky. We've got two and a half hours together in this car, you damn well better believe I will pester you nonstop the whole way if you don't."

Wrinkling my nose, I sighed. "Fine. It's FWB. Are you happy? I caught the feels, but I don't think I can be with him."

"Why the hell not? Does he have a crooked dick?" Katie asked. I glanced over at her, my jaw slack.

"No, he does not have a crooked dick." In fact, his dick was damn near perfect. It was thick and long, veins in all the right places, and he sure knew how to use it.

"Then what's the problem?" she demanded, practically vibrating in her seat with excitement. She was so happy for me. For years, Katie had been trying to nudge me toward the dating scene.

"I have more issues than National Geographic and *I know it*."

"So check that shit at the door," Katie said, waving her hand dismissively.

"You know, it's *really* not that easy," I grumbled. If it were, I'd have already done it.

"Maybe not," she amended, her smile reserved. "But so long as you're upfront with those issues, it'll be fine. Now tell me...*who is FWB?*"

"I can't tell you."

Katie scoffed at me. "I have some theories." She sat back in her seat, tapping her finger against her chin. "Would you like to hear them?"

"No."

"At first I thought it was someone you worked with...but that can't be right. It's definitely somebody I know," she continued thoughtfully. "Steve?"

"Winters? No," I almost laughed. Out of all my brother's friends, Steve was the enigma. He was a bit of a hermit. I could see why Katie's first guess was him—we were similar in that regard.

"Could it be...Travis?"

I said nothing, biting my lower lip and stealing a glance at my friend. I hated outright lying to people I cared about, but I didn't want to confess it out loud either.

"It *is* Travis!" she exclaimed with excitement. "That explains the night at Flanigan's. You took off right after he showed up."

"Yeah, well," I sighed, my breath escaping in a loud whoosh.

"*Travis* is FWB?" she repeated, still absorbing that information. "When did it actually start?"

I drew in a deep breath, lifting my right hand off the steering wheel to lift up my water bottle and chug back a sip. My throat felt impossibly dry. "The day after my mom's funeral."

"Shut the front door! So when you came over to talk to me about friends with benefits, *Travis* was already your friend with benefits?" she exclaimed. She was in a state of stupefaction. In all our years of being friends, I had never truly shocked Katie. I nodded, guilty. "Please tell me *everything*."

We were driving through a section of fifty-foot tall rock cuts that were a part of the Canadian Shield. Traffic was light, given that most people were heading up to cottage country, not into the city, but I still didn't trust that I wouldn't start bawling my eyes out and have to pull over.

"I'll tell you everything later, when I'm not driving. Preferably when I'm drunk," I finally said.

"Fair enough," Katie sighed, leaning back in her seat. She was quiet for several moments, watching the scenery pass by while she mulled over my confession. "So...why the secret?" she asked, and I knew she was feeling hurt I hadn't trusted her with this news sooner.

"I was afraid of being judged, or that Brock would end up finding out and that he'd be mad about it."

"Why'd you even *pick* Travis if you were worried about Brock's reaction?" Katie questioned, prying into the inner workings of my mind.

"Well—you've *seen* him. He's hot, and charismatic...and I

don't know. I guess I thought I could use Travis to help me move on from...well. *Him.* And he did—does when we're together, anyway. But things were easier when we were just... friends with benefits. When I had no expectations and he had no expectations. At the end of the day, we don't make sense. At least not in the long run," I admitted.

"And why the hell not? I think you guys would be great together."

"He's gone more often than he's not, he's *famous*, and he could get any woman in the world. Why would he settle for me?"

"He wouldn't be settling, you idiot." She firmly slapped my shoulder, glaring at me.

"Hey! I'm driving," I scowled, nodding toward the highway in front of me.

"Sorry, but it ticks me off when you say stuff like that," she frowned, affronted. "You're gorgeous, and you're the nicest person I know. You work hard and you're loyal. You're a catch, Becky Miller. When are you going to see it?"

"Ugh, okay fine. I'm a catch, are you happy?" I said, exasperated. "It still doesn't change the fact that we won't work forever, and I don't think I'm willing to put my heart in his hands. I could fall for him, but I don't know if he's *really* prepared to catch me."

Katie shook her head venomously. "I don't agree with that outlook. No relationship has a guarantee of forever. Look at Ben's mom and dad; she died young. They didn't get a whole lot of time together, but the years they did have were magical. You've just got to hope for the best and work at it."

"That's a morbid outlook," I remarked, her words saddening me.

"It's the truth," she insisted. "The regrets that haunt us the most are the things we never did, the risks we never took. For the record, I think you're being a huge baby."

"Maybe I am," I laughed, Katie's candor easing the tightness in my chest.

THERE WAS something liberating about a night out with just the girls. Strangers—women and men alike—were buying our drinks and celebrating Tessa's upcoming wedding almost as hard as we were. The inflatable penis Elle insisted Tessa carry around was pleasing everyone we encountered. At first, it was mortifying, but it quickly became more and more hilarious with each drink we tossed back.

The drinks helped ease my typically reserved nature, and soon I found myself out on the dance floor, moving my hips in time to the music.

Katie and I were at the bar when I looked up and saw him. I was almost certain his likeness was summoned by alcohol and my inability to stop thinking about him.

Our eyes locked from across the crowded room, and I inhaled deeply. The pull was too much.

"What the hell is he doing here?" I asked Katie, gesturing to where he stood with a slight nod of my head.

"I might have texted him...from your phone...when you were getting ready at the hotel, and *maybe* I pretended to be you and asked him to come," Katie cackled, pleased as punch with herself. She snapped her fingers at the bartender, summoning him. "Two shots of Peach Paradise please!"

Travis was situated in the middle of the dance floor, alone in a sea of people. Nobody was paying attention to him, he had a black baseball cap on that obscured most of his face and wore a long sleeved black Henley that covered the tattoos on his arms. He knew how to blend in with the crowd, and blended without notice from the other drunk patrons.

His words from the other night fluttered around in my head,

intoxicating me with allure, mixing with the many drinks, creating a cocktail of bad decisions.

I wanted him, even though I knew I shouldn't. I trusted him, even though my brain cautioned me not to.

The bartender placed two shot glasses down in front of us and I tossed one back, needing the liquid courage.

"I'll cover for you," Katie promised. "Go!" She gave me a gentle shove, coaxing my legs into moving. I walked to the dance floor, my heart pounding in my chest.

With this being the last stop of the night, the girls were so drunk they could scarcely stand. I wasn't worried about them recognizing him, especially not with Katie helping to redirect their attention.

His eyes were on me. As Luke Bryan's *Games* thrummed through the speakers, I swallowed hard and closed my eyes, moving my body to the beat, propelled by alcohol and need.

I opened them a moment later, my eyes landing on his. I danced for him, the kind of dance I've only ever done in the privacy of my own home, when no one was around. I had the attention of those around me, but I didn't even care about that. I didn't even see them. My focus was locked on Travis.

His eyes were burning, the intensity of them arousing me, lighting every nerve ending on fire and driving me further into the rabbit hole we'd created for ourselves.

He started to stalk toward me, his broad shoulders parting the sea of bodies. When he reached me, I turned and fell against him, the two of us moving together with perfect rhythm. My ass pressed against his groin, and he used his hand to move my hair off the nape of my neck. He kissed it, his cap brushing against my cheek as his lips brushed across my flesh.

My back was flush with his chest, and I could feel his heart racing. The frantic thudding matched my own speeding heart.

We danced together like that, our bodies melting into one another and grinding with the flow, until he pressed his erection firmly against my ass. I gasped as he brought his lips to kiss the shell of my ear. "Come with me," he said, loud enough for me to hear him over the music.

He pulled my hand, leading me toward the street. "I can't, the bachelorette party!" I shouted, coming to a stop. I tried to tug my hand free from his. I couldn't leave the girls, even though I really wanted to. *Could I?*

I was tipsy enough that the alcohol in my system eased my massive fears of letting him in, and I knew that was dangerous. When I woke up in the morning, I'd undoubtedly regret being so unbound.

But what if I didn't regret it? Katie's words from earlier taunted me, spurring my desire to close my eyes and jump.

"We'll come right back," he said urgently, turning toward me and pulling me against his chest. He released his hold on my hand, his hands drifting to grip my hips. He lifted me against him, pressing his erection against my core. My thong was embarrassingly damp, my need for him a rush of heat I knew he could feel, and still I was undecided. He closed his eyes for a moment, drawing in a ragged breath. "Or I'll just start kissing you in the middle of this dance floor, and that will only lead to a very inappropriate display of public indecency."

Astonished, I blinked up at him. His eyes were open and fixed on mine, the ravenous look in them made me ache with desire. I believed without a doubt that he meant each word. I allowed him to take my hand and lead me outside.

There was a black Hummer limo with dark tinted windows and a man leaning against it. "Give me the keys and have a walk to the pizza shop down the street, Rob."

The bodyguard wordlessly tossed the keys to Travis and obeyed him without looking back. He hit the unlock button on the remote and opened the door, pulling me in after him. He closed the door behind us, locking the entire thing with the remote before he set it aside. His eyes remained on me the whole time; his expression full of intent and promise.

I moved to the seat across from him, tugging at the hem of my dress as I tried to ignore the desire coursing through my veins.

He moved closer, placing his arms on either side of my thighs. The way his eyes racked over my body was stimulating in a way that was almost poetic.

Tugging his shirt over his head, I ran my hands along the ridges of his abs. I was swollen with desire, and I knew it wouldn't take much. The intense way we'd danced together had sparked an insatiable fire within me, and the fervent way he looked at me had me shivering with need.

We came together, our lips meeting frantically. His tongue brushed across my bottom lip, tasting me. "You taste like *peaches*," he said, sounding tortured.

His thumb brushed across my swollen bottom lip. The gesture was so gentle, so reverent, it stole the breath from my lungs.

But then, the mood shifted, becoming heavy with desire. His hand tangled in my hair, and he used it to guide my lips to his. My hands worked on unbuckling his jeans. Travis stopped kissing me, grinning against my lips as he shifted to help me.

He shimmied out of his jeans like he'd done so a million times before. My stomach lurched when the intensity of just how much that thought stung. I was certain this wasn't Travis's first time in the back of a limo, although it was mine.

I stumbled over that thought, wondering how I was supposed to complete with all the beautiful women he'd encountered, and all the beautiful women he would encounter in the future.

But then I couldn't breathe, all of my negative thoughts and insecurities flushing out of my system as Travis's lips danced with mine. He pulled me on top of him, unzipping my dress. He tugged the material down, freeing my breasts. I moved against him, and he moaned as the tip of his thickened cock stroked against my centre. I sank down on him without thinking. Both of us stilled except for him pulsing inside of me and my walls squeezing him in response. I shifted a bit, and Travis exhaled sharply.

"We need a condom," I bit my lip, the feel of him skin to skin with me so was so erotic. I never wanted it to end. It felt as if my eyes were truly rolling into the back of my skull. I didn't move. I couldn't.

"I'm clean," Travis assured me, his eyes searching mine. "Are you on the pill?"

I nodded, biting my lip enough to almost puncture the skin. The responsible Becky insisted I hop off and dig for a condom, or halt the sexy-times...but the reckless Becky wanted to keep going, and she hadn't been out to play in a long while.

And I believed him, because his eyes were so open and raw, and I knew he really wouldn't put me at risk. He'd proven that time and time again. Not so much with his words, but his actions. It was in all of the things he didn't say.

So I started to move my hips, riding him slowly. His head fell back against the seat, and he moaned. A moment later, he cupped my breasts in his hands and brought his lips to them, taking each of my nipples in turn into his hot mouth. He flicked at the swollen peaks as I rode him fast and hard.

I felt my orgasm rushing over me in waves. My body pulsed around him, and Travis took control, guiding my hips with his hands. His brow scrunched up, and he stared up at me like he was seeing a glimpse of heaven. His fingers pressed into my hips as he thrust into me as far as he could and roared out his release.

Hearts pounding, we collapsed against each other. My head landed on his shoulder, and he brought his hand up to stroke the flesh on my thighs. I trembled, drawing in a shaky breath. I felt as if I'd fallen to earth from the stars.

He leaned forward with me to grab a towel and a bottle of water from the bar. He poured some water on the towel and used it to clean the evidence of our joining from between my legs. My eyes closed, tears threatening to spill at his tender touch. I breathed through it, collecting the broken pieces of my heart together, and opened my eyes.

"They're probably looking for me," I said, climbing off of him, feeling shame-faced. This night was supposed to be about the girls—about Tessa, and I'd snuck off for a quickie.

"I'll help you find them," Travis offered, grinning at me as he pulled up his jeans. The action reminded me of my earlier thought, about how many times he'd hooked up in the back of a limo. I felt sick.

I had no right to feel sick. Travis had only done what I'd told him to do—live his life the way he always; had an unattached bachelor roaming from one corner of the world to another.

"It's okay." I avoided his eyes as I adjusted my dress and attempted to zip it up. Travis's hands took over, effortlessly tugging it up.

I wished it was easy to let go of all of my fears and fall completely into him. Instead, I held myself back, retreating the moment I let him in.

Travis seemed to know where my thoughts had gone. He cupped my cheek with his hand, gently guiding my eyes to his. "You're beautiful. Did you know that?"

"Thanks," I said hesitantly. I climbed off of him, feeling an achy breathlessness. I searched for my underwear, finding it in the cup holder between the seats across from where we'd been. "Well...they're probably looking for me," I said looking back toward the club, regrettably.

"Alright, let's find your party." Travis put his cap back on before he opened the door and stepped out. He waited for me with his hand extended, his eyes twinkling. He tugged down on the bottom half of my dress, his fingers brushing against the back of my thighs, sending little tingles of awareness shooting to my core.

After paying the bouncers off to let us back in, we walked into the club. Travis lingered by the closed coat check and watched as I made my way across the dance floor back to the bachelorette party. Most of the girls were too inebriated to have noticed my absence. He nodded at me as I slipped unnoticed back into their fold. Katie shoved a shot glass in my hand, winking at me with a self-satisfied smile on her face.

"I told them you were making a call to check in on Aiden," Katie giggled in my ear. "They don't suspect a thing."

"Thanks." The deceit still made me uncomfortable, but less so than it would have had I had to carry it by myself.

"Here's to love!" she toasted loudly, raising her glass high and winking at Tessa.

"Hear, hear!" everyone shouted, raising their own glasses before tossing them back. The liquid burned the back of my throat, and my eyes instinctively went to the last place I'd seen Travis. He was gone, but my flesh singed where he'd touched me, as if imprinting his hands to memory.

MY MIND WAS SPINNING and spiraling in millions of interwoven paths, filtering from one concern to the next. My therapist often referred to these as "obsessive thoughts", and urged me to try different coping methods to redirect them.

I let Katie drive home the next day, while I sank into the passenger seat. I was running on fumes, exhausted from struggling to stop the obsessive thoughts.

Every time I closed my eyes, I saw him. I felt him, the way he'd touch me...and I wanted everything he promised. But I was afraid, afraid to start something and be left wanting. At least I still had my pride, and I wasn't all that sure it would remain intact if Travis were to grow bored of me.

It's why I'd been so insistent that we wait until after the wedding to start seeing each other. And even after that, I wanted to keep things quiet for a while. I wanted to tell my family in my own time, and I didn't want to risk the possibility of being an even bigger target to gossip.

But already, I'd lost control.

"What's wrong?" Katie asked, pulling me from my pity party. "You've been kind of down all morning, did the visit with Travis not go over well?"

"It's not that," I shook my head, recounting how wonderful he'd been. My reactions had little to do with Travis himself, and everything to do with my lack of trust in people in general.

"So what's the problem them?" she asked, turning to look at me with her brows pinched together in confusion.

So many thoughts entangled my mind, and I couldn't pause them, no matter how badly I wanted to. They came out in a muddled rush.

"I want to feel the way he makes me feel. I don't know how to describe it but...he's never made me feel like a victim, or damaged by my past," I admitted. Katie drew in a deep breath, she knew how important that was to me; to be seen as something other than the damaged girl I was.

"Does he know about it? Like, all of it?" she asked, her eyes darting to mine.

"I don't know. If he does he's never brought it up," I shrugged.

"Don't you think it's something you guys should probably talk about?" she suggested

"I'm scared to show him my scars. I'm scared that when I do, he'll start to see me like a victim."

Katie looked at me again, her eyes aching. "You're a survivor,

Becky, not a victim. You've finished school, you've got a great job, and family and friends who love you. You survived, and you thrived. You are literally the strongest person I know."

Her words brought forth fresh tears, and she began to cry too. I nodded to acknowledge the progress I'd made. It hadn't been an easy road, but I was proud of the leaps and bounds I'd made since everything happened.

"If I let him in, I'm afraid that I'll lose everything I've worked for. My independence, my dignity..." I trailed off helplessly. "I don't like feeling insecure, or giving him the power to destroy me. I don't want to close myself off to love, but I guess I just don't know how to open myself up to it, either," I admitted.

Katie's hand reached out across the seat to take mine. She squeezed it gently before she released it to hold the steering wheel.

"Trust takes time to build," she assured me. "But in order to build it...you've got to be honest about your thoughts and feelings. If he's the right guy—and my Spidey senses tell me he is—then he'll understand and he'll help you work through it."

CHAPTER TWELVE

ravis

I COULDN'T STOP THINKING about her, running Friday night over and over again in my mind. What we'd shared in the limo had been heavy, and it had shifted something between us.

I'd never gone bareback before, but the moment she'd sank down on me, I didn't want it to stop. It was heaven in its purest form. But that level of trust was something she'd never given me before, and I knew it unsettled her.

After four days of hearing nothing from her, and not seeing her at all around town, I was beginning to worry. I gave in and texted her.

I want to see you again soon.

It didn't take her long to reply.

Sorry Travis, I can't this week. I'm working every day and I have to help Tessa and Elle with last minute wedding things.

I sat at the island in my kitchen, sulking at my phone.

During my tenth read through, Mom walked into the kitchen and gave me a peculiar look.

"What's gotten into you lately?" she asked, walking around the length of the counter and pausing before me. She leaned against the counter, resting her arms on the marble surface. She was dressed in her uniform, ready to head out to her Thursday evening shift at the diner. "You've been sulking since you got back from Toronto."

"I have not," I retorted, even though I knew that's exactly what I had been doing. I was desperate to talk to her, to make sure that she was okay—but it wasn't a conversation I wanted to have over text message, and I knew she wouldn't appreciate me showing up on her doorstep. I'd risk running into Braden.

"Who's the girl?"

"What girl?" I asked, feigning surprise. Mom saw right through my bullshit and arched a brow. I deflated a little under her scrutiny. "Becky Miller."

"Becky Miller?" Mom repeated, recognition flickering in her eyes.

"The one and only," I sighed, scratching at the back of my head as I scowled down at my phone.

"How long has this been going on for?"

"On and off for the last four years or so," I admitted. "It was supposed to be a one-night stand, but every time I come home we hook up again."

Mom didn't look impressed with my answer. She thought I played the field, and I didn't like to give her any additional reasons to believe it. She didn't like players, and rightfully so. My sperm donor had been a player. I didn't begrudge her jumping to that conclusion, not with the tabloids blasting my latest escapades, but most of that stuff was fabricated.

They painted me as the country play boy, always with a new girl on my arm. Most of those girls the paparazzi caught me with were friends or fans, and I definitely hadn't had sexual relations with any of the ones I'd been pictured with in the last two years. I was completely hung up on Becky.

She was my favourite song that I wanted to play over and over again and get lost in the chords.

"Before you give me shit, Mom, please know that it's mostly Becky's idea."

Becky clung to her rules with all she had. In the past, we'd avoided being around each other and the group at the same time. When we couldn't avoid it, we had to keep our distance. She didn't want me talking to her, fearing that someone would pick up on what we were doing behind closed doors.

She didn't want me coming by her house in case one of her brother's saw me, or in case she had to explain my presence to Aiden. She wasn't comfortable with my place for the same reason.

"Like I believe that," Mom scoffed, rolling her eyes.

"It's true." My mother's lack of faith in me stung, but I only had myself to blame. "She wanted the one-night stand, and she was the one who wanted to keep whatever we have going for us a secret. She's terrified of commitment and dodges any attempt I make at moving things forward with us," I sighed heavily, my eyes darting to the sliding doors that led to the wrap-around porch overlooking the lake.

Mom was quiet for several long moments; I could feel her eyes on me. "Just be patient, Travis. You've never been good at waiting...but it sounds like Becky needs your patience."

I didn't have to ask my mom how she knew that. Mom raised me all alone, without any assistance from family. She didn't have one, and my bio dad hadn't stuck around long enough to even give her a last name. Mom's childhood wasn't the greatest, and I knew she struggled to trust men too. If she was taking the time to give me advice, I'd take the time to listen to it.

"I'm being as patient as I can." Mom was right: patience was never my strong suit. I was the kind of guy who preferred to go out and get what I wanted. It wasn't so simple when it came to Becky. It had to be on her terms—it was the only way she'd feel comfortable.

———

MY MASK WAS SECURELY in place when I rolled up the private road that led to Brock's cabin and the beach. I eased the Mercedes to a full stop. Braden was the first person I encountered when I approached with my loot.

"Way to be inconspicuous." He shook his head as he eyed my Mercedes, but I knew he was impressed. Braden was a mechanic and had always loved tinkering on vehicles, but I doubt he saw flashy six-figure sports cars often at the shop. Most people around here drove trucks or cars that could handle the massive dumpings of snow each winter.

"This *is* inconspicuous," I shrugged, grinning. "I could have brought the Porsche." Braden's eyes brightened. He loved that thing, and so did every car nut within hearing distance.

Gordon sauntered over and threw his arm around my shoulders in greeting. "Where are your bodyguards tonight?" He asked with a shit-eating grin on his face.

Being famous enough to merit having bodyguards around could be frustrating—especially when your old best friends razzed you.

Paul was already back in Nashville, and Rob was still holed up at the motel he'd rented. Neither one of them were really needed for regular crowd management anymore, now that the stampede was over and tourism had begun to slow down.

"Not here. I figured we were far enough out in the middle of nowhere that nobody would come across us," I answered.

"Fair enough, besides—they're *kind of* buzzkills," Gordon snorted, tossing back the rest of his beer.

"You're telling me," I sighed in agreement, taking in the transformed waterfront. String lights illuminated the entire beach area. Several chairs were arranged around the fire pit, with the fire already burning. The picnic tables were weighed down with food and there was an old wheel barrow with a wooden sign that read *Beer Barrow*. I nodded at Grady, Tommy, and Ben in greeting before my attention zeroed in on Brock.

"Hey! Groom guy! What the fuck is with this backwoods sausage fest!? Aren't we supposed to celebrate your dwindling time as a free man by ogling strippers and shit?" I asked, placing the brown paper bag I'd brought down on the table and embracing my best friend in a one armed hug.

"Guess I got enough of a stripper show when you brought the Vegas escorts by Flanigan's," Brock responded smoothly, his lips twitching with a repressed grin. *Fair enough.* I tried not to wince at the reminder. "Hey, Grayson—this is my buddy Travis. Travis, this is Grayson Dixon."

Recognition flashed as I appraised Brock's friend, Grayson. His face and his name both seemed so familiar to me, but I'd met so many people over the course of my career that it was impossible to place him. "Hey, do I know you from some-where?" I asked, tilting my head as I tried to figure it out.

"By proxy, yes," Grayson replied, his eyes narrowing as he gave me a rather menacing scowl. His reaction to my question helped me place him, so I let it roll of me like water on a duck.

"Ah right, you're Everly's man right?" Grayson clenched his jaw and nodded once, the only response I could expect to get from him, if my memory served me right. "How the hell is she? Haven't seen her in a while! I think the last time I saw her was at the 2014 Music Awards."

"She's good," Grayson replied unwillingly, uncomfortable and pissed off at my line of questioning. I had to resist the urge to chuckle at him for seeing me as a threat.

Everly and I had done a few charity concerts together in the past. She had impressed me with her talent, and the fact that she hailed from a small town east of Toronto hadn't hurt. She'd been very down to earth, and we became easy friends. But friends was all we ever were. She was fun and creative...but she had also been tragically distracted...as if her heart had been elsewhere. Two years ago, her sister died in a car crash and she left the music scene.

"Everly Daniels was the lead singer of *Autumn Fields*," I explained, catching Brock and Braden's bewildered expressions as they watched our exchange. "Will she be at the wedding?"

Grayson was silent for a moment before replying. "Yeah, she will."

"Fucking eh! It's a small world after all," I joked, laughing. Grayson seemed less than thrilled with me, so I picked up the brown paper bag that contained one very expensive bottle of aged whiskey. "Anybody want a shot?"

BY THE END of the night—and after we'd consumed nearly the entire bottle of aged whiskey—Grayson had warmed up to me. I couldn't stop thinking about how good it would be to turn the first-dance song I was going to sing solo into a duet with Everly as we sat around the fire pit slinging beers and smoking darts.

Once the idea came to me, I couldn't let it go. Becky *loved* Autumn Fields, and it was a miniscule way I could show her I cared about her—I *saw* her, and I paid attention to the little things—like her CD collection in the car.

Plus, it benefited me. My music to date had mostly been about having a good time, but I was considering changing direction. I'd slipped in a few more romantic songs on my latest album, and I was toying with the idea of doing a duet. It was something I'd never done before, but the song *was* meant to be sung as a duet.

Everly's voice had a folksy quality to it, and from a musical standpoint...we complemented each other nicely. It'd be a good test run to see how I sounded in a duet, before I made a massive fool of myself in the studio.

Some of the guys had retreated into their tents, but a few were fishing off the docks. Neither Grayson nor I felt like fishing, so we sat around the fire talking about how I knew Everly. We had a bit of a heart to heart, where I told him that I'd only ever seen Everly as a friend and a talented artist.

"Yeah, she's talented," he said, nodding in agreement. He stared into the fire and took another swig of the hundred year old whiskey we'd been drinking. He smiled a little, shaking his head as if he couldn't believe how lucky he was.

"Do you think she ever misses it?" I asked. Sometimes, the thought would cross my mind. There was a time when I had truly believed I wouldn't give it up for anything. But I knew without a doubt that I would give it up, if that's what it took.

"Without a doubt," Grayson admitted quietly. "She still writes and sings, and we've talked about it before and she calls it her prolonged pause. She wants to be home for Cadance, and she's not ready to go back. Not yet, anyway."

Leaning forward, I dipped my chin forward. "Do you think she'd help an old friend woo the girl of his dreams?" I asked hopefully.

"How?" he asked distrustfully.

"By singing a duet for the first dance song at Brock's wedding."

"I'll ask," Grayson said after a moment of consideration. "But no promises. Everly's never met Brock before. She's basically only coming because she knows we're friends. I don't have many of those," he half-laughed. "I'm a bit of a dick."

WITH ANOTHER FIVE days to kill before the wedding, I grew restless. I could hear the countdown in my head, and I needed to escape for a bit, so I took my mom to Nashville for a few days. Being in such close proximity to Becky and unable to see or talk to her was driving me mental. I needed to put a border between us for a few days, or I knew I'd blow our cover and jeopardize it all.

Mom had never been to Nashville, and it was fun seeing it all through her eyes, seeing the pride that reflected in them when she listened to the tracks on my new album in the studio.

I stopped in to see my usual stylist to get my hair cut for the wedding. I had it buzzed short at the sides, keeping it a little longer on top. My curls went with the shorter cut, but it was so much cooler in the thick humidity and summer heat.

We returned the night before the rehearsal dinner, and I counted down the hours until I saw her again.

The day before the wedding, everyone was supposed to meet at the Armstrong's farm to set up and do a trial run of the ceremony. After that, everyone would head to The Dock for the rehearsal dinner.

I showed up early, hoping for a chance to talk to Becky, but she came last with Aiden in tow, who immediately darted over to the field where Tessa's horses were grazing.

She grabbed a stack of linens and started to arrange them over the tables. I followed her, catching the other end of the tablecloth with my hands. I helped her direct it over the table and make sure that the sides were even in length.

"Are you okay?" I asked lowly, my eyes drinking in the sight of her, searching for an answer as we went about our task. We'd managed to cloth three tables before I could no longer hold back the flood of questions I had.

"I'm fine," Becky responded, her gaze traveling across the room, noting where everyone was in relation to where we were. She shifted from foot to foot, her cheeks flushing prettily.

"Good, good," I grinned. "Tomorrow's the big day, huh?"

"Yep," Becky said, her lips popping on the 'p'. She continued to avoid my gaze, moving on to the next table.

"Come home with me after?" I said with a wink and a smile that was far too hopeful.

She swallowed hard, finally dragging her eyes back to mine. The fury that swirled within her irises took me by surprise. "What, lose interest in your blonde friend so soon?" she demanded hotly.

"What are you talking about?" I asked, confused. She cast a nervous glance to where her brother stood with his bride-to-be.

"This is exactly why I called things off," she muttered, shaking her head at me in disappointment before she turned on her heel and stomped off to help Elle with the centerpieces. I gaped after her, completely at a loss.

I wanted to follow her, beg her to talk to me and let me know what I did to piss her off so much, but I knew that would only aggravate her more, so I backed off and focused on doing my part. I continued to spread the tablecloths and set out the centerpieces.

Sue Thompson put her fingers to her lips and whistled loudly. "Alright folks! Pastor Bruce is here. It's time to do that trial run!" she called out, her voice projecting easily across the gleaming dance floor. We all shuffled outside to the field where we'd set up for the ceremony.

Gordon's father and two brothers had set up the white chairs and the aisle while we'd set up the reception tent, and it looked great.

I had been to a lot of completely over the top weddings—celebrities with millions of dollars to spare had no qualms with spending a sickening amount of money. None of those weddings would hold a candle to the set up at the Armstrong farm for tomorrow.

Gordon and Tommy had created a wedding arbor made

from thick birch branches which sat almost twenty feet away from the bush. It was minimalistic and somehow, completely perfect...completely Tessa and Brock.

It was beautiful, but all I could focus on was Becky's hostility and her remarks. "Who's my blonde friend?" I whispered while we waited for our turn to take a spin down the aisle.

"Like you don't know," she whispered back angrily. She wouldn't look at me.

"I don't, actually. Care to enlighten me?"

"We are not talking about this right now," Becky hissed.

Pastor Bruce motioned us to move forward. Taking her arm, I escorted her down the aisle, my mind still whirling with the accusations she'd tossed at me. Becky didn't look too pleased either. "Don't forget to smile! This is a joyous day," Pastor Bruce said, and both Becky and I forced smiles.

I had done something to disappoint her, that much was clear. But as I racked my brain, I couldn't figure out *why*. I'd given her space because she said she was busy.

I released her arm and went to stand with Brock and Braden, my throat constricting as I watched Becky take her place beside Elle near the arbor. A few years ago, commitment and marriage weren't even on my radar, and suddenly it was all I could think of and the person who'd finally sparked that interest and possibility seemed hell-bent on running every chance she got.

AT THE REHEARSAL DINNER, Becky made sure to sit as far away from me as she possibly could, focusing all of her attention on literally everybody else but me.

I sat on the opposite side of the table, between Gordon and his cousin Caroline. Caroline was a slight little thing, long fair hair, delicate features, big green eyes and a dusting of freckles across her nose and upper cheeks. We'd met a few times before, when she'd come to Parry Sound for a summer visit, but I'd never paid much attention to her before.

"I hope you don't mind me sitting here," she breathed, blinking up at me flirtatiously.

"It's all good," I shrugged. I could feel Becky's eyes burning a hole in the side of my head. Turning, I caught her watching. She looked away the moment we locked gazes, but I'd seen the hurt in the depths of those cobalt blue eyes.

The evening was full of toasts and boisterous celebrating, but I couldn't really get into it. I was happy as all hell for Brock and Tessa, but at a complete and total loss for how to handle the precarious situation with Becky.

My phone vibrated in my jeans. I pulled it out of my pocket, noticing I had a text message from Katie. All it contained was a link to an article on a celebrity gossip website. I clicked it, seeing several blurry pictures of me in Nashville. Then I read the headline;

Notorious playboy country singer Travis Channing was spotted back in Nashville earlier this week with a blonde beauty.

I snorted, shaking my head and sliding the phone back into my pocket. I looked up, catching Becky's eye, and shook my head slightly. I was equal parts amused and pissed off.

Of course she'd seen the article and would have taken it the wrong way, but it stung that she'd sooner throw up walls than talk to me about it.

Shortly after dinner was served, Becky got up and headed to the bathroom. I waited a minute before standing up and walking to the hallway where the bathrooms were located. I leaned back against the wall, resting with my foot on it.

The hallway provided enough privacy that even if someone from our table looked over, they wouldn't see us.

A moment later, the door swung open and she stepped out. She paused when she saw me waiting in the hallway.

"What, Travis?" she demanded, crossing her arms. My expression somber, I stepped away from the wall.

"I just wanted to let you know that the woman I was pictured with in Nashville is my mother, Becs. If you're looking for a reason to be pissed at me, you'll have to find another one," I told her.

Her eyes flashed with regret and embarrassment, and she dropped her gaze to the floor, unable to look at me.

I stepped a little closer, tipping her chin so she'd finally look at me. "You are the only woman I've been with in two years."

"But…I thought…" she trailed off.

"That I was carrying on with every girl I met?" I filled in the blanks she'd left, smiling sadly. "I tried to—you told me to, and I thought I meant what I said about not wanting commitment. I *did* mean it, when I said it. But…you were all I wanted, and you're still all I want. One day—sooner or later—you're going to believe that."

It took everything I had to pull my hand back and walk away, but I knew I needed to give her space to process.

CHAPTER THIRTEEN

ecky

After the rehearsal dinner, we headed to the Armstrong's farm while the groomsmen went to Brock's cabin. Tessa invited all of the bridesmaids to spend the night at her family's farm so that her cousin, Caroline, could do our makeup and hair in the morning.

I brought Aiden with me to Tessa's, knowing that sleeping arrangements at Brock's would be even more cramped than they were at the Armstrong homestead.

"Why couldn't I go with Uncle Brock and Uncle Braden?" Aiden asked when I tucked him into Tessa's bed.

"Because, you're going to bed now anyway. You've got an important role tomorrow, and you need your sleep," I responded, kissing him on the forehead. Aiden was the ring bearer, and he'd been excited about it ever since Brock had asked him.

"Okay," he said, yawning. He was already half asleep. Once

his head touched the pillow, it would only be a matter of minutes before he drifted off. He'd always been that way. "Love you, Mom."

"Love you too, Aiden. Goodnight baby," I whispered, kissing his cheek before I snuck out of Tessa's bedroom. I closed the door gently and headed back downstairs.

In my absence, the girls had spread out sleeping bags and pillows. I paused by the railing, watching the scene play out before me with a small smile on my lips. I'd never gone to a slumber party before, and I'd imagined this is exactly what one would be like.

Elle was passing around glasses of wine, and everyone was chattering with excitement.

"I can't believe tomorrow is *finally* the day!" Tessa exclaimed. She was sitting cross legged on the floor with a large glass of wine in hand.

"I know! How are your feet?" Caroline giggled, shoving Tessa's foot with her toes.

"Toasty warm!" she grinned.

Katie motioned for me to join her. She'd spread out a sleeping bag for me beside hers, and held out a glass of wine for me. I sat down, accepting the glass gratefully. It had been a hectic, stressful last few days.

"I told you there was more to the story than meets the eye," Katie said low enough for only me to hear. My eyes flickered over to Caroline and Tessa.

I felt embarrassed whenever I looked at Caroline. I'd jumped to my own conclusions when I'd seen the pictures of Travis with a blonde woman in Nashville, and when Caroline had sat down beside him...I'd actually thought *she* was the blonde woman in the photos.

When Travis cornered me outside of the bathroom to tell me the woman was his mother, I realized how foolish I'd been. None of those pictures had suggested a sexual relationship, but

I'd let the so called article get into my head, like the insecure fool that I was.

"We'll see," I sighed. "This is what I meant when I said I had way too many issues. Travis isn't going to want to stick around."

"I call bullshit," Katie retorted quietly. "He's really into you." I paused, thinking about our exchange in the hallway of the restaurant a few hours before. He'd been so sweet, so reassuring, although I knew my accusations had wounded him.

Getting comfortable, I laid-back with my head on the pillow. My limbs were heavy with exhaustion, and it wasn't long until I drifted off, the sound of quiet chatter a welcome lullaby.

THE CEREMONY HAD BEEN BREATHTAKING, there simply wasn't another way to describe it. I was forever grateful that Caroline had brought her airbrushing kit and used waterproof mascara. Had she not, I likely would have cried off all of my makeup watching Tessa and Brock as they stood beneath the arbor and vowed to love each other in sickness and in health.

I ached with sadness that Mom was missing out on this beautiful day, but I knew she'd want us to enjoy it. When Brock had asked me to stand in her place and dance with him during the mother-son dance, I'd been honoured, and though I'd had to hold the tears back from slipping down my cheeks the whole time, I felt her presence with us.

Valerie picked up Aiden around nine to take him back to her house for the night so that I wouldn't have to leave the reception early. I watched her taillights disappear down Tessa's driveway before turning back to the reception tent.

Tessa was standing on her tippy toes, trying to peer around with an urgent look on her face. I walked over quickly. "What's wrong?"

"We have ten minutes before we do the bouquet toss, and I

can't find Elle," she answered. I'd just been outside to see Aiden off, but I hadn't seen Elle. Of course, I hadn't been looking for her either.

"I'll find her, don't panic," I said, gently squeezing her arm. I gave her a reassuring smile before I released her.

"Who are you looking for?" Travis asked, appearing at my elbow when I was searching faces at the tables. We'd walked down the aisle together and posed together for photographs, but we hadn't gotten an opportunity to talk to one another. But I was still aware of him.

"Elle, or Alex. Or even Braden at this point," I sighed. I didn't have a good feeling about all three of them missing at the same time.

"I just saw Alex leave the tent," Travis supplied. "Want me to help you find them?"

"No, that's alright," I told him, my lips curling up in the hint of a smile. "If they come back, tell them we're going to do the bouquet toss soon."

"Will do," Travis answered, his eyes twinkling. "Save me a dance, okay?"

"Maybe," I smiled back, relieved that he wasn't angry about the way I had reacted when I found out about his Nashville trip and assumed the worst.

I stepped out of the tent, spotting Elle and Braden standing just before it. "There you guys are!" I said, slowing when I saw Elle's tear streaked face. "What did you do?" I demanded, glaring at my brother.

"It's not his fault," Elle interrupted, trembling. "I-I think Alex and I just broke up."

"Oh Elle, I'm sorry," I said, hugging her. I shot Braden a suspicious look. He was totally at fault. I'd warned him to leave her be, and of course he hadn't listened. Not that I'd expected him to.

"What's happening inside?" Elle asked, immediately slipping

back into her maid-of-honour hat. I recognized the avoidance tactic.

"We're getting ready to do the garter and bouquet toss," I answered cautiously.

"Great," Elle exhaled. I turned to head inside, assuming they'd be right behind me. Tessa was still waiting by the stage. She approached Elle and they talked for a minute. I wandered over to stand beside Katie near the dance floor to wait for the bouquet toss.

Little White Church played while Tessa walked out to the middle of the dance floor and stopped, standing with her back to the crowd of single women behind her, myself included. She looked over her shoulder and grinned wickedly before looking forward again. Tossing the bouquet over her head, it sailed through the air and into Sue Thompson's hands.

"Who's the lucky guy, Sue?" Tommy joked. Sue waved her hand, her face red with embarrassment. Tommy called all of the bachelors to the dance floor, and I moved to stand off to the side. I passed Travis, and the back of his hand brushed against mine. He winked at me, clearly enjoying himself and the open bar.

Kenny Loggin's *Danger Zone* blasted out of the speakers as Brock dropped to his knees and put his hands behind his back. His head disappeared beneath Tessa's dress, and he painstakingly removed the garter with his teeth. He stood up, flinging it over his shoulder. It flew straight at Tessa's dad and landed on his shoulder.

"Was that intentional?" Tommy asked, laughing. Bill buckled forward and laughed deeply.

I chuckled, shaking my head. "You know, that's not a bad idea..." Katie said thoughtfully from beside me. "Bill and Sue, I mean."

"Everybody knows Bill never got over his wife," I responded.

Katie shrugged. "If I ever died, I wouldn't want Ben to be married to my memory. I'd want him to move on."

"You can't force people to move on," I sighed, watching as Braden took Elle's hand and lead her out on the dance floor.

Before Katie could respond, Ben grabbed her from behind. "Dance with me, wife," he said, his lips close to her ears. She laughed and sent me an apologetic look.

"Go on, have fun!" I told her, smiling. I was content to watch everyone around me enjoy themselves.

My eyes found Travis's across the dance floor. He brought the beer he was drinking to his lips, taking a deep sip. He licked his lips sensually, his eyes full of promise and lust.

"You look like you needed a drink," Sam exclaimed, appearing out of nowhere and offering me a tall glass. I'd seen her sitting at the ceremony and during speeches, but I hadn't had a chance to talk to her.

"That I do," I sighed gratefully, reluctantly pulling my eyes away from him. I smiled at Sam and took the drink from her. "It's good to see you again! How have you been?"

Sam looked beautiful in a deep purple lace dress, her brown hair curled and held back in intricate braids.

"I've been good! Quite the wedding, huh?" she remarked, watching everybody on the dance floor. Tommy was wearing his tie on his forehead, dancing like a baboon.

"Yeah, it is," I smiled, relieved that everything had gone so wonderfully for Brock and Tessa. Sure, we'd had a few hitches— like the slight tear in Tessa's dress after the last bathroom trip, and the whole Alex and Elle situation. It was the first wedding I had been a part of, but I'd heard a lot of horror stories from the girls at work.

"That first dance song was incredible, wasn't it?" she asked, her eyes darting back to mine and twinkling.

"Yeah, it was incredible." My gaze drifted back to Travis. He sat at a table with Brock's old friend from work, Grayson, and his fiancé—Everly Daniels, the lead singer of one of my favourite bands. To say I'd been shocked when I saw her walk up to the microphone to join Travis in a duet was an understatement. I hadn't even known my brother knew her, let alone that she'd be coming to the wedding to sing with Travis.

They'd sounded incredible together, and I'd been reduced to tears while I watched my brother and his new wife spin around on the dance floor and listened to their soulful duet.

"Did you figure it out with him yet?" Sam asked tentatively.

I bit my lip and shrugged with one shoulder, glancing back to her. "Not really. Did you figure it out with Tommy?"

"Not really," she responded with a small laugh. "He still looks at me like a friend."

"But he invited you to the wedding. That has to mean something."

"I was coming anyway," she laughed, then sighed. "It means he didn't know who else to ask and didn't want to show up alone," Sam shrugged. "It's cool though, I have a secret addiction to weddings. They're so beautiful and dream-like."

"Well, I'm glad you came," I told her earnestly.

"Sam! Come dance!" Tommy called out, waving her forward.

Sam downed her glass of wine and gave me a timid smile. "At least everybody's drunk enough to not notice how terribly I dance."

"And with Tommy as a partner, I'm sure you'll look like a pro," I laughed, watching as Tommy did the sprinkler. She smiled, shaking her head as she walked out to join him.

THE NEXT FEW hours slipped by quickly, and around midnight, Tessa and Brock left for the airport. Soon after, the night started to wind down as more and more people began to leave the dance floor. Tommy and Sam left when she could no longer stand, and Katie and Ben had taken off shortly after. Gordon, Annaka, Grady, Paige, and to my complete surprise—Bill and Sue—were still tearing it up on the dance floor.

My feet were throbbing and my cheeks hurt from smiling and laughing so much. I had danced a lot, although not with Travis. I'd wanted to, but I hadn't trusted myself to keep it PG, and I wasn't ready to come out in the open with whatever it was we were doing.

Our eyes met from across the dance floor, and the look within his hazel depths had me putting my glass down and turning to leave the reception tent. His desire roared through me, tangling with mine and adding fuel to the fire within me. I knew if we met out on the dance floor, I wouldn't be able to keep my hands off him. The seven glasses of wine I'd consumed throughout the night made certain of that fact.

I could hear someone following me, and I knew without looking that it was Travis. The gravel crunched beneath his dress shoes, and he came to a stop just behind me.

"Come back to my place," he whispered, catching a curl and tucking it behind my ear. I couldn't help but melt against him, the feel of his lips on my neck made me grind my ass against his thickening erection.

I turned into his embrace, my hands tightening their hold on his crisp dress shirt. "Okay," I whispered. He kissed me. I responded ardently, my tongue dancing with his, my teeth gently biting into his bottom lip. My need was blinding my ability to take things slow.

"I want you so fucking bad, it actually hurts," he told me.

"Let's get out of here then," I said, swallowing hard as I gazed up at him. I was drunk enough on him to not care where we ended up, so long as we were together.

"Rob's already pulling the car around," Travis admitted with a sly grin, his hands massaging my ass as he tugged me closer to him. "Come on," he added, seeing the slick Escalade pull out of its parking spot. He grabbed my hand and we hopped into the back seat without a backwards glance.

I half expected him to maul me on the drive to his place, but Travis kept a respectable distance between us. His arm was slung around my shoulders, and my head rested against it, my chin turned to look at him while he watched me with quiet reverence.

He lowered his lips to my ear, his tongue gently flicking out to lick along my lobe. "I can't wait to see that dress on my floor," he whispered.

CHAPTER FOURTEEN

 ravis

"Travis Channing."

"Kimberley Channing," I said, matching my mom's stern voice with one of my own. I arched a brow at her, trying to keep the arrogant grin from my lips, lest I earn a slap in the back of the head.

"I already told you to stop spending money on me," she lectured, hands on her narrow hips. Mom had always been thin, especially back when I was a kid. She'd sacrifice everything on her plate so I could have a full meal in my belly.

"Mom," I sighed, bringing my hand up to massage my temple. I was a little hungover, my head was pounding from lack of sleep, and I was more than a little desperate to get back up to my bedroom. But naturally, Mom had no pity for me and had gone straight for my metaphorical balls when I'd gone downstairs to grab some coffee. "Can we talk about this later, please?"

I glanced toward the stairwell that led to my bedroom. Originally, that room had been used as an entertainment room, but I'd liked the fact that it was separate from all the other bedrooms. It had made sneaking Becky in the night before really easy.

"No, we're talking about it right now," she insisted, pressing her hands down against the marble countertop and forcing me to pay attention to her.

"Fine," I said, pressing the brew button on the coffee maker while I arched my brows at her. "I paid for your schooling to a program of your choice because you're smart and you deserve to have a career."

"I have a career," Mom sounded a little hurt, but she masked it well enough. Most people wouldn't have even detected it, but my mom was one of my best friend's, and I knew her. "I like my job, Travis. I like the people I meet."

Mom had worked as a waitress at a diner on the outskirts of town practically my whole life. She'd gotten pregnant with me when she was fifteen years old, knocked up by some guy that left town before she could even tell him about me. As a result, I grew up poor. Mom worked as hard as she could, but it was never enough. We often had to choose between paying rent and buying groceries. Shelter was important, especially during the cold Northern winters, so that came first.

But even though we struggled financially, my mom was an amazing mother. No matter how exhausted she was, she'd take time to play with me. She would throw a ball around in the backyard with me, and teach me how to cook using the limited ingredients in our cupboard. She taught me how to ride a bike and she was always singing, always dancing. Mom had a beautiful voice, and she passed that on to me.

When I was twelve, I vowed that one day, I'd change everything about her life. I'd take care of her so that she wouldn't have to work so hard to barely get by.

And that's exactly what I did. I worked my ass off so that one day, I could buy her a nice place to live in and make sure that she never went without anything ever again.

Some say I stumbled into fame, and maybe that's true. When I was eighteen, I entered a talent show and scored a record deal, not from the producers of the show, but from a Nashville recording office that liked my voice and my songs and saw potential in me.

I worked my ass off every moment of my life to get where I was. Going from rags to riches made me feel invincible. The first thing I did after my first album went platinum was purchase the beautiful cottage on Lake Rosseau, where my mom lived year round. I came back for a couple months here and there, but I had mostly bought it for her.

At first, it wasn't easy getting Mom to move from the prefabricated trailer I'd grown up in. She insisted that she didn't want me to spend my money on her. I had to tell her that it was a great way for me to build up equity and that I couldn't be there to manage the grounds when I was on tour ten months out of the year. I told her that I'd rather have someone I trusted living there than have to hire someone else to take care of it.

Only then did she agree to move in, but she kept her waitressing job, and I wanted her to do something more. I knew she was capable of it, and I lived in constant fear that I'd end up losing everything about this life I'd built. Stars fall all the time, musical careers die off and people fade into the background like they were never there. I didn't want her to go back to life the way it was before if that ever were to happen to me.

"Just think about it, okay?" I sighed, turning back to face her. I knew how much she loved waitressing. She was comfortable there, she knew the job and excelled at it. She was afraid to fail at something new, and that's what this was all about. I knew she wouldn't fail, I knew she'd do amazing because my mom was smart and quick. My mom was a fighter.

But Mom lacked a formal education, and while she'd gotten her GED when I was in high school, she still felt like she wasn't good or smart enough for more.

"I don't want to think about it, I want you to get your money back and invest in *your* future," she said firmly, her green eyes focused on my face.

"Maybe you could take a business course, or restaurant management. But we really do need to talk about this later, okay?" I said as the coffee finished brewing, the scent of it filling the room. I glanced back toward the stairs, hoping that my house guest wasn't trying to sneak out on me.

Mom looked down, noticing the two cups I'd set in front of the press. She caught me looking toward the stairs again. "I take it one of those isn't for me?" she arched a brow, pursing her lips.

"No, a friend crashed here last night," I admitted, trying not to grin.

"A friend that you're fetching coffee for? Must be one of the female variety," Mom called me out.

"Hey, now," I argued, grabbing the coffee pot from the cradle. "I would fetch a coffee for Brock if he asked. Gordon though, he'd be on his own. He's a prick."

"Watch your mouth Travis Joseph Channing before I wash it out with soap," Mom threatened, wagging her finger at me. She *hated* when I swore. It didn't matter how bad the curse word was, she'd flip her lid every single time.

"I think I'm a little old for that, Mom," I chuckled. "But I'll try to watch my tongue."

"Is it her? On second thought, don't answer that." Shaking her head, Mom turned around and walked away, leaving me to it. "We'll talk later. I'm going to the grocery store," she said over her shoulder. She made a show of grabbing her purse and closing the door.

Chuckling, I poured the coffee and splashed some cream and sugar into one, leaving the other black. I made my way back to my bedroom and nudged the door open with my hip. I closed it as quietly as I could manage with my foot, then padded across the room to my bed.

Sunlight poured in through the windows. Her dark hair was spread out across my white pillow. Her thick lashes rested against her cheeks, and she breathed softly as she slept, her chest rising and falling with each breath. She was gorgeous, and nobody else compared.

I came to a stop at my side of my bed, setting both mugs of coffee down on the night table. *My side of the bed*, it was an odd thought for me, one that made me take pause and look back down at her naked, sleeping body. Before her, I *liked* playing the field. The whole damn *bed* was my side, and I liked dating super models and actresses. It felt good, powerful, even...but four years ago I realized how empty the whole thing was.

She was beneath my skin, embedded in my heart. She couldn't see it, though. She didn't believe I was capable of being the relationship type. That much was obvious from her reaction over the Nashville photos.

She didn't trust me to catch her when she fell.

But I would, and I'd spend every day proving it.

Crawling into bed beside her, I laid on top of the sheet and brushed my hand across her naked shoulder, her skin smooth beneath my fingers. She inhaled, a soft smile spreading to her lips. "Quit staring at me, Travis."

Her voice was groggy from the amount of moaning I had her doing last night, and it made me grin.

"Can't help it," I told her, my thoughts running amuck with memories of her beneath me.

"I look like crap," she moaned, pulling the white sheet up over her head. I tugged it back down and rolled on top of her, pressing my body against hers. I was already hard again, already aching to be back inside her.

"You don't look like crap," I told her, a sly smirk on my face. "You look like you just had the best lay of your life."

"That's because I did," she murmured, her cheeks flushing.

With the wedding over, there were no more excuses to hide behind. I wanted to claim her as mine in every way, and I'd risk the potential beat down if it meant at the end of the day, I could crawl into bed and fall asleep with her in my arms.

The allure of single life no longer appealed to me. I wanted to build something real with her, and I'd stop at nothing to prove it.

I pressed my hard length against her pelvis again, my Calvin Klein pajama bottoms and the sheet the only things preventing me from sliding into her. I felt her nipples pebble through the thin sheet against my naked chest, and I throbbed. I kissed her slowly, moving my body against hers. She broke away, breathlessly. "I have to go," she told me, her voice full of regret. Her eyes bore into mine, panic and desire and adoration swirling around together, confusing me and intriguing me all at once.

"You're going to have to wait until I'm ready to drive you home," I reminded her, nudging her nose with mine. "Rob drove us back here, remember?" I murmured against her lips. She hummed in response and I kissed her again, softly tasting her and trying to coax her into relaxing. She kissed me back for several moments, her mouth hungrily moving against mine. Then she shuddered, and her hand pressed against my chest as she turned her head.

"I need to go," she insisted, dragging her eyes back to mine. I could see panic within their blue depths, and it saddened me until she continued. "I need to pick Aiden up," she said, pushing at my chest. "And I think it'd be better if I *didn't* have you drop me off...in case Braden is still at the house."

"I thought we were going to start telling people after the wedding?" I frowned, confused.

"Brock should be the first person to know, and I don't want

to trouble him on his honeymoon," she said, biting her lip. "Besides…I think we should try dating for a few weeks *without* everyone knowing, to see if it's even something we want to do."

"Oh, dating you is something that I definitely want to do, and I want everybody to know it," I responded cockily, pushing my pelvis into hers to drive the point home. Becky smiled and lifted her head, pressing her lips against mine softly.

"I'm not ready to tell anybody yet, Travis," she admitted reluctantly, her eyes searching mine.

"Why not?" I was trying to be patient and understanding, but it was hard when all I wanted to do was shout from the rooftops that she was mine and I was hers.

"Because I'm afraid it will ruin it," she confessed.

"How would telling our family and friends ruin it?" I asked her, looking down into her eyes.

"Everyone will have an opinion," she pointed out. "And I don't want to hear those opinions. It's the first time I've even been in a relationship since…well, you know."

"Right, well I'll give Rob a text," I said quickly, rolling off of her. I didn't want to push her too far too soon, and I understood her reasons.

I sat on the edge of my bed and fired out a text message to my bodyguard, Rob, telling him to meet me out front with a car to take her home. He also doubled as a driver when I needed him to. I grabbed the black mug of coffee, downing it in three huge gulps. I handed the other mug to her and fell back into my bed, reading Rob's reply. "He'll be here in ten."

I could feel her eyes watching me warily as she took a tentative sip from the mug she was holding. "Are you mad?" she asked me.

"No, I'm not mad," I replied, turning to give her a reassuring smile. I wasn't mad, but I was feeling a little bummed out that she was leaving so soon. I had illusions of spending the rest of the day with her, tangled up in my sheets.

"Good," she breathed as she got up, bringing the sheet with her. She set the mug down on the other night table, her eyes scanning the room before she spotted her dress. It laid crumbled on the floor by my door. She walked over to it and picked it up, shimmying into the tight little number. I walked across the room to pull the strap up over her shoulder.

Moving her tangled hair out of the way, my fingers brushed along her spine, my breath fanned across the nape of her neck. Her skin erupted into goose bumps. I kissed the sensitive spot between her shoulder and neck, loving how she tasted.

"Alright, he should be here by now," I told her, pulling away.

I walked her to the front door, grabbing her hand before she could open it. I pulled her back to me for one lingering, bittersweet kiss. I could feel her heart racing through the pulse in her wrist.

I opened the door for her. Rob was waiting beside the black Escalade, his sunglasses in place. I knew I could count on him to get her home safely.

"Shit...my car," Becky looked up at me with panic stricken eyes. She'd left it at the Armstrong's the night before, and I knew she was dreading showing up with Rob to pick it up. That wouldn't go unnoticed by any of the Armstrong's, if they were to catch her.

Which is one of the reasons why I had already taken care of it. The other reason? I wanted to make her life a little easier in any way that I could. "Rob drove it back to your place last night. He slipped the keys into your mailbox," I told her.

"How?"

"He went back for it after dropping us off. He took a cab from your house back to the Clayton's to get his car."

"That's amazing! Thank you both," she breathed, her shoulders relaxing. "I'll see you at the farm," she added, pressing her lips tentatively to mine before she slid out from under my arm and walked out to the car. Rob opened the back passenger door, letting her climb in before he closed it. I remained in the doorway, watching as the Escalade pulled away and trying to stomp down the pessimistic feeling sitting in my gut.

I understood it better than anybody, but it still sucked that we had to keep this secret for another week. It felt like we'd spent years being each other's secret. I wanted to break free of that, but she was right; we needed to tell Brock first.

I walked back inside, letting the door slam behind me. I had to shower and get ready to head over to the Armstrong's farm to help clean up the aftermath of the wedding reception. A part of me kind of wanted to sit at home and sulk with my guitar, but I had an obligation as one of the groomsmen. Braden would kick my ass if I bailed, and I knew I'd see Becky there.

Besides, there was no sense in sulking. At least Becky had acknowledged that we were something, even if she didn't want to share that knowledge with the world. I was happy to live in a private bubble with her a while longer, but I knew I'd want to solidify things between us before I returned to Nashville in September.

I was in and out of the shower within five minutes and dressed within two. I pulled my Under Armour cap on over my wavy, damp hair and grabbed my keys and wallet. Mom was in the kitchen unloading groceries.

"Want any help with that?" I asked, grabbing an apple from the bag.

"I can handle it," she replied, putting away the carton of eggs she'd bought. "What are your plans today?"

"I've got to go help clean up from the reception. Then who knows, maybe I'll stick around and see what everyone's up to, or maybe I'll just come home," I shrugged.

Mom nodded, giving me a loving smile. "Is Becky still here?"

"No, she left about half an hour ago," I answered.

"Oh," she looked a little put out by that. "I was hoping she'd stick around for brunch."

"She has to change and pick Aiden up," I explained, and Mom nodded with understanding.

"Another time then," she mused.

"Might be a while Mom, we're only just starting to figure things out and I don't think she'd be comfortable with any sort of meet the parents type situation," I warned her, kissing her on the forehead.

"I know. I'm just excited," Mom smiled. "I've been wondering when you're going to settle down and give me some grandkids."

"Whoa," I backed away slowly, my hands in the air and my eyes wide. "Slow your roll Mama C." She laughed lightly as I practically sprinted from the kitchen and toward the garage. I couldn't get out of the house quick enough.

CHAPTER FIFTEEN

I TRIED to quietly sneak inside undetected after I had Rob drop me off at the end of the street. Braden's truck was parked in the driveway, so I knew he was home. I tried to quietly sneak inside undetected, hoping that he would be sleeping when I got in. But, I had no such luck; he was standing in the kitchen making coffee.

Hunter barked a few times when I opened the door, then came over to me to investigate, his large wet nose sniffing at my legs. Brock and Tessa must have dropped him off early in the morning before they drove to the airport.

He peered around, as if searching for Aiden. When he realized I was alone, he let out a heavy sigh and nudged my hand with his head.

Aiden had been so excited to dog sit for his uncle, and I'd completely forgotten about the damn thing. Even *if* Braden wasn't in the kitchen staring at me like I had eight heads, I would have been outed by the dog. Absently, I stroked the fur on his face.

"Where have you been?" Braden asked me, suspicion lining his features as he took in my frazzled state. My hair was a mess, my dress was rumpled and it was very obvious that I'd been somewhere I shouldn't have been.

"None of your business," I responded through narrow eyes that dropped down to the two cups in his hands. "Who's here?"

"Elle," he grinned, elation lighting up his blue eyes. Braden and I had similar eyes, *Miller blue*, as my mom used to call them. Aiden had inherited them too, while Brock's eyes were more of a stormy gray colour.

"Braden," I sighed, exasperated. I knew that they'd been dancing around each other for weeks, but I couldn't help but worry that if things didn't pan out the way he wanted...all the progress he'd made for himself over the last few years would be wasted. He was doing well, and I didn't want to see him fall back into old habits.

The easy smile on his face faded slightly and he frowned, locking his jaw. "Look, I won't tell you how to live your life if you don't tell me how to live mine, got it?"

Wordlessly, I nodded. He had a point. I had made plenty of mistakes of my own. Braden nodded too, satisfied with my response, and headed back down to his basement bedroom.

I stood there, thinking about the hazel eyed, sweet talking country singer that had somehow managed to steal a very large piece of my heart.

Glancing at the digital clock on the microwave, I jumped into action when I realized I had less than twenty minutes to get ready before I was supposed to be at the farm, and I still had to pick up Aiden.

But I couldn't go *anywhere* looking the way I did; especially not when I could still smell Travis on me.

Travis wanted to start telling people about us, but I was

worried. I wanted to see how things progressed between us before announcing it.

From a risk assessment standpoint, Travis was a *major* risk, but even knowing that…I couldn't stop my heart from racing with excitement and throbbing with renewed hope.

I knew I still had plenty of issues to overcome, and I wasn't entirely sure where I would even begin there…but I'd woken up in Travis's bed that morning with my chest bursting with possibility and hope. It had felt amazing to wake up with his arms around me.

I dressed quickly, forgoing makeup and tossing my damp hair up into a clip. When I came out of my bedroom, Elle was waiting in the kitchen for me. She was dressed in her bridesmaid dress, her cheeks flushed with embarrassment.

"I was wondering if I could hitch a ride off of you, and maybe borrow something to wear…" she said, trailing off sheepishly. I felt for her, having done the walk of shame myself that morning.

"Yeah, sure," I smiled at her. I disappeared back into my bedroom to grab a dress I knew would fit her. It hadn't fit me in a few years, but I'd clung to it because it was a pretty floral print. "Here you go," I told her, handing the dress out to her.

She smiled at me as she took it. "I'll be back in a second," she promised, disappearing back downstairs.

I had always liked Elle. My apprehension about her being with Braden was mostly due to the fact that I wasn't overly confident that *Braden* was in a good place mentally for a relationship. I knew that Elle was struggling too, and I didn't know if Braden could handle that.

And, I was self-aware enough to know that I was projecting a little.

"Are you okay?" Elle asked, her brown eyes squinting in concern as she placed a hand on my forearm. I hadn't even realized I'd gapped out while waiting.

"Yeah, sorry. Just tired," I apologized, grabbing my purse. "Are you ready? Is Braden coming with us?"

"He'll be along shortly..." Elle bit her lip. "I kind of told him we needed to show up separately."

"Ah," I exhaled, nodding with understanding. After all, I had the same arrangement going on with Travis.

"It's just, Alex—"

"It's okay, you don't need to explain it to me. Trust me, I get it," I sighed again.

"Are you picking Aiden up?"

"Yes," I answered. "Valerie has plans with her family, and I know he'll want to say hi to Spirit," I smiled, referring to Tessa's horse. Aiden loved going to the farm to see all the animals—especially the horses.

I opened the front door and stepped out onto the porch, reaching inside the mailbox. My fist closed around my keys. Pulling them out, I ignored the curious look Elle sent me and continued walking to my car.

Braden was standing in the driveway beside his truck, waiting. Hunter sat in the cab, looking regal and self-satisfied as he peered ahead, panting. Brock usually took Hunter everywhere, and he'd come to expect the same treatment from the rest of us.

"He slipped out when I opened the door, and apparently is insisting on coming with. Not my first choice for shotgun," he joked, looking at Elle with pointed longing.

"Better you than me," I replied, climbing into my car. "At least Elle won't shed all over my seats."

"I just might," she grinned, putting her large sunglasses on. She blew Braden a kiss and slid into the passenger seat. Starting the engine, I backed out of the driveway.

The Jefferson's lived about ten minutes away from us in a modest two-story house. The yard was well maintained but littered with bicycles and foot balls, the evidence that three rowdy growing boys lived and thrived there. I pulled up the driveway and put it in park, leaving the car running before I jogged up the walkway and rang the bell.

Valerie answered with a smile. "Becky! Come on in. How was the rest of the wedding?" she asked.

"It was great! Thank you for watching him last night, Valerie." I returned her smile with one of my own as I stepped inside.

"It's my pleasure, Aiden is no trouble at all. If anything, he keeps Max in line," Valerie replied. She turned her head and hollered up the stairs. "Aiden! Your mom is here!"

I could hear several sets of feet tromping around upstairs, and ten minutes later Aiden was barrelling down the stairs with his backpack and pillow. "Hi Mom!"

"Hi buddy!" I said, crouching down to give him a hug. "How was the sleepover?"

"AMAZING!" he exclaimed, his eyes bright and excited. "We watched a scary movie!"

"Ghostbusters," Valerie whispered with a wink.

"That's great, bud," I smiled. "Do you have everything?"

"Yes. Are we going to the farm?"

"Yep," I answered. Aiden whooped and practically flew out of the door. "Thanks again, Valerie! I'll see you tonight at practice!" I said, waving at her before I closed the door.

It didn't take us long to get to the farm. When we pulled up, Elle's mom was already directing the helpers on where to go. The second the car rolled to a stop, Aiden flew out, heading immediately for the front pasture, where the horses were grazing lazily in the mid-morning sun.

As we approached, Sue fixed her daughter with a wry stare, arching a brow. "Bout time you two showed up! The party rental place will be sending a truck here within the hour. We've got a lot of decorations to put away. Did Tessa say what she wanted to do with the centerpieces?"

"I know what she wants to keep," Elle replied, ignoring the rest of her mom's statement. "We'll get started on that."

Braden pulled up when Elle was talking to her mother. Hunter jumped out of the cab and looked around, sniffing the air for a moment. He caught sight of Aiden and Alyssa on the wooden fence, both of them holding out bits of long grass to the horses, and ambled over to them.

Avoiding looking in the general direction of Elle and her mother, Braden instead headed over to where Gordon and Tommy were busy grabbing all of the rental chairs from the ceremony. He set to stacking them up against the fence near the barn.

I resisted the urge to snort—Braden wasn't fooling anyone, lest of all Elle's mom. The two of them had been inseparable all evening, and it was obvious they'd left together.

I wondered if it was obvious I'd left with Travis too. Before I could worry too much, Elle grabbed my arm. "Come on. Let's get this done—I need to sleep off this hangover."

We walked into the reception tent and started packing up decorations. We lined up the centerpieces on Bill's front porch for the time being and when Krista stumbled into the tent looking as hungover as I felt, Elle set her to work folding linens.

Heavy truck tires crunching against gravel had my heart thrumming in my chest at the possibility of it being Travis. I'd known I would see him again, and I knew it was foolish, but I was excited about it. The accompanying swell of disappointment when the white party rental truck rolled up would have been embarrassing if I'd confessed to it, but instead I suppressed it and continued on with the task at hand.

Then he actually *did* show up. He parked his truck and climbed out, his eyes meeting mine from across the vast space that separated us. He smiled at me, that secret smile that made my insides feel all tingly.

I brought the linens I was carrying over to the party rental truck, trying to keep my face impassive as I walked by him. Travis jogged after me, and I shot him a warning look. "What are you doing?" I asked him, my voice barely above a whisper as I handed the linens to an employee.

We were hidden by the party rental truck, but that didn't mean we wouldn't be discovered by anybody else who needed to drop linens off.

"I just wanted to talk to you for a minute, if that's alright?" he arched a brow, a daring smile dancing upon his lips. Hiding how I felt from *him* was a challenge in itself, especially now that we were *together* together, and still hiding it.

Still, I softened my features and offered him a small smile. "Quickly," I told him, ever powerless when he looked at me that way.

"I want to see you again tonight," he said.

"I can't, Aiden has soccer," I replied, disappointed about it. An emotion I couldn't pinpoint passed through Travis's eyes before an easy smile graced his lips. "I'd say come over after Aiden's in bed, but..."

"Braden," he finished for me, sighing. It might make things worse for Brock if Braden were to find out before him.

"Call me later, okay?" I said, looking at him wistfully before I turned on my heel and walked away.

WHEN THE JOB was finally done and the party truck was kicking up dust as it drove down the Armstrong's driveway, I breathed a sigh of relief. Weddings were *exhausting*. I wanted to sleep for a thousand years, and I silently prayed that nobody close to me would get married again any time soon.

But it *had* been beautiful, whimsical, even. It had been the kind of wedding every little girl should dream of having. Small and intimate, with friends and family coming together to make sure everything went off without a hitch. There'd been a few close calls, but we'd pulled it off in the end.

"Are you heading off now?" Sue asked, catching me as I attempted to sneak away without drawing Travis's attention. After our quick conversation by the party rental truck, he'd proceeded to watch me whenever nobody else was looking, which only made my nerves feel more frazzled. "There's burgers and sausages on the grill if you're hungry!"

"Yeah Mom! Can we stay for a while, please?" Aiden pleaded, appearing at my elbow. "I'm starving and Alyssa wants to show me the treehouse her grandpa built!"

"Alright, we'll stay a little longer," I relented, my shoulders dropping in surrender. "But don't forget, you've got soccer practice tonight." Aiden cheered and raced off after Alyssa, heading toward the back of the house.

"Can I do anything to help?" I asked Sue awkwardly, feeling a little out of place. She threw her arm around me and grinned.

"You can help me fix a salad," she said warmly. She squeezed me quickly before releasing me, and the familiar pang throbbed within my heart. I felt it whenever I missed my mom, which was a lot lately. Elle was lucky—what I wouldn't give for one more conversation with my mom. I wasted too many years being angry at her for things she couldn't change, instead of appreciating her for all that she did for us—especially after everything with Richie.

As I followed Sue into the Armstrong's house, I couldn't help but wonder what Mom would think of Travis, of us. Would she be happy about it?

Sue went to the refrigerator and began to grab things we would need for the salad. I rinsed the lettuce, tomatoes and radishes while she started chopping some green onions.

I'd been in the Armstrong's kitchen a few times before, when Tessa had insisted we join them for holidays, and I'd always found it warm and welcoming. It was impossible not to feel that sense of home, here, so I set to my task and relaxed.

"Did you two have a good night last night?" Sue asked casually, effectively slicing through my ease.

I froze, looking at her warily. "What do you mean?"

"I wasn't drinking all that much," she informed me, a knowing little smile on her lips. "I saw a lot more than everyone thought I saw," she added with a laugh. My mouth opened and closed like a fish, as I searched for something to say.

"Don't worry, I know how you Millers like your privacy… your secret is safe with me," Sue said after I'd taken too long to respond. She went about chopping the radishes. "But, I will say that I'm happy to see it. It's about time you let someone else in. I know you've had a rough past, but you aren't meant for a spinster's life, and I'd hate to see you reduced to that."

I'd always admired Sue Thompson. She didn't need a man, and never had. It had always been just her and Elle. I'd wanted to be like her, content with my family and friendships, and in a lot of ways…I was.

But Travis had unlocked something inside me, a hope that I couldn't seem to push back inside.

Sue seemed to be waiting for me to say something, so I cleared my throat. "We're just seeing how things go, for now."

"Playing it safe," she nodded with understanding, dropping the freshly chopped radishes into the salad. "But don't play it *too* safe, you hear?"

"Okay," I said, confounded. I wasn't used to parental advice. Mom had never been one to tell us how to live.

"He's a good man," Sue informed me. "I know his mother, we went to middle school together, and we've kept in touch over the years," she added, seeing the confusion on my face.

"I know he is," I replied.

Sue smiled with satisfaction, grabbing the large salad bowl.

She gestured to the mason jar of homemade dressing on the counter with a tilt of her head. "Mind grabbing that for me?"

SINCE MY CONVERSATION with Sue in the Armstrong's kitchen, my mind wouldn't quit spinning and spiraling in millions of interwoven paths, filtering from one concern to the next.

When I sank into the plush sofa in Dr. Rootham's office on the Wednesday after the wedding, so many things ensnared my mind, and I couldn't pause them, no matter how badly I wanted to. They came out in a muddled rush while I recounted the last few weeks, barely pausing to take a breath.

After getting through a huge chunk of my mental list, Dr. Rootham made me expand on my developing feelings.

"When I'm with him, I can trust him. There's just little moments that sting, little waves of insecurity that make me question what we're doing," I finished, wondering if anything that I'd said during the course of our half hour had made any sense at all. But, when I looked at Dr. Rootham, she was nodding with understanding.

"Trust takes time to build," she assured me. "Open communication is important, have you told him about Richie yet? Your fears?"

I winced, thinking about how I'd shut him out yet again. It hadn't been intentional, of course, but between my work schedule, Aiden's soccer, and my moody younger brother—we hadn't been able to get together since the night of the wedding.

We'd texted and spoken on the phone several times a day, but it wasn't enough…and it didn't feel right, talking about those things on the phone. I'd hoped I would be able to see him at least once, but Braden hadn't been doing too well either, and the knowledge of that sat heavily on my shoulders. I was genuinely worried about him.

Elle had gone back to Barrie after the wedding. At first, he'd believed she was tying up loose ends and that she'd be back in a few days. But she didn't come back when she said she was going to, and she hadn't returned any of his phone calls.

I couldn't get away, but I also couldn't invite Travis to my place and run the risk of Braden coming home. It was important to me to tell Brock first, before anybody else found out.

But the clock was ticking, and our opportunity to spend time together was dwindling, and I was to blame.

"I'll take that as a no," Dr. Rootham summarized from my body language. Her eyes drilled into mine, willing me to listen... to hear. "You've come so far, Becky. The effort you've put into your recovery is astonishing, but it still seems like you're punishing yourself for falling for an abuser."

"I am," I nodded, not even bothering to resist the truth of her statement. "If I knew how to stop it, I would...but..." I trailed off, shrugging helplessly. I've always been exceptionally hard on myself, I've always shouldered the blame...tried to carry it myself. It was who I was even before Richie, before he dismantled my heart and my spirit.

"When you find yourself thinking that way...try to redirect your thoughts," she urged. "You persevered. You came out of a horribly traumatic situation a stronger person, a person who knows what they will and will not tolerate from a prospective partner. Trust your intuition, Becky."

CHAPTER SIXTEEN

*ravis*

I HAD BEEN HIT with a wave of inspiration after my night with Becky. That night, spent with her in my arms, in my bed, had felt so...intimate. So right.

I'd spent the last few days as a recluse, waiting Thursday while I worked on some new lyrics I had rolling around in my head. I was also dodging the persistent phone calls from my manager, demanding to know when I'd be back in Nashville. I'd already told him six times that I'd be back in five weeks, but Tom was still hoping I'd change my answer. He wanted to get a start on the new record, only there wasn't anything to start.

I had nothing worth sharing. Yet, anyway.

The song that I'd been working on seemed too personal, too emotional, and I wasn't ready to share it. My public image was beers and trucks, not love ballads. But, singing with Everly Daniels at the wedding had me convinced a ballad wasn't such a bad idea, that maybe it was time to take my music in a new direction. I could think of no better time to do it than when I went on stage at the Grand Ole Opry in September.

By Wednesday, I knew I needed to get out of the house, so I met the guys for half priced ribs and a couple of beers at Flanigan's. The regular group consisted of Gordon, Tommy, Grady, and Brock. Sometimes, Steve would randomly show up. Sometimes, Braden would show up, if he didn't have anything better to do, only he'd drink a coke in place of beer.

Steve, Braden, and Brock were absent this week. Brock was still on his honeymoon, Braden only really came when Brock was there, and nobody knew what Steve did when he wasn't hanging out with us. On this particular night, it was just Gordon, Grady, Tommy, and me.

"You know what I don't get?" Gordon said, pausing to take a sip of his beer. He sat across the table from me at Flanigan's.

"What?" Tommy demanded, irritated at the long pause.

"I think its bullshit that you live in that bad ass mansion on a sick lake and you never throw parties there," Gordon said, his tone accusatory and his focus zeroed in on my face.

"My mom's there," I shrugged. "I don't want to put her out."

"We wouldn't be! Mama Channing can sling some beers with us," Tommy grinned, waggling his eyebrows suggestively. The *your mom is hot* jokes would never stop coming, and I couldn't even get mad at them for it. Gordon and Tommy had lost their mom when they were kids, so any *your mom* revenge jokes would be cruel. They knew it and used it to their full advantage, of course.

"It's not just her. Last time I let you douchebags talk me into throwing a party, some dumbass put the address on Myspace and an extra three hundred guests show up. We had paparazzi swarming the gates for months afterwards," I reminded them pointedly.

"Okay," Tommy said, raising his finger to stop me right

there. "That was *years ago*," he argued, rolling his eyes. He'd been the one to stupidly put up the address on his public Myspace.

"It's true, Tommy has learned the error of his ways," Gordon nodded, smirking.

"I couldn't come home for *months*," I laughed. "I had to hire twenty-four hour ground security to make sure people would leave my mom alone."

"Why does it matter?" Grady asked, coming to my rescue.

"It doesn't, not really. I was just thinking that we should have a final *hurrah* party," Gordon shrugged, taking another swig of his beer. "Before you leave for Nashville again and Tessa and Brock leave for Toronto. Get everyone together one final time." His words seemed ominous, like we'd never all be together again.

I pursed my lips and mulled it over: Gordon made a fair point. It *would* be cool to throw a party, and my cottage was a pretty good location for it. Private, remote. Enough space to host everyone comfortably.

"I'll have to run it by my mom and see what she says."

"Oh man, it sounds so ridiculous when you say that—like you're still living in your mom's trailer and she's still ironing your shirts on the kitchen table," Tommy laughed.

"Yeah, except it's *his* place and he pays people to iron his shirts," Gordon ribbed, joining in on the laughter.

"Don't be dicks," Grady scolded. "She lives there, it's her home too."

"We know," Tommy rolled his eyes.

"I'll see what I can do," I promised.

Grady downed the rest of his beer and stood up. "I'll catch you guys later, let me know what's happening with the party."

"Where are you off to?" Gordon asked, bemused. Grady didn't usually tap out that early.

"Paige's," he grinned. Tommy pretended to crack a whip, making the accompanying sound and all.

"Is it really that bad to be whipped?" I voiced. "What's the harm in making your girl happy?"

"No harm in that," Gordon nodded with agreement and glanced at me with mild suspicion.

Tommy wrinkled his nose. "There's a difference between making your girl happy and having to hand in your man card because you left guy's night early to watch Gilmore Girls with her," he said, waggling his eyebrows.

"Fuck off," Grady laughed, flipping him the bird. "And for your information, we're watching Game of Thrones."

"Still, you're bailing out early for Netflix and Chill."

"Ignore my little brother, Grady," Gordon said, putting Tommy in a headlock. "He doesn't ever get to the *chill* part of Netflix before his date runs for the nearest exit, so he wouldn't understand how awesome it is. Chill means sex, Tommy, and a man has needs. If Grady's gotta dip out to get his wick wet, that's fine in my books."

"Gee, thanks, Gordon," Grady frowned as he shook his head. "Maybe I just prefer her company to yours." Tossing a couple of bills down on the table, he cast one more unamused scowl in our direction before leaving.

When he'd gone, Tommy wandered over to the only pool table in the bar that was littered with beautiful girls. Gordon and I watched while he tried to pick up a few of them, being his regular goofball self. The girls giggled under his attention, but none of them acted interested in the pool lessons he was offering.

"I hope he's not asking them to rub his cue again. I told him that was a terrible pick up line and to never use it again, but he's not that bright," Gordon remarked. I laughed, shaking my head.

My phone buzzed in my pocket, and I pulled it out to check it. I hadn't seen Becky since the day after the wedding, but we'd been texting nonstop.

She didn't want to risk anybody seeing us before we told

Brock, and Braden was in a foul mood after Elle returned to Barrie so she had no one to watch Aiden. I'd offered up a solution in my mom, but Becky had venomously refused it. She said she didn't know my mom well enough to ask that of her, and she felt weird about it.

I understood, but in the same breath...my feelings for her weren't temporary.

The message wasn't from her—it was from one of my producers. I ignored it, shoving it back into my pocket without reading it. I couldn't get my mind off of Becky, and the last thing I could think about in that moment was *work*. My knee bounced up and down, my aggravation rising. I had half a mind to just show up on her doorstep, just to see her and be with her for a few hours, but I knew that'd go over about as well as bathing a cat.

"Why the long face, pretty boy?" Gordon mock-pouted, still razzing me.

"No reason," I straightened.

"See, I'm not buying that," Gordon said decisively. "You've been acting weird all summer."

"How the hell have I been acting weird?"

Gordon pinned me with a considering stare. "That's a long list bud. Let's see...there was the whole twin thing, you showed zero interest in either one of those girls and they were *so* willing. Then there's the wedding—you didn't bring a date, which is so not like you. I was so sure you'd bring *two* dates that I bet Grady. I lost fifty bucks."

"Fake tits are overrated, no matter how willing they are. And I didn't bring a date to the wedding because I didn't know anybody who wouldn't accidentally slip the details to the paparazzi," I answered.

"That's never stopped you before."

"This was my best friend's wedding," I reminded him through narrowed eyes. "I wouldn't chance ruining his big day."

Gordon hummed, clearly not believing me. "Whatever you say."

We were silent for a few moments, watching while Tommy struck out with one girl and moved on to try his luck with the next.

"What pissed you off the most about Brock and Tessa being together?" I asked, the question spilling from me before I could think it through. "Was it just that he broke the code?" In high school, Brock and Gordon had enforced a bro code specifically regarding their sisters; they were completely off limits.

"Is this about Becky?" he asked, glancing back at me, a slight smile on his lips.

"What? No."

"Travis, there aren't any more sisters in the group. It's either about Becky, or it's about Tessa. And if it's about Tessa—"

"It's not about Tessa, for fucks sakes Gordon," I grumbled, pissed that he'd cornered me into being more honest than I'd intended on being, and pissed that I'd walked straight into it.

Gordon laughed richly. "I knew that all along. I saw you guys leaving the reception together."

"Fuck off," I growled.

"I did," Gordon smirked, looking extremely pleased with himself. "Annaka and I slipped out to…relieve some tension, if you know what I mean, and we saw you guys climbing into the Escalade."

"Seriously?" I deadpanned.

"Seriously. If the Escalade's a rocking, don't come a knockin'," Gordon joked.

"Can you stop fucking around and answer the question?" I asked, my aggravation rising. "What pissed you off the most about it?"

"I didn't know his intentions," Gordon answered simply. He leaned back in the booth, resting his arm along the back of it. "I mean, we all went years without seeing him or talking to him, and suddenly he was back in town and sneaking around with my sister? It was shady."

"Well we didn't exactly have his back when it all went down," I reminded him. "At least, not as much as we should have." I had tried calling Brock a hundred times after I heard about the arrest, but he hadn't returned a single one of those calls. Nobody else had known the details, either...just that Brock was doing jail time for aggravated assault.

Turns out he had every reason to beat the ever living crap out of Becky's ex after he put her in the hospital.

Thinking about it made me grip my beer a little tighter. I'd never heard the whole story, and never from Becky—but what I did know made my blood boil with rage, and it made me feel ashamed too. Ashamed that I hadn't reached out to her, ashamed that I'd given up so easily on Brock.

"I know," Gordon nodded with agreement, pursing his lips. He wore the same regret I did.

"So if Brock had *told* you that he was interested in Tessa, you would have been cool with that?"

"I probably would have punched him in the fucking teeth," he shrugged, grinning. "But, then I would have been fine with it. I *am* fine with it. I see how he looks at her, how he treats her. He loves her with everything he has, and I know he'll take care of her."

I exhaled, rubbing at my jaw. "Basically, no matter what I do, he's going to rearrange my face."

"I didn't say that. Brock's not me, and Becky isn't six years younger than us. I saw Tessa as a little girl still, and it freaked me out that my friends didn't." Gordon paused, shivering as if that thought disgusted him.

"In Brock's defense, it was his first time coming home in years, and *I* was struck by how stunning she is. Honestly, I didn't even realize I was talking to your sister until she told me. She looks and acts older than she is," I commented.

Gordon scowled at me. "Shut up, Travis, or I'll rearrange your face myself." I laughed in response, glad I'd managed to get under his skin a little. He'd pissed me off first, and that was kind of how our friendship worked.

"What the fuck are you chicks talking about?" Tommy demanded, flopping down in the booth.

"Strike out so soon?" I grinned, laughing when he shot me the finger.

We shot the shit for a while longer, mostly talking about Gordon's renovation company and Tommy's inability to hold down a job. It wasn't long until we called it a night.

I had just put the keys in the ignition of my truck when my phone rang. Fishing it out of my pocket, I couldn't slide my finger over 'answer' quick enough when her name and picture flashed across the screen of my phone. "Hello?"

"Hey, it's me," she said hesitantly. "So…I actually managed to find a sitter for Aiden tomorrow evening. Katie offered to have him over for a sleepover. So, if you still wanted to—"

"Fuck yeah I still want to," I interrupted. She laughed, the sound like music to my ears. "I can pick you up at seven."

"I'd rather meet you somewhere, if you don't mind," she said. I could hear the uncertainty in her voice.

"My place?" I suggested.

"What about your mom?"

"It'll just be you and me," I answered, the plan already forming in my mind. I knew that she would have no problem giving us privacy for the night. "Meet me at my place at seven. I'll text you the address."

JUST AS I EXPECTED, my mom had no qualms with making herself scarce for the night. She jumped on my suggestion to go see a movie.

When she left the house, I started cooking dinner. I knew Becky didn't want to chance anybody seeing us and outing us before we had the chance to tell her brother, so I figured a romantic night in would do the trick.

I didn't want to make it too complicated, so I made baked honey mustard chicken with a touch of lemon, scalloped potatoes and green beans. Becky pulled up with ten minutes left on the timer, and I watched her through the window while she seemed to give herself a pep talk before exiting her car.

Her nervousness made me smile. I was glad I wasn't the only one whose nerves were in overdrive. This would be the first official date the two of us had ever had with each other. Skinny dipping in lakes or meeting up in hotel rooms for an afternoon delight aside, I mean. Those couldn't be classified as dates.

I met her at the door, throwing it open before she had a chance to knock.

"You look stunning," I told her, my eyes eating her up. She was wearing a floral print dress with a low neckline that made all the blood in my body travel south. She hadn't even set foot inside yet, and my need to have her was overwhelming.

But tonight wasn't about sex. It couldn't be, I already knew we connected on that level and I wanted her to know that I saw her as more than walking sex.

"Thank you," she blushed prettily, stepping inside the foyer and looking around.

"Do you want a tour? We were a little preoccupied the last time you were here," I pointed out, taking her hand. She nodded, and I led her around the main level. Just as we were walking back into the kitchen, the timer went off.

"It smells amazing," Becky remarked, watching while I removed the tray from the oven and put it on the stove top.

"I hope it tastes amazing too," I winked, throwing the oven mitts down on the counter before I put my hand on the small of her back. I led her out the sliding doors to the patio, where we'd be eating. Candles illuminated the table for two, and wine chilled in a bucket. I pulled a chair out for her, holding it while she sat. "Wine?"

"Sure, just a little though," she replied, her fingers toying with the layered material of her dress.

"I'll be right back," I said after I'd filled both our glasses. When I returned with two plates, Becky was staring out at the lake.

"You've got a beautiful view," she commented, smiling at me when I set her plate down.

"I agree," I responded, my eyes still on her when I sat down. I didn't think I could pull my eyes away from her if my life depended on it. "You're beautiful, Becs."

Her cheeks flushed and she smiled with just the corner of her lips. "Thanks."

***

AFTER DINNER, we went for a walk so I could show her the grounds. The stone pathway that led to the dock was lit up with little solar lights, and the dock itself had twinkle lights weaved around the posts, reflecting off the lake and illumining the wooden dock in a soft glow. I may have taken a page out of Elle's book, hell-bent on making this a night to remember for the both of us.

"Wow, it's breathtaking," she murmured, looking out at the moon over the lake. Becky closed her eyes at the sound of the loons calling to one another, smiling like it was the most beautiful thing she'd ever heard.

"It really is," I agreed. "I do love it out here. It's one of my favourite places to be."

"In all the world?"

"In all the world," I answered honestly.

She let out a contented sigh, slipping off her shoes before she sat down on the end of the dock. She dipped her toe in to test the temperature before submerging both feet.

I pulled off my shoes and socks and rolled my jeans before joining her. The water was refreshingly cool.

"I've got to ask," she said, glancing at me with a subtle smile on her lips. "Who taught you how to cook like that?"

"My mom," I answered honestly. "She believes everyone should know how to cook a decent meal."

"She's not going to like me very much, then," she cracked a small smile. "I can cook basic meals, but I botch almost all breakfast foods—save for cereal—and I can't bake at all. Aiden practically cries whenever I try."

"If I can be taught, you can be taught," I laughed.

We sat in silence for a little bit, both of us finding our footing with one another. It should have felt odd going from knowing exactly what we were, to figuring out how to be something different—but this felt *right*.

"Tell me more about little Travis," she asked, lips kicking up in another hesitant smile. I could tell she was still a little uncomfortable in this date like setting, but she seemed to be enjoying herself.

"I hope you're referring to me as a kid," I joked, arching a brow at her. She laughed, her smile growing and her blue eyes sparkling.

"Obviously I'm not asking about your dick," she shot back. I laughed, unable to resist kissing the tip of her nose. "I remember that one talent show you did...but when did you start singing?"

"My mom says I've been singing longer than I've been talking. We had this old record player, and stacks of old country records. We didn't have TV, so we sang a lot," I answered with a reminiscing smile. I shrugged. "What about you? When did you decide you wanted to become a nurse?"

"After Aiden was born," she answered, her jaw tensing a little as she gazed out at the moon over the lake. "I met this incredible nurse on Aiden's first day in NICU. She changed my life."

"I think you did that all on your own," I murmured, hoping she'd continue.

She turned her head to meet my eyes, offering me a small smile. "I wanted to be like her, to help women going through such a scary, devastating time find their footing. I wanted to help babies that needed the extra tender touch, the fragile ones —like Aiden. I'm still working my way up, obviously...but that's the end goal."

I brought my hand up to cup her face. "You amaze me," I told her softly. I kissed her then, my lips brushing against hers reverently. It completely blew my mind, all that she'd been through and all that she strived for despite of it.

Becky was silent strength and determination, and a whole lot of heart. To pursue the career she had after enduring the past she'd had was unfathomable.

I ended the kiss sooner than I would have liked. I was trying to be a gentleman, but my cock strained against my jeans, protesting the loss of her lips on mine.

My desire to have her warred with my desire to know everything about her.

"How do you become an NICU nurse?" I asked, running my hand along the side of her ribs. She yawned sleepily as her flesh broke out in goose bumps.

"Time and experience. I've been an ER nurse for almost a year. I have to prove my worth first. Plus, I'd have to move. The hospital here isn't equipped to handle NICU babies. They all get transferred to Toronto or Barrie," she answered.

"So you'd leave one day?"

"I don't know about that," she admitted. "I want to say that yes, I would leave here, but I've always lived here...and I don't know how I feel about selling the house. I know there are a lot of bad memories there...but there are a lot of good ones, too.

Aiden took his first steps in that house. His growth is measured on the same trim around the same doorway that my mother tracked my brothers and I. And after...Richie, it became my refuge, where I rebuilt our lives."

I held her a little closer to me and kissed her forehead. "There's no rush," I said. "There's no expiry date on dreams."

We talked about our hopes and dreams for a while longer, and I admitted that I was thinking about changing direction with my music. "I think your fans would love it," she assured me when I confessed my reluctance to shake things up.

"I'm worried my fans will hate it and I'll become irrelevant," I admitted. "I know money isn't everything, but growing up without any makes me appreciate it more."

"Your garage full of flashy cars suggests otherwise," Becky pointed out with a playful grin.

I chuckled self-deprecatingly and splashed water at her bare legs with my foot. "Smart ass. I save triple what I spend, and if I needed to, I could sell all of those cars and this house and still live comfortably."

It should have been weird, sitting there revealing the hidden bits and pieces of ourselves to one another, but it was as natural as breathing. Every little morsel she offered, I ate up, and I laid it all bare for her. Anything she wanted to know, I answered.

Around eleven, when she was yawning more than she was talking, I stood up and offered my hand to her, helping her stand. Her arms went around the back of my neck as she gazed up at me.

"I had a lot of fun tonight, Travis," she said, her eyes sparkling in the moonlight.

"When can I see you again?" I asked, feeling very much like my heart was caught in my throat.

She thought about it for a few minutes. "Brock and Tessa get home late on Sunday night. She's got to work at the clinic on

Monday, but I'll invite them over for dinner so I can tell them about us." She looked a little nervous, but determined.

"Did you want to tell them together, or…"

She bit her lip and brought her right shoulder up in half a shrug. "I haven't decided yet. I really don't know what would be better."

"Well you let me know," I told her. "I'll do it however you want."

CHAPTER SEVENTEEN

ecky

RAIN PELTED against the thick glass panes of the living room window the next afternoon. I was sitting on the sofa, leaning forward and contemplating my next move in the rather intense game of Jenga that Aiden and I were playing.

It was a dreary day, and Aiden was bummed out about it. He'd wanted to go up to the property for the day, and instead we were stuck inside, exhausting all means of entertainment at an alarming rate. My son could be amused for a little while with Lego and video games, but he preferred being outside.

I carefully selected a wooden block, using my index finger and thumb to slowly pull it out. The tower wobbled dangerously, so I slowed my movements, letting it settle again.

Thunder boomed, startling me, and pieces of the tower flew everywhere.

"Jenga!" Aiden giggled. I smiled at him indulgently.

"You win this round," I said as he began to pick up the pieces. I fought a yawn while he set up.

When I returned home from my date with Travis late last night, Braden still wasn't home. I didn't get reception at Travis's house, so I had missed a call from Krista. She left a voice mail, letting me know that Braden's truck had been parked outside of Flanigan's for hours.

I'd waited up for him, fearing the worst—that he'd started drinking again. When he finally walked through the front door, I sagged with relief when I realized he wasn't drunk, but our conversation had done little to ease my concerns.

He admitted that sometimes, the thirst overwhelmed him. After that, he decided to head to Brock's cabin for the next few days. He took Hunter with him, at my insistence. I didn't like the idea of him all alone in the state he was in.

A new game of Jenga began, but as I expected, it didn't hold his interest for very long. "I'm bored, can we go somewhere?"

"It's raining really badly, Aiden. I'm pretty sure most of the roads are flooded," I told him. I stood up again, racking my brain. "We could play Pie Face."

"But, you said that was only on special occasions," Aiden's face lit up with excitement. Usually, I didn't volunteer to play that game. It was needlessly messy, and the clean-up was a pain. But Aiden loved it, so I was determined to suck it up.

"Well, being bored on a Friday night counts as a special occasion, doesn't it?" I asked, looking over my shoulder as I pulled the game out from the front hall closet. Just as I was pivoting to head back into the living room, someone rapped on the door.

Elle had stopped by earlier, looking for Braden. Thinking that it was her again, I opened it quickly, worried that something had happened.

But it wasn't Elle, it was Travis, and he was even more

soaked than she'd been. "Hey, so...could I borrow your phone?" The rain was coming down in thick rivets.

"What's wrong with yours?" I asked, stunned and almost a little irritated to see him standing there. Last night's date had been incredible, and I was looking forward to many more of them...but I wasn't ready for *this* particular step. I cast a worried glance into the living room at Aiden.

"I took the Porsche out for a spin, and I forgot it on the counter when I made a sandwich," he admitted sheepishly. The sound of his voice had me turning to look at him again. "It's raining pretty badly, I need to see how the access road is."

"Of course, come in," I stood aside to let him pass and closed the door, looking at Aiden.

When Aiden realized who was in our house, he jumped up with excitement. "Travis! What are you doing here?"

"Seeking shelter from the rain," Travis laughed lightly. "Mind if I borrow your phone, little man?"

"It's in the kitchen, I'll show you!" Aiden said with importance, leading the way. Ever since they had raced the day we'd gone ATVing together, Aiden had talked nonstop about how cool Travis was.

"Remember to give Travis his privacy while he makes the call," I reminded him. Aiden nodded, returning to the living room with an excited grin on his face.

"Can we ask him to stay and play Pie Face with us?" he asked in a hushed voice, his eyes pleading with mine.

My breath caught in my lungs, and I hesitated, recognizing the urge to throw up my walls and protect our hearts. But, if I was going to start building trust, I needed to stop running.

"I'll see if he wants to. Tidy up Jenga and set it up," I instructed, passing the box to him. I walked into the kitchen, catching the tail end of Travis's conversation.

"Alright Mom, you be safe too. I'll figure something out. Don't worry about it. Yeah, I'll wait until it slows down a bit.

Love you too, bye." He flushed a little when he saw me standing there, almost like he was embarrassed to be caught telling his mom he loved her. I thought it was sweet.

"Everything okay?" I asked, arching a brow and leaning against the doorway, my arms folded across my chest.

"The access road is flooded," he replied, pushing his wet curls out of his face. "Look...I can head to Gordon's. I'm really sorry for showing up. It was getting worse out there, and—"

"It's okay," I sighed. I didn't want him to leave, not when his access road was flooded. "You don't have to leave if you don't want to. Aiden wants you to stay and play some board games with us," I shrugged, biting my lip. This situation was entirely new to me, and I had no idea how I was supposed to find my footing.

"Really?" he grinned with elation. "Yeah, I'd love to. I'm a little soaked though," he added, glancing down at his jeans with apology.

I arched a brow with amusement. A puddle had formed beneath his feet on the linoleum.

"You can borrow some of Braden's clothes and I'll toss yours in the wash," I suggested hesitantly. "But, you're here as a friend today, okay?" I added, keeping my voice hushed as I glanced through the service hatch into the living room. Aiden was tidying up the Jenga game to make room for Pie Face.

"Of course," Travis agreed willingly.

"All set up!" Aiden called out.

"Okay, we'll be right back bud. Travis needs to borrow some of Uncle Braden's clothes. Why don't you grab the whipped cream?"

"Whipped cream?" Travis repeated, sounding perplexed as he followed me down into the basement.

"It's for the game, Pie Face," I explained, my lips twitching with a smile.

He waited by the stairs while I rooted through my brother's

dresser drawers, finding a pair of old sweat pants and a t-shirt I hadn't seen him wear in months. I handed them to him, looking down when his hands covered mine.

"I can put them in the wash, you know," he told me, his lips kicking up in a humoured smile. "I do know how to do my own laundry."

"Our machines are old school," I replied. "And they need a special touch to work. You can change in Braden's bathroom," I pointed in the direction of the bathroom, wishing I could join him.

"You don't think *I* have a special touch?" he asked, his voice deep. He brushed some loose tresses of hair from my face.

"Go change," I laughed, pulling away because I knew if I didn't, we wouldn't be able to stop. Last night, Travis had been the perfect gentlemen. To say that I'd expected sex was an understatement; that's what the two of us did best, after all.

Travis smirked, knowing where my thoughts had gone. He changed quickly, and insisted on carrying his bundle of soaked clothes to my prehistoric washer. I wasn't kidding about our washing machines, they were almost as old as I was and they'd only lasted as long as they had because of Braden's mechanical skills. As it was, the dial button was broken so we had to twist it with pliers.

Once the washer was running, we went back upstairs. Aiden had grabbed the aerosol can of whipped cream from the refrigerator and was impatiently waiting in the living room for us, bouncing on his heels. He held it up with an excited grin on his face. "Travis, you're first!"

I closed Aiden's door gently. He was having so much fun with Travis, so I'd let him stay up a little later than usual. He'd been so tired that he almost fell asleep on the couch during the game of Monopoly.

Pausing in the hallway, I stared into the living room with my mouth agape. Travis had been busy cleaning while I was putting Aiden to bed. The games we'd played were stacked up neatly on the coffee table, and our plates from the frozen pizza I'd made for dinner were gone too.

He was waiting for me on the couch, and he patted the vacant space beside him, motioning for me to join him. I was bone tired, so I sank willingly into the cushions, curling up into his side.

"Not exactly how I imagined our first time using whipped cream together," he remarked, a playful smile on his lips as he looked down at me. "But, excellent none-the-less."

I snorted with laughter, then flushed with embarrassment. He titled his head down to mine, capturing my lips in the sweetest, briefest of kisses imaginable. He caught himself, wincing with apology. "Should I not have done that?" he asked with uncertainty.

I felt bad. I could see what my hesitation was doing to him, and I didn't like it. He was cautious, afraid to rock the boat lest I hightail it away like all the times before. I had to admit, he was right to worry.

"You know…when you first showed up, I was a little mad," I admitted, adverting my eyes. I was trying to take everyone's advice to heart. I knew we couldn't build trust if I didn't start giving him more of myself. "I was scared, more than anything… and I still am. It's not just my heart in this, Travis. It's his too," I looked at him as my eyes filled with tears that I refused to shed.

"I know that, Becs," Travis assured me, his hand came up to cradle the side of my face. I leaned into it, biting down on my lip, trying to hold back the floodgates. His eyes didn't leave mine, and they didn't waiver. In that moment, I knew he did.

That knowledge stilled the erratic racing of my heart. "I see that now," I told him, my eyes dancing with his. My chest rose and fell, the air thickening between us. "I'm in therapy. I go weekly. What he did…it affects me every day still," I admitted, baring my truths to him…baring my soul.

Pain flickered in his hazel eyes, and he nodded slowly. "It breaks me. What happened to you, to Aiden. I wish I'd—"

"It wasn't up to you to save me, and it wasn't up to Brock either. It was up to me, and I did it, Travis. I was leaving him that day. My bags were packed, and my keys were in my hand. I was going home. I *came* home," I said, needing him to understand something that I'd only just come to understand myself.

I drew in a breath, smiling softly at him. "And you make that bearable. I can forget, for a little while. You give me hope again, and it's scary and invigorating all at once," I laughed, brushing away the wetness from my cheeks.

He gazed at me with wonderment. "You're my home, Becky. This thing may have started out as sex, but it's kismet."

I kissed him then, exhausted by words and overwhelmed with need. I climbed onto his lap, my fingers weaving through his curls. I straddled him, our lips and tongues clashing in the most breathtaking way.

His fingers gripped my ass, and he let out a low moan as I ground against his erection, seeking relief of this deep ache within me.

He pulled away, laughing a little, his eyes never leaving mine and the molten desire never fading from his. "I'm trying to do the right thing and not make it all about sex, but damn it Becky, I want to bury myself so deep in you that you feel me for days afterwards," he all but growled.

"Can't it be a little bit about sex?" I asked innocently, bringing my lips to the side of his neck, just below his chin. His cock twitched in response, and I smiled into his neck.

He stood, taking me with him, his fingers gripping me tightly. My legs wrapped around his waist, finding purchase there. "Is this still your room?" he whispered, nodding to the door on the far left of the hall.

I nodded, biting my lip. "You remembered that?"

"Let's just say you took centre stage in more than one of my adolescent fantasies," he said, the corner of his lips darting up in a playful half smile.

TRAVIS LEFT in the early hours of the morning, knowing that I didn't want to throw a new relationship in my son's face without talking to him about it first. He kissed me on the cheek, leaving me in the warmth of my bed with a contented smile on my face, a lightness in my heart and plans to meet up with him later.

Friday's storms had given way to sunny skies, and I knew that Aiden would want to go to the property. At nine o'clock, I heard him stirring so I got out of bed myself. I put on a pot of coffee and tossed a couple of waffles in the toaster for Aiden and some toast for me.

He ambled down the hall, sitting heavily in one of the worn kitchen chairs. He yawned, wiping the sleep from his eyes. "Can we go to the lake, Mom?"

"Sure!" I smiled, smothering his waffles in butter and syrup. "Breakfast first," I placed his plate down and went back for my raisin toast.

"Can we see if Travis wants to come?" he asked in between hurried bites.

"I think Travis has plans today, but we could ask Max," I replied. That appeased Aiden, and he smiled widely at me.

"Okay! I can't wait to tell Max that Travis played Pie Face with us!" he exclaimed. I wrinkled my nose, and his expression fell. "What?"

"We probably shouldn't tell *anybody* that Travis was here," I said, drawing in a deep breath.

"Not even Uncle Braden and Uncle Brock?"

"We'll tell them when the time is right," I assured him.

We finished breakfast and grabbed everything we'd need for the day, stopping off at Max's to pick him up. The boys were boisterous the entire drive to the property, filled with excitement and energy. I rolled up to the beach, and had barely put the car in park before both of them had leapt out and were racing toward the water.

I set up my chair and grabbed the worn paperback I'd been trying to read for the last several months, setting up camp with my bare feet on the cooler. I had high hopes of scoring a tan.

Keeping half an eye on the boys splashing around in the lake, I exhaled, breathing in the fresh air and taking in my surroundings.

Since our grandfather had died, the care of the waterfront had fallen to the wayside, and for a while there—it'd been a little overgrown. With Brock back for weeks at a time, he'd managed to do some cleaning up and had added sand to the beach, restoring it to its former glory.

"You guys are here early," Braden said, startling me. My paperback fell to the ground when I jumped, and I leaned sideways to grab it.

"Yeah," I said, gratefully accepting the cup of coffee he'd brought out.

Braden stole the cooler from beneath my feet, moving it a little so he could sit beside me and still look out at the lake. "I was talking to Brock last night. Their flight gets in at midnight."

"I know, I spoke to Tessa the other day. They're coming over for dinner on Monday," I responded, my stomach lurching uneasily. I was a grown woman—I knew that, but my brothers were the only family Aiden and I had left, and I wanted them to approve. I couldn't help but worry a little that they wouldn't.

"Yeah," he replied, looking at me curiously. "Am I not invited?"

"Of course you're invited, you live there too," I answered, arching a brow.

"What about Elle?"

I arched a brow. "Are you guys back together? I thought she wasn't answering calls..." I trailed off, remembering the look of steely determination on Elle's face the night before. I knew she was back in town, but I didn't know the context.

"Yeah, we are. She forgot her phone at home, and tying up her loose ends took longer than she expected. She messaged me on Facebook a few times, but I don't ever go on Facebook," Braden shrugged with a rueful grin. I knew he was thinking about all the energy he wasted being upset.

"Okay, well dinner's at seven, I'll pick up the food and you're barbequing," I added, knowing that's what he was waiting for.

Braden's grin widened.

"Don't be surprised if I bring a guest, okay?" I remarked, thankful that my sunglasses hid my eyes.

Braden's eyebrows shot up with surprise. "Is this the mystery dude you were with the night of the wedding?"

"We're not talking about it now," I retorted, my lips pulling down in a slight frown.

"I'll take that as a yes," he laughed, his eyes twinkling a little. When his laughter faded, he looked at me again. "Does Aiden know?" he asked, peering out at the lake. Aiden and Max were taking turns jumping off the floating dock.

"He's been introduced as a friend," I replied. "It's better that way, so I'd appreciate it if everybody didn't make a big deal about it in front of him. Save your commentaries for when he's not around."

"Don't worry, we'd never put you on the spot. Besides, it's a good thing, Becky. I'm glad you've decided to date again and I'm sure Brock will be too."

Yeah, until he sees who I'm dating, I thought.

TESSA PURSED her lips at me thoughtfully. She was sun-kissed and glowing, her week in paradise having done wonders for her complexion. "I just don't know why you're keeping it a secret. Why can't we know his name?"

She leaned against the counter, watching me scoop out the potato salad from the plastic container into a serving dish. I wouldn't deny it came from the grocery store if I was asked, but I didn't want to advertise my lack of skills in the kitchen.

"You'll know it soon enough," I replied evasively, glancing at the clock over my stove. Travis would be pulling up at any moment. A small part of me deeply regretted inviting him tonight, and I wondered if perhaps it would have been easier to just tell everybody individually, without him there.

The welcoming committee out front did little to ease my anxiety. Brock and Braden had decided to stand on the front yard and check out the roof, as the next thing on Brock's hefty to-do list was replace the leaky, rotten shingles. Of course, this gave them a wonderful vantage point of both the neighbour-hood and the driveway from where they stood on the front lawn. They would be able to spot Travis before he even hit my street. I hoped they would have hid in the backyard, manning the barbeque.

Elle stood at the other counter, making a Caesar salad. She glanced over her shoulder at me, a knowing look in her eye. I wondered if Sue had let anything slip to her. If she did, Elle was doing a wonderful job keeping the secret.

The distant sound of the rumbling diesel engine had my head swivelling, and I stepped out onto the porch just as Travis's truck came into view. I could see the confusion and surprise on both of my brothers faces from where they stood. Braden turned to speak lowly to Brock when Aiden flew across the yard to greet Travis.

"No freaking way!" Tessa exclaimed, turning to me with the widest grin on her face. "Travis?! How? *When?*"

"It's a long story, I should probably tell it another time," I said, casting a pointed look toward the driveway. Travis was stepping out of his truck, a bouquet of flowers and a bottle of champagne in his hand.

My suspicion of Elle's knowledge was confirmed by the unsurprised smile on her face. She tucked a strand of her wavy dark hair behind her ear and smiled. "That's awesome! I'm happy for you guys!"

I breathed a little easier, feeling their genuine excitement for me.

Brock, on the other hand, was noticeably less thrilled about it. He had a hard set to his jaw and a somber look on his face.

Luckily, Braden heeded my warning from the other day. He put his hand on Brock's bicep to slow him down enough to say something. Brock nodded reluctantly, and although the air was still thick with tension, he stopped stalking toward Travis.

I watched warily while Travis and Aiden started walking up the sidewalk to the house. Travis didn't seem the least bit uncomfortable. Aiden was chattering happily to him, reminiscing about the night of the storm, all the while being his smiling, charismatic self. He paused before Brock and Braden, tucking the champagne under his arm and shaking each of their hands in turn. "Hey man! How was the Dominican?"

"Great," Brock replied, his tone clipped.

"Alright, let's get those steaks on the barbeque, fellows," Tessa instructed, breaking up the terse moment and giving her husband a pointed look.

Travis let my brothers walk ahead, and paused before me. The smile on his face was genuine contentedness, and his eyes swept tenderly across my face. "Hey Becs," he murmured, his eyes pausing to rest on my lips. "These are for you, and I brought champagne to celebrate the newlyweds. It's non-alcoholic, so Aiden can partake in a toast too," he added, making me fall for him a little more.

I accepted the bouquet from him, and held my breath when he purposely brushed the back of his hand against the back of mine when he passed. The subtle gesture had my heart stuttering.

Taking a stabilizing breath, I followed him inside.

CHAPTER EIGHTEEN

ravis

DINNER WAS A LITTLE BIT AWKWARD. Brock really wasn't at all stoked about me being there, but he put his best foot forward for Aiden. His smiles seemed a little strained, and he avoided looking directly at me, but he wasn't the kind of guy to cause a scene and Tessa seemed to keep him grounded.

They left after dessert, once they'd given Aiden gifts they'd bought for him in the Dominican, after telling us that they were still jet lagged from their trip. He hugged Becky before he left, but he barely cast a second look in my direction. I figured he'd be pissed for a bit, so I tried not to let it get to me.

Shortly after they left, Elle and Braden dipped out too, claiming that Elle's mom needed help with something. I figured they were trying to give us some privacy.

"Alright Aiden, it's bed time!" Becky instructed after everyone had gone. Aiden and I were playing Minecraft. I'd always been big on video games when I was a kid, but I hadn't had my own gaming system until I started working part time at the gas station near the diner where my mom worked. I'd saved up for months to buy the first generation Xbox. I still had it, I'd held on to it for nostalgic purposes.

"Awe but I wanted to stay up with Travis!" Aiden pouted. "We're building a rollercoaster."

"You'll see him again soon, but he's going home too. I have to work in the morning," she replied. "Come on, let's go."

Aiden let out a loud sigh, but stood, setting his controller on the table. "Bye Travis," he murmured, still rocking the pout.

"Later bud," I couldn't help but smile. Becky mouthed at me to wait, and followed him down the hall. I shut down the system and went into the kitchen to clean up the post-dinner mess. There wasn't much of one, Tessa and Elle had cleaned up the majority of it before they left, but I still didn't want Becky getting stuck with the rest of it.

Twenty minutes later, she returned to the living room and sank down beside me on the couch. I wrapped my arm around her shoulders, pulling her against me and breathing in her sweet scent.

"What are you doing this weekend?" I asked. While she'd been busy putting Aiden to bed, I'd been plotting. I wanted to spend as much time with the both of them as I could before I had to return to Nashville.

"Nothing really. Aiden has a game on Sunday, but aside from that...we'll probably just go to the lake," she shrugged, unconcerned.

"Why don't you come to my place? We'll take my boat out. It's been a while, she needs a tour," I chuckled. "I think Aiden would enjoy it."

"He probably would," Becky nodded deliberately, likely weighing the pros and cons of such a venture with me. I held my breath, worried that she'd say no.

"Can you be ready around nine?'

"That shouldn't be a problem. I'll bring some sandwiches," she smiled.

I pressed my lips to hers, tasting her like I'd gone weeks without doing so. She let out a quiet gasp, barely audible, and all but melted into me. I pulled away for a moment, resting my forehead against hers while I looked into her eyes.

Biting her lip, Becky moved so that she was straddling my lap. She ran her hands through my hair—tugging it at the roots a little before she kissed me again. My hands went to her ass, gripping it and grinding her against my thickening erection.

THE NEXT MORNING, I drove out to Brock's cabin. I knew he would be there working on the dock, given by what little was said during dinner.

When I pulled up the private access road, I saw him over near the dock. Brock had his table saw set up on a picnic table to the right of the beach, and was cutting new pieces of wood to replace the rotten boards.

He didn't hear me approach, and I waited until the saw was off to make my presence known. "Hey man, need a hand?" I asked, extending the proverbial olive branch to him.

Brock looked at me over the shoulder. I could tell he was a little pissed still, but I needed to resolve this weirdness between us. "You still do manual labor?" he shot back, purposely hitting me below the belt.

"It's been a while but I'm sure it's like riding a bike," I shrugged, stepping up to the table. We worked in silence for a while, making sure we had all the pieces we'd need cut and piled by the dock.

I'd been Brock's friend for over two decades, and I knew he was the kind of person that preferred to work through things silently. He didn't speak again until we'd finished the task at hand and stood back to admire our work.

The rotten boards were all replaced, and the dock looked more stable than it probably had when it was first built forty-years ago.

"So, you and Becky huh?"

"Yeah," I nodded, my eyes serious.

"When did it start?" he asked, his brow furrowing.

"Full disclosure? Four years ago." I inhaled deeply, shoving my hands in the pockets of my shorts.

Brock's jaw clenched, and he nodded slowly, absorbing that detail.

"Look, before you punch me in the teeth...can I just say something?" I asked. His only response was to look at me expectantly. "I really care about her, Brock. She's all I think about, she's all I want."

"What about the twins you brought to town a few weeks ago?" Brock brought up darkly, his tone as unforgiving as his eyes.

I winced. "Yeah, that was a dick move. But I never touched either one of them, or anyone else for that matter. Becky's the only one I've been with for the last few years."

Brock must have seen the honesty behind my words, because he nodded, some of the tension leaving his body. "So, what now? Aren't you leaving in a couple of weeks?"

"Yeah, but I still want to make things work with her, and I will. Technically, we've been doing the long distance thing for a while," I shrugged.

He nodded slowly. "I still don't know how I feel about this, man. I'm pissed you didn't tell me sooner, and I'm not going to lie—I'm uneasy about the whole thing. Becky's been through so much, and both of them deserve someone who's going to be there...you know?"

"I am here," I frowned, not really catching his meaning.

"You're on the road a lot, Travis."

"You're gone for months at a time too," I pointed out, my brow furrowing with aggravation. "And I'm not planning on being gone for such long periods of time. I want to come home more, and she gives me a reason to," I shrugged.

"What about Aiden?"

"Him too. I know they're a package deal, and he's a great kid."

Brock sighed deeply, nodding again, this time with begrudging acceptance. He clamped a hand over my shoulder. "Just know that if you hurt either one of them, I'll rip your pearly white teeth out."

His statement was so serious, but I barked out a laugh. "I'd expect nothing less from you," I responded, feeling lighter than I had in years.

I WOKE up early on Saturday morning, eager for the day to start. I couldn't wait to spend it with Becky and Aiden, and I hoped they liked my idea to go to Bala, a little hamlet tucked on the southwest shores of Lake Muskoka. It was one of my favourite places to visit, and home of the best ice cream parlour I'd ever been to.

After breakfast, I headed out to the boat house to get things ready for our day trip. I'd had the Sea-Doo Sportboat for several years now, and I'd taken a serious love to exploring the Muskoka lakes and the towns offshore. The boat was perfect for touring the lakes, fishing, and water sports. It was an all-in-one kind of boat, but it hadn't seen a lot of action as of late.

In recent years, I hadn't really been able to make time for boating, and I didn't realize how much I'd missed it until I was back on *Treble Times* hull, tucking the cover into a storage bin at the stern of the boat.

Named for both my love of music and fishing, the *Treble Times* was also a nod back to growing up in poverty.

Catching movement in the corner of my eye, I watched as Becky and Aiden made their way down the steps toward the dock. Becky was dressed in a pair of shorts and a tank top over her bikini. Her hair was in a ponytail, shoved beneath a trucker cap. She held a wicker basket in her arms and had a beach bag over her shoulder.

Aiden was a few steps ahead of her, carrying life jackets over each of his shoulders, his face white with a layer of sunscreen. "Whoa! Is that your boat!?" he exclaimed, his eyes widening as he took it in.

"Sure is," I said, standing up to my full height. "Welcome aboard!" Becky waited while Aiden slipped on his life jacket and hopped onto the boat with surprising agility. He strolled straight over to the helm, tentatively brushing his fingers across the steering wheel with a look of esteem.

"Aiden, you know better than to touch the steering wheel," Becky reprimanded. He quickly withdrew his hand and flashed me an apologetic smile.

"Sorry!"

"It's okay," I laughed. "Maybe I'll let you steer it, once we get out on open water—if your mom's okay with it."

"Cool!" Aiden exclaimed, flashing a toothy grin at me.

I extended my hand to Becky to help her climb aboard, knowing that she didn't need it but wanting to provide it anyway. She flushed, gracing me with another secretive smile. "We'll see how many boats are out today."

Taking the basket off of her, I double checked to make sure that Aiden's back was still turned before I allowed my hand to brush across her ass as she walked by, giving it a little squeeze before I dropped it to my side. She sent me a look over her shoulders, one that warred between reproach and desire.

I tucked the basket away securely and inwardly groaned.

Touching her had been a mistake, because now all I wanted to do was touch her. Instead, I hopped out of the boat and untied the ropes before I returned to the helm and started the engine. Becky and Aiden were checking out the seats at the bow.

"Sit wherever you want, you can always switch it up if it gets too windy," I told them as I turned on the stereo. I pulled away from the dock, easing into the speeds I knew it could handle.

It was a calm day, and the boat cut smoothly through the wake as I pointed out my favourite areas along Lake Rosseau. I lived a fifteen minute boat ride from the Indian River, which connected Lake Rosseau to Lake Muskoka through a lock system in Port Carling.

Each summer, tourists flocked to the lock system to watch it in action. Becky seemed a little wary of the people gathered around the locks, but nobody was paying close enough attention to who was in each boat. They weren't looking for celebrities.

Besides, I'd always felt safe with my anonymity when on the water.

We dropped anchor just off Rossclair for lunch before continuing to the southwest shores of Lake Muskoka, to Bala. After docking at the public harbor, we walked into town for ice cream. A few people looked at me curiously, as if they found me familiar but couldn't place where they knew me from, but nobody said anything.

Ice creams in hand, we strolled through town, toward the falls carved straight out of the Canadian Shield. Bala Falls truly were one of my favourite sights in Muskoka.

We finished up our ice creams and then started walking back to the harbor.

"Are you my mom's boyfriend?" Aiden asked as we walked. His question caught both Becky and I off guard. I looked at her for help, honestly perplexed at how she wanted me to respond.

Her lips tugged up in an encouraging smile, and she nodded a little, her left shoulder rising in a tiny shrug.

"Would you be alright with that?" I asked instead of answering.

Aiden was reflective for a moment, mulling over my question with a serious look on his face. "I think so," he finally said. "But, only if you don't do any of that gross kissing stuff."

"Wouldn't dream of it," I winked. "Girls have cooties."

On our way back I let Aiden steer, taking over again to get us through the locks and back to Lake Rosseau.

The sun was just beginning to set when we finally got back to my cottage. I steered us directly into the boat house before turning off the engine and hopping out to tie it to the dock.

"It's pretty late, did you guys want something to eat before you head home?" I offered, hoping the answer would be a resounding yes.

She smiled at me. "Thanks, Travis, but we better get going. We had a wonderful day, didn't we Aiden?" she asked, sending an imploring look to her son.

Aiden nodded hurriedly. "Yes! Can we go out on your boat again?"

"Whenever you want. Next time we'll go tubing," I replied, relieved that they'd both seemed to have a good time.

"Really?" Aiden's face shone with excitement as we all moved toward the stairs. "Can we Mom?"

"Sure," Becky smiled, opening the rear door so he could climb in. She turned to me while Aiden got settled in his seat and pulled the strap across his chest. "If you're free Thursday night, why don't you come over for dinner?"

"Sounds good," I grinned.

"And you can come to my soccer game tomorrow if you want!" Aiden added, looking up at me with wide blue eyes so much like his mother's. I glanced at Becky to gauge her reaction. She was smiling.

"It's at Kinsmen park," she explained. "The game starts at eleven."

"See you then," I told them both.

I WAS a little early getting to the park the next morning. I'd even stopped for two cups of coffee. After I found parking, I texted Becky to see where she was. She messaged back a moment later, telling me that they were on their way.

It wasn't even eleven, and it was already 26 degrees, and even hotter in the cab without the air conditioning on. I waited outside beneath the shade of the tree I'd parked near. Becky pulled up ten minutes later, sending me a frazzled smile as she parked and practically leapt out of the car.

"Hurry Aiden, you've got to go warm up with your team," she said, holding the door open for him. He jumped out, waving at me with an ecstatic grin on his face.

"Give 'em hell kid," I nodded, holding out my hand for a high five as he raced by. When Becky started to move toward the soccer field, I took her hand and pulled her toward me. "Morning, beautiful," I smiled, bringing my lips to hers for the kiss I'd longed to give her the night before, but hadn't out of respect to Aiden's wish about the kissing.

She kissed me back for an agonizingly long moment before she pushed against my chest with her hand. "Travis, someone could see us," she scolded, although her lips twitched with the smile I'd brought to them.

I glanced around pointedly. The occasional person arriving might see us, but we were mostly shielded from prying eyes by my truck and the large maple tree in front of it.

"Fine, I'll save the kissing for when we're alone later," I promised her, reaching to grab the coffees off the tailgate. I passed one to her, using my free hand to close the tailgate.

"Thank you," she all but purred. Taking a heady sip and moaning like it was the most delicious thing she'd ever had, she made it incredibly difficult for me to keep my hands to myself as we walked to the bleachers, but I managed.

Becky sat down on an empty bench, and I joined her, our thighs were pressed against each other. I sent her a secretive wink, waggling my eyebrows at her over my Ray-Bans. She laughed lightly, shaking her head at me, her eyes focused on the field before us.

The teams were getting into position, coaxed by their coaches and referees. Watching kids play sports always amused me. Some of them were intense, while others barely paid attention to the game.

Aiden proved to be one of the kids completely focused on the game. He played central midfielder, and cut across the field with the ball with such skill and ease, it was as if the ball was an extension of him. I had no idea seven-year-olds could play like that.

"Shit, he's good," I told her, my brows raising.

"Excuse me...Travis? Is that you?" a woman's voice asked at the same time I felt a finger poking me in the back of the shoulder. I turned my head, my eyes narrowing behind my glasses while I tried to place why the speaker looked so familiar. "It's me! Kristen Base! Well, Kristen Landry now!" she giggled, flashing her wedding ring at me.

"Oh hey Kristen! It's good seeing you again," I smiled politely.

"What are you doing here?" she asked, seemingly oblivious to the striking beauty I was sitting beside.

"I came to watch my girlfriend's son play," I explained patiently, grinning at Becky. "You remember Becky Miller, right?" Kristen arched an overly plucked eyebrow at me.

"I thought you were dating that supermodel...the one in

your latest video? What's her name again?" Kristen's nose wrinkled as she thought. "Serena! Serena Gold!"

"I've never spent any time alone with Serena. She was just in the music video," I responded, my tone significantly less friendly than it usually was.

"Could have sworn I saw pictures of the two of you in Nashville," Kristen smiled coyly, her eyes returning to Becky. My lips twitched into a smile when Becky snorted, trying unsuccessfully to hold back her laughter. Of course, she knew what photos Kristen was referring to.

"Nope," I shrugged.

"Oh…well that's nice," she said, her tone contradicting her word choice. She assessed Becky quickly before dismissing her. "Well it was good seeing you again! Maybe you'll stick around after the game, we always take the team out for ice cream to celebrate. Win or lose."

"Maybe," I responded, turning my attention back to the field in front of me. I slipped my fingers through Becky's, bringing her hand up so I could kiss it.

CHAPTER NINETEEN

ecky

It didn't take long at all for the gossip websites to start retweeting a photo circulating of Travis and me at the ice cream parlour in Bala. The photographer had managed to snap a few pictures on their phone as the three of us walked away from the shop, ice creams in hand, but most of them were blurry. The only photo with any clarity had been the one of us paying at the counter, with Travis's hand on the small of my back, but thankfully my cap had obscured most of my face.

To my knowledge, they hadn't figured out who the 'mystery woman' was, but I knew it was only a matter of time, and I was determined not to stalk the websites. It would only fuel into my paranoia, and I wanted to enjoy what little time Travis had left in Ontario.

After work on Tuesday, I picked Aiden up from Max's house before driving to the grocery store to pick up a few things for dinner.

I made it halfway through our shopping excretion before the skin on the back of my neck started crawling. I felt like someone was watching me, but every time I looked over my shoulder, I saw nothing alarming. Just regular people grocery shopping, like us.

"Mom! I asked if we could get chips like *ten times* now!" Aiden whined, drawing my attention back to him.

"Sorry Aiden, but no. Chips are expensive and unhealthy."

"Uncle Braden lets me get them," he muttered, rolling his eyes.

I normally would have scolded him, but I said nothing, that prickly feeling back full tilt. I swung around, catching someone's back as they rounded the aisle and disappeared. I told myself I was just being paranoid, and continued to push my cart forward.

Aiden sulked as we made our way to the checkout. While we waited in the line, my ears caught the sound of my name. I looked over, seeing Melanie Clayton and Kristen Landry standing in front of the magazine rack. I'd gone to high school with both of them and still had to endure Kristen's presence during Aiden's soccer games.

Suddenly, it made perfect sense—why I felt like someone was watching me, because they definitely were, and they weren't being discreet about it at all.

In high school, they alternated between being outright cruel to me and overly sweet. It depended on when Brock was around, really. If he was there—they were nice. Fake nice, but nice. If he wasn't there, they gossiped and tittered about me. They were adeptly skilled at making me feel like a social pariah. Still were, apparently.

It was Kristen's second time this week trying to cut me back down to size. She hadn't been too thrilled to see Travis at the game on Sunday, because he'd been with me. I'd forgotten all about their brief fling together until that moment.

But, the way Travis had reacted to her made her comments bounce off me.

"I couldn't believe it myself when I saw," Kristen was saying. She glanced up, caught me looking at them, and smirked before turning her head. "I mean, *Becky Miller*? Why her?" she lowered her voice a fraction, but I could still hear her. That was the point, though. That was always the point with those two.

"I know, I don't get it," Melanie tittered, shaking her head. I looked away, flooded with embarrassment and anger. "Clearly, she's just a gold-digger."

"That'll be a hundred and thirty-five dollars and thirty-eight cents," the cashier said. I pulled my card out of my wallet and paid. Moving my cart toward the end of the conveyer, I started putting the groceries away.

"Maybe it's a pity thing," Kristen mused, peering at me again with consideration, watching while I loaded up the bags with my purchases. "He always did like charity work." I stiffened, aggravated.

I was tired of petty immature women who made me feel terrible about myself and I was sick to death of being the subject matter of choice for gossip. If Aiden wasn't with me, I would have stomped over and given them both a piece of my mind, but I was trying to teach him to ignore bullies and rude comments. No matter where you lived, there was always at least one person who felt the need to rain on other people's parades.

Melanie and Kristen's hostility didn't change the fact that Travis and I were together. Their lack of approval meant very little to me, and I knew with his career, I'd need to do my best to tune them out.

When I turned to tell Aiden to follow me, he wasn't waiting beside the cart. He was marching over to Melanie and Kristen. "You aren't nice!" he scolded them, his brow furrowed with anger, his little hands clenched tightly in fists that he held at his sides. "Travis doesn't pity us, but I bet he'd pity you! You're horrible and—and you're UGLY!"

"Aiden, come here," I told him sternly, flushing at the attention we were receiving from the other shoppers. "It's not nice to call people names."

"They're calling you names and saying mean things!" Aiden pointed out hotly. Several shoppers glanced over, watching the scene unfold with hungry eyes. I stood taller, lifting my chin.

"*We* don't call people names, and *we* don't say mean things. If they decide that's how they want to treat other people, they will find themselves very lonely one day. That won't be us, bud," I said, not caring that everyone else could hear me as well. Melanie and Kristen gawked at me, but I barely spared them a second glance.

Aiden's shoulders sagged as he walked back to me. He turned to face Melanie and Kristen. "I'm sorry for calling you ugly, but you're still horrible."

"Aiden!"

"I'm sorry for calling you horrible *to your face*."

"Good enough," I sighed. "Let's go."

Kristen gasped, completely affronted. I shot her a look that conveyed exactly what I thought of her before we walked out of the store.

I pushed the cart through the parking lot with one hand while I rested the other on Aiden's shoulder. He sniffled, looking up at me with wide blue eyes full of hurt.

"I hate how mean people are," he said, his voice heavy with sadness.

"You can't focus on how mean people can be," I told him gently. "You have to focus on the good. There are some real jerks in this town, Aiden, but you'll encounter people like that wherever you go. So long as you surround yourself with good people, you'll be okay…and there are a lot of good people in this town too."

"What about you?" he asked me, still looking at me like I held all of the answers to life's complicated questions. "Doesn't it make you sad?"

A few years ago, Melanie and Kristen's words might have destroyed me. Every year, my skin thickened a little more and I cared less and less about the opinions of people who didn't like me. It wasn't always easy to let the comments roll off my back, but I'd gotten better at it, especially the last little while.

"Sometimes," I answered truthfully. "But at the end of the day, I know I'm blessed." I stopped walking and pulled him against my side, kissing him loudly on the top of the head.

Aiden laughed, his arms wrapping around my waist. He hugged me tightly, staying that way for a moment longer than he typically did.

"I heard something this afternoon," Katie said, pausing to swirl her glass of wine around. We were sitting in the living room, Katie in the old armchair that nobody ever sat in, Tessa on the other side of the couch with me and Elle sitting crossed legged on the floor.

They'd finally roped me into doing the girls' night that Tessa and Elle had threatened me with after finding out about Travis. I'd told Katie to come along, thinking that I would need an ally against the other two. Gauging by her tone, I wondered if I would come to regret that.

"What's that?" I asked, reaching forward to grab a small handful of popcorn. According to Tessa, girl's nights had to include boxed wine, five different candy selections, and popcorn. If Aiden wasn't already in bed, he'd be livid at me.

"That Aiden told off Kristen and Melanie at the grocery store yesterday," Katie finished, arching her eyebrows at me.

"He did," I nodded, trying not to smile.

"Really? What happened?" Tessa asked, her eyebrows raising in surprise. Aiden was gentle and kind-hearted, he didn't often have outbursts.

"He overheard the things they were saying about me, and he went off on them for being mean. He also *might* have called them ugly, which wasn't cool but—"

"If the shoe fits," Elle muttered. "They *are* pretty ugly, personality wise."

I shrugged, nonplused. "Whatever, I'm beginning to realize that I don't actually care what they think."

"Cheers!" Katie proclaimed, lifting her glass.

Not long after that, the girls roped me into talking about the trip to Bala Falls.

"Is he still leaving in September?" Elle asked.

Adjusting so that I was sitting with my legs tucked beneath me, I lifted one shoulder up in a shrug. "We haven't really discussed it yet, but I'd imagine so. I can't picture him walking away from music, and I don't want him to."

"People make long distance relationships work all the time," Tessa said with a dismissive wave of her hand. She wasn't concerned about it, but I was.

The feelings I'd been so worried about catching were beginning to afflict me, to the point where the very idea of going months without seeing him made me feel absolutely dreadful.

"You should definitely have *that* conversation soon," Katie interjected, giving me a pointed look as if she knew where my head had gone.

"I will. He's coming over for dinner on Thursday, and we'll talk after Aiden's in bed," I informed her.

"Are you cooking?" Elle asked, her lips twitching with amusement. I nodded, and she grinned. "Better tell him beforehand, then."

USING OVEN MITTS, I carefully removed the lasagna I'd spent the last two hours trying to cook. Tessa had sent me the recipe, insisting that not even I could mess it up. I'd been extra careful to follow her instructions perfectly.

I set it down on the stove top, hoping that it tasted as good as it looked. Cooking wasn't really my forte, but Travis had already prepared a fancy meal for me and I felt that it was my turn to make something other than frozen pizza. Knowing how he felt about cooking made me want to try harder.

Knuckles rapped against the door, and I called for Aiden to answer it. Travis was right on time. I grabbed the shiny silver spoon holder off the stove, using it as a mirror to make sure I looked okay. My hair was a little messy in the high ponytail I'd thrown it in, so I did my best to smooth it out.

"Is your mom home?" a voice that definitely wasn't Travis's asked. I froze for a fraction of a second before darting out of the kitchen and down the hallway to the front door. Aiden held the door open, frowning while he stared at the stranger in front of him.

"Yes. Who are you?"

My heart dropped into my stomach when I came face to face with Richie for the first time in over eight years. "Aiden, go to your room please."

"But Mom!"

"Now!" I barked, my hands trembling. I normally wasn't one to yell, and Aiden's eyes widened with surprise. I gave him a look and he scurried down the hall to his room. I braced myself, raising my eyes to look at the monster that had terrorized me for years.

Richie didn't look like the carefree boy I'd fallen for all those years ago. The constant use of hard drugs had aged him. His hair was thinning, his skin was sallow, and he was dressed in torn jeans and a black t-shirt that fit loosely over his wiry arms.

His cheeks were sunken in, but the same cruel dark brown eyes still looked back at me, a glint to them that I didn't trust.

"Long time no see, Becky," the sound of his voice made my skin crawl.

"You can't come within thirty feet of either one of us," I said, surprised to find that my voice wasn't shaking as badly as I expected it to. "Leave right now, or I'll call the cops."

"I'm not leaving until I get what I came here for," Richie shrugged, enjoying the panic he was causing. The colour drained from my face, and I stared at him with astounded horror.

"And what's that?" I demanded.

Richie cast a glance through the door, down the hallway where Aiden had disappeared. He smiled slowly, a cruel smile that made me feel cold straight into the marrow of my bones.

"Let's be real Becky…I want nothing to do with the kid. I have zero interest in being a dad, but when I found out you hooked yourself a millionaire country singer, well. Let's just say an opportunity arose that I couldn't resist."

"What opportunity?" I asked through my teeth.

"I need money, and if I don't get it…I will make your life a living hell."

"How much?"

"Fifty-thousand should be more than enough," he answered, smiling at me with yellowed teeth.

"You're out of your mind," I seethed. "I don't have that kind of money."

"But your boyfriend does," Richie pointed out. "You have one week to decide. Either I get my money, or I get the kid." Finished with his threats, he turned and began to walk down the driveway to the sidewalk to a gold Sunfire parked against the curb in front of my house.

Something in me snapped. I grabbed the wooden baseball bat from the front hall closet and chased after him. He heard me coming and turned, a look of pure amusement on his face that only served to fuel my anger.

"You are a vile piece of shit, Richie Anderson, and I'm not afraid of you anymore. You're not going to get *anything* from me, and I swear to god if you come sniffing around here again—"

"You'll what?" he laughed. "Hit me with the bat? I'm so scared Becky, so scared." He stepped toward me, and I pushed the end of the bat against his Adams apple, a venomous look in my eyes. I didn't care that we were on the sidewalk in front of my house, that my neighbours could potentially see this drama unfolding.

"You should be," I promised him, my eyes narrowed. "I'm not the timid girl I was back then, Richie. I'm not going to let you walk all over me, I'm not afraid of you anymore."

"Maybe you should be," he said, pressing his throat against the bat. His eyes were wild, almost deranged. When he laughed, my blood ran cold in my veins, but I held my ground...pushing the bat a little harder against his Adam's apple.

The sound of a diesel engine pulling onto my road had us both looking toward the end of street. Richie made a run for his car when Travis's truck pulled into the driveway. I stared at the licence plate, repeating the seven letters and numbers over and over in my head until I knew it was embedded in my memory.

I closed my eyes for a moment, my heart still pounding with adrenaline. I could hear Travis's truck door shut.

"Who was that Becky?" he asked from behind me. I turned to face him, trying to slow my breathing. Travis had never met him before, as he'd already been long gone pursuing his music when Richie moved to town. But the horrified expression on my sheet white face was an answer enough.

"Richie," I muttered, watching as Travis's eyes darkened at the mention of his name. He put his hands on the side of my arms, holding me.

"Are you okay? What did he say? What did he do?" he demanded, assessing me for damage.

"It doesn't matter. I'm calling the police." I pulled away from his embrace, my eyes stinging with tears, and stopped when I caught sight of Aiden as he stood on the front porch, eyes wide with fear. I had no idea how much of the last several minutes he saw, but the need to comfort and protect him propelled me forward.

"Mom?" he asked, his voice tiny and unsure as I stopped before him.

I dropped the bat as I sank to my knees to take him in my arms. "It's okay, Aiden."

"Who was that? Why did you send me to my room? Why were you chasing that man with a bat?" Aiden asked, his questions coming out in rapid fire succession.

I'd imagined this horrible scenario a thousand times before, in a thousand different ways. I'd hoped that he would leave us alone, but I should have known that he'd be back.

"It was a bad person," I choked out, my voice raw. I couldn't tell him the whole truth, not yet anyway. "But, he's gone now. I'm going to have to report it to the police though, to keep other people safe. Why don't you go play Xbox?"

"Okay," he said, his voice lacking its usual enthusiasm when I told him he could play.

I squeezed his shoulder gently before returning to the kitchen for my phone. I dialed 911 and waited, each dial tone like an electric shock to my system.

"Hi, yes. My abusive ex just showed up at my residence and made threats."

Miraculously, I managed to relay the information without falling completely apart, keeping my voice as low as possible to avoid alarming Aiden.

Travis had brought him into the living room and I'd heard

him tell Aiden that everything was going to be okay and not to worry about it. He put on a video game to distract him.

The dispatcher told me officers were on their way to take a report. I hung up the phone and Travis came into the kitchen, wrapping his arms tightly around me. I buried my head into his shoulder, fighting to breathe. The knowledge that I'd have to recount it all to them when they arrived sat heavily on me.

I remained in his arms for a few moments before I pulled away, drawing in a pain-laced breath. I rubbed at my collar bone and turned my head, looking back out into the living room.

Aiden knew his father wasn't a good person and that was why he wasn't involved in our lives, but he didn't know just how terrible his father was. I'd wanted to protect him from it, because I knew the knowledge would shake him. I worried that it would ruin his innocence, or at least a portion of it.

"We should call your brothers," Travis said, bringing my attention back to him. My hand pressed harder against my chest.

"I can't, Travis," I bit my lip, shaking my head. "If Brock finds out, he'll go after Richie again and he's got a record already. I don't want him back in jail, but I'm not about to let Richie blackmail me either."

"What did he want?"

I dreaded this question, and the last thing I wanted to do was answer it. "He wanted money from me, and lots of it...or else he'd come after Aiden."

The tick in Travis's jaw was back, and his usually warm eyes hardened. "We're not letting him anywhere near Aiden, Becs. Or you."

The doorbell rang, and my feet refused to move toward it. Travis seemed to understand, and he took it upon himself to open it to two police officers.

AFTER THE POLICE officers took my statement, they assured me that they'd be on the lookout for a vehicle that matched my description. I opted to press charges against Richie for harassment and extortion, because I knew that he wasn't going to go away on his own.

Officer Browning had assured me they would call with any updates, but I wasn't feeling so sure. Richie had a devious glint in his eyes, and I knew he was willing to do whatever it took to get what he wanted.

I watched the police cruiser pull out from our driveway before I turned my head. "Aiden, please start getting ready for bed. I'll be there in a few minutes."

He nodded, abandoning the video game he'd been half-heartedly playing without complaint, and said goodnight to Travis before making his way down the hall to the bathroom. I could hear the tell-tale sound of the sink running as he brushed his teeth, followed by a pause and the flush of the toilet.

Facing Travis, I opened my mouth to thank him—but no words came out. While I was busy talking to the police officers on the back porch, he had heated up a plate of lasagna for Aiden and kept him busy.

I couldn't seem to formulate words to thank him—but he inheritably seemed to know how grateful I was. He stepped toward me, taking me in his arms and planted a kiss on my forehead.

"I understand why you don't want to tell your brothers, but..." he trailed off, leaning back a little so that he could look me in the eyes.

"But what?" I demanded harshly, stepping away from his embrace. I didn't mean to snap at him, but the whole situation made my body and head thrum with anxiety.

"I don't like the idea of them not knowing. How can they be

diligent if they don't know he's back?" Travis explained patiently, his eyes imploring me to listen.

I hesitated. He had a point. I didn't think Richie had any friends in town still, but someone could recognize him. Telling my brothers would prepare them in case they caught wind of his return, or happened to see him themselves. I shuddered to think what Brock would do without fair warning.

"You're right," I relented, my shoulders deflating with a sigh. "I'll text them and ask them to come over."

"I'll call them, you go tuck Aiden in," Travis said, pulling me back into his arms. He kissed my lips softly and looked at me with reverence. "You are not alone, Becky. You don't have to handle this by yourself. I've got you."

I nodded, giving him the tiniest smile I could muster before I turned and walked down the hall, knocking lightly against Aiden's door before I opened it. He was sitting on his bed with his legs crossed, dressed in his pajamas, just waiting for me. He looked up when I opened the door.

"I'm sorry I took so long," I apologized, drawing in a deep breath as I walked across his room and sank down on his mattress. I reached out, brushing his fringe out of his eyes. "Are you okay?"

"Yeah," Aiden nodded, unsmiling. "Who was that man really, Mom?"

I took a moment to glance around my son's bedroom. It was still decorated in the dinosaur theme he'd picked when he was three. I had to close my eyes for a moment, trying to prepare myself for this conversation.

"Remember how I told you that your biological father wasn't a good person, and that's why he wasn't involved in our lives?" Aiden nodded, his brow furrowing with confusion. "When I was pregnant with you, he hurt me really bad. I had to go to the hospital. He went to jail."

"Was that him?" Aiden's blue eyes were full of worry, and I

hated that we had to have this horrible conversation. I hated that this was our reality, but I knew *not* telling him wasn't an option. He'd already seen—and likely overheard—too much. I nodded, my eyes watering. "Why is he back? Is he going to hurt you again?"

"I don't want you to worry about that. I am safe, so are you. The police are going to take care of it to make sure he doesn't come back. They're going to take him back to jail."

Aiden was still young enough to believe that the police would solve any issue, because they were the good guys, so my words were able to console him. Pulling his bedding down, I helped him get comfortable before laying down beside him. "I love you, buddy," I whispered, kissing him on the tip of his nose.

"I love you too," he said, the last word stretching with his yawn. When I went to stand, he grabbed my arm, his eyes pleading with mine. "Can you stay until I fall asleep, Mommy?"

"Of course," I whispered, laying my head back down on his pillow, facing him. My heart ached for the fear and displacement he must be feeling. I hated Richie with an intensity that alarmed me. I hated him for everything he'd taken from me, and from Aiden.

I had finally gotten to a place where I was beginning to accept the past for what it was, mainly because Aiden had no recollections of the terror. But, with Richie's return and his threats, he'd invited fear into our home once again.

This time, my fear didn't cripple me. It motivated me. I still felt it coursing through my body, but it didn't render me immobile. I knew what to do in order to protect myself and my son.

Aiden fought sleep, his eyes growing heavier by the second. Within five minutes, he was snoring softly.

I kissed his forehead and pulled myself out of his bed, careful not to disturb him.

Voices drifted down the hallway as I quietly closed Aiden's

door. Brock and Braden had arrived, and from the sound of it, Travis had given them the news.

Brock saw me first, and moved toward me with a pained look in his stormy eyes. He hugged me tightly before releasing me. "Are you okay?"

"I'm fine," I said, my spine stiffening with resolve. "Or I will be fine...I'm sure Travis already told you that Richie's back, but I called the police to report it. Please...don't go after him."

I was asking for a lot, but I hoped that both of my brothers listened. Richie seemed almost desperate, and he hadn't cared at all about breaching the restraining order, which told me he would go to drastic measures. I wasn't sure what kind of trouble he'd gotten himself into, but I didn't know what he was capable of and I didn't want my brothers in the crossfire.

Brock paced the living room like a caged animal, brushing his long hair behind his ears. His muscles were coiled with tension and anger that rolled through him. "You can't expect me to do nothing about this."

"That's exactly what I expect from you," I shot back, standing my ground. "You just got married, Brock. You're building a life with Tessa, you don't need to go to jail again. Let the police handle it."

"She's right, Brock. As much as I want to gut him myself, we can't intervene like last time," Braden voiced from the armchair. His words spoke of reason, but he was every bit as pissed off as Brock was. Braden was more inclined to think with his fists, too.

I stared at my surprising ally, nodding.

"Fine, we won't hunt him down. But I can't promise that I won't tear him limb from limb if he comes anywhere near you or Aiden," Brock said decisively. "And until the police find him, I don't want either one of you alone."

"That's probably for the best," I agreed. I hoped that the police would find Richie before he tried anything, but I couldn't afford to be naïve either. Richie was dangerous. "I'm going to take a few personal days off work."

"What if you left town for a bit?" Travis suggested. I turned to look at him. "You and Aiden could stay with me."

"I don't want to run from my problems," I frowned, although the idea was enticing.

"It's not running from your problems, it's removing yourself from harm's way," Travis argued, stepping forward and closing the distance between us. He framed my face with his hands, his eyes searching mine. "It'll give the police time to find him. Even if it's just a couple of days."

"I don't want to put out your mom."

"You wouldn't be, the house is big enough," he assured me, his lips lifting in a small smile. He was worried. "It's got a gate and a security system, and cameras overlooking the grounds."

"We'll talk about it later," I murmured, uncomfortable with my brothers watching our exchange. I was indecisive, swaying between wanting to escape for a few days and not wanting Richie to chase me away from my home, my job, and our life here.

BROCK LEFT AROUND ONE O'CLOCK, and Braden reluctantly retreated to the basement shortly thereafter. Braden had to work in the morning and couldn't afford to take time off, and I'd had to practically throw Brock out. Both seemed wary of leaving me alone, despite my insistence that I was okay.

And I was, for the most part. My heart still raced with fear, and time passed agonizingly slow as I waited for the police to call me.

I kept nodding off on the couch, and I woke up to Travis carrying me to my bedroom. "Stay," I murmured into his chest, half asleep and completely unwilling to relinquish the warmth of his arms.

"Okay," he said lowly, brushing his lips across mine tenderly before he broke away to climb into bed with me.

I curled up in his arms, resting my head against his chest. The steady thrum of his heartbeat eased the panicked racing of mine. I couldn't help breathing him in while he rubbed my back.

"Travis?" I asked.

"Yeah babe?"

"I'm glad you're here," I whispered, nestling closer to him as I allowed a few tears to fall. I feared so many things in that moment, but being with him wasn't one of them—and I wanted him to know that. Usually, I was too busy running scared from how incredible he made me feel. Tonight, something had realigned within me, and I was leaning on him, drawing strength from him, thankful for his presence in my life, instead of denying it or running from it.

"I'll always be here," he told me, kissing the top of my head.

Having him there didn't stop the nightmares, but each time I woke up gasping for air, he was there, chasing them away with his reassuring caresses, and reminding me that I wasn't alone... making the dark a little less lonely.

CHAPTER TWENTY

ravis

I woke up to a vacant space where Becky should have been. I sat up quickly, looking around the semi-dark room.

She stood near her dresser, pulling a pair of denim shorts up her thighs. Her hair was wet from a recent shower, cascading down her back, a dark contrast against the milky white of her skin. She hadn't put on her a shirt yet, so I was gifted with the sight of her black lace bra. She turned her head when I sat up.

"What are you doing?" I asked, my lips twitching a little as I watched her pull a shirt over her head.

"Couldn't sleep anymore. I'm usually up at this time anyway," she shrugged, collecting her hair and pulling it out from under her tank top.

Tossing the sheets off me, I stood up, loving the way her eyes tracked every movement, loving how they widened slightly as they roamed my bare chest, dropping to where my shorts hung low on my hips.

Despite how hot it had been last night, I'd left them on—worried I might get caught in a state of undress.

I crossed over to her, putting my hand on her hip and tugging her toward me. "Hey, it's going to be okay...alright?" I told her softly. Tilting her chin up so that I could look at her with the little light that came through her blinds from the streetlamp outside. "The police are going to find him, and we're going to keep you both safe in the meantime."

She collapsed into my arms, resting her head against my chest. She didn't cry, but I could tell she was affected by my words from the rapid rise and fall of her chest.

Before everything happened yesterday, I had every intention on telling her exactly how I felt about her, just in case there was any doubt still in her mind. I knew we had to address the elephant in the room...the tours, the distance, and what that meant for us.

I knew what it meant for me—but I needed to make sure she was on the same page.

Naturally, we hadn't been able to have that conversation yet. Richie was still out there somewhere, and none of us knew how dangerous he really was. He didn't seem to mind terrifying women and children, but he'd run like a bat out of hell when I pulled up.

"I need a coffee," she finally sighed. She held on a little tighter for a moment, then pulled away, gracing me with a small smile. "Do you want one?"

"Yes please," I replied, bending over to grab my t-shirt that I'd tossed on the floor at some point during the night. I pulled it on, following her as she crept quietly from the bedroom. She paused by Aiden's door, opening it soundlessly. I heard her exhale softly before she closed it and continued down the hall to the kitchen.

When the coffee finished brewing, I fixed us both a cup before returning to the table. Becky had her phone in her hand, she was staring at the zero missed calls with dejection. I put my hand over hers, prompting her eyes to rise. "They'll call."

I heard movement on the basement stairs, and a moment later, Braden came up, quietly shutting the basement door behind him. He was dressed in coveralls for work, his eyes puffy from lack of sleep.

He walked over to the coffee pot and poured some into a travel mug. "I'll try to get off early tonight," he said, his voice gravelly from lack of use.

"I'll be around," I pointed out, my brow raising. Braden nodded, relief filtering across his face.

"Call me, okay? With any updates at all," he added, pausing to squeeze Becky's shoulder before he headed to the front door to put his work boots on. A few moments later, the door closed behind him, leaving Becky and I alone in the quiet of the kitchen.

My fingers twitched with the urge to pick up the phone and call the police station to see if there were any updates on Richie's whereabouts. Becky must have had the same idea, because a moment later she reached for the card Officer Browning had left and dialed the number.

"Hi, yes. This is Becky Miller. I spoke to you yesterday... I was just wondering if you'd found him yet?" she paused, listening to whatever it was that the police officer said. "Yes, I understand. Thank you."

She hung up, a dejected look on her face. "What if they don't find him?" she wondered out loud, looking up at me.

"One way or another, they will," I promised. I'd make sure of it.

BROCK AND TESSA pulled into the driveway at eight o'clock in the morning, along with Hunter, waking us from the unintentional nap we'd taken on the couch. I'd fallen slept sitting up with my head on the back of the couch, and Becky's head in my lap.

The moment they cleared the threshold, Hunter took off down the hallway and laid outside of Aiden's door, almost as if he was guarding him.

Tessa immediately went to Becky and hugged her tightly. Her amber eyes were overwrought with emotion.

"It's okay," Becky breathed, patting her sister-in-law on the back. "I'm okay."

"Really?" Tessa sniffled, appraising Becky carefully. Aside from the exhaustion on her face, she was calm. Tessa sat down on the sofa, her eyes still heavy with worry.

"How's Aiden?" Brock asked.

"He's okay, still sleeping," she answered. "He knows what's going on, maybe not in great detail—but he knows that Richie is his biological father. I didn't want Richie to be the one to tell him."

When Brock and Tessa were busy talking to Becky, I slipped out front to make a couple phone calls of my own.

First, I called Rob. Out of everyone I knew in the security business, I trusted him the most.

"Hey man, look. I'm going to need your discretion on what I'm about to tell you. I don't want the label knowing, and I definitely don't want the paparazzi getting wind of anything. I know it's kind of your off-time, but I'll pay you," I said after he answered.

"Alright. You have my word. What can I help you with?" Rob asked.

"Becky's abusive ex came back yesterday, he's made some threats and the police are looking for him. When they find him, they'll charge him with breaching a restraining order, uttering threats, and extortion."

"Extortion?"

"He wanted eighty grand to leave town and leave Becky's son alone, and promised he'd be back for Aiden if he didn't get it within the week," I explained, looking out down the quiet street.

"So you want additional security duty, for her and the kid?" Rob clarified.

"Yes, but be discreet about it. I don't want him to see you. I also need some numbers for private investigators. So far, the police haven't found any leads on where he is, and I don't want either one of them to worry. I'd rather see him behind bars as quickly as possible."

"I know a guy. I'll text you his number," Rob replied. "And I'll be there within the hour, maybe less."

"Thanks man," I sighed, disconnecting the call. Before I could go back into the house, Brock stepped outside, a conflicted look on his face. "Hey...what's up?"

He let the door close behind him before crossing his arms to face me. His jaw ticked with aggravation. "I'm getting tired of waiting. I think I should go to all the local bars. See if anybody's seen him."

"You can't do that man," I shook my head. We had a history of being brawlers, when it came to protecting the people we cared about, and with his criminal record, Brock had to be extra careful. "I got a number for a private investigator, I'm going to give him a call, and I've hired Rob on security duty. He's going to tail Becky and Aiden, make sure he's everywhere that they are. Richie won't get anywhere near either one of them," I added confidently.

"How much is that going to cost?" he asked, his gray eyes appraising me.

"Does it matter?" I retorted, arching a brow. I wasn't about to put a price tag on Becky and Aiden's safety.

Tessa opened the door and poked her head outside. "Hey, breakfast is ready. Come in and eat," she said. Leaving the screen door open, she walked back into the kitchen.

Brock and I exchanged a terse look before heading inside.

———

TWO DAYS PASSED without any sign of Richie. Rob's private investigator, Winston, was on the case, and we'd learned a lot about what brought Richie Anderson back to Parry Sound. Mainly an astonishing debt with the wrong people. But so far Richie hadn't left a trail to his current whereabouts. Aside from coming over to Becky's, he hadn't checked in with anybody else. None of his old friends had seen him, and he hadn't been to any of the local bars.

Becky was trying not to let the Richie situation disrupt Aiden's life too much. She'd been taking him to his soccer practices all week, but she was struggling with letting him do anything without her.

On Sunday, Aiden had a soccer game, and Brock's plan was go as a united front. Becky had a different plan.

"It won't work," Brock argued, shaking his head after she'd pitched her idea to us the night before.

"But it might," Becky argued. "If I take Aiden to the game, alone, and if he's watching...Richie's more likely to approach me. If he approaches me, he comes out of hiding, then the police can arrest him."

"As much as I don't like it...I think she's right," Tessa voiced, Elle nodding along with her in agreement.

"He already knows what's waiting for him if you guys catch him, and I don't think he'd sign up for that again," Elle said, fixing both Braden and Brock with a pointed look. "It's more than likely that he'll wait until she's alone."

"It sounds risky," I frowned, not liking the idea at all. There were too many variables, too many opportunities for Richie to hurt either Becky or Aiden.

"I just want this to stop," she admitted, her jaw trembling a bit. My hand found hers beneath the table, and I squeezed it gently.

And so, it was agreed. Becky would take Aiden to his game alone, and I was going to tail her with Rob, because she was nuts if she thought I'd let them out my sight for one hot minute.

Rob and I were in the black Honda he'd rented, parked in the parking lot across from the soccer field with the air conditioning blasting when my phone rang. "Hello?"

"Mr. Channing? It's Winston," the clipped voice said. I had no idea if Winston was a first name or a second name, he'd never found it imperative to tell me. Either way, Winston was the polar opposite of Rob. He was short and lean, with one of those faces that faded straight out of your head. He was inconspicuous, which probably served him well when he was on someone's trail. "I've managed to locate where Mr. Anderson is staying. He's at the Sound Inn."

"Is he there now?" I asked, sitting up straight, my hand gripping my phone tighter. I knew exactly where that motel was, as it was one of the places Becky and I had used to secretly hook up at. I could get there in ten minutes.

"No, cameras saw him leaving in the gold car around midnight. He hasn't been back, but he hasn't checked out yet."

"Keep me posted, and do me a favour and drop an anonymous tip to the police department," I said, ending the call to go back to watching the field.

I could make out Becky's dark hair against the faint pink of her tank top as she sat in the bleachers, but the kids on the field all blurred into one as they zipped and raced around. Sometimes, I'd catch glimpses of Aiden's number before he flew off down the field again.

Rob was focused on the sidelines, his dark eyes scanning up the periphery.

Nothing out of the normal happened for the entire game. No strange men lurking on the sidelines, no gold cars driving past the field. And yet still...there was something in the air, an unsettling feeling that made the hairs on the back of my neck stand up.

Aiden's team won, and Becky took Aiden out for ice cream to celebrate with his team, like they always did following a win.

Rob turned the engine on, waiting until Becky's car pulled out of the parking lot before he kicked it into reverse. "Wait," I said, a flash of gold catching my eye as a Sunfire pulled out a few parking lots over, following Becky's car. "That's him!"

I grew more and more sure each moment that passed that the driver was Richie. He kept two car lengths behind her, and waited until Becky and Aiden had gone inside the ice cream parlour to pull into the parking lot.

Through the windows that lined the front half of the ice cream shop, I could see the blue uniforms of Aiden and his teammates.

Richie was nearing the sidewalk that led to the doors, and I knew we didn't have much time to spare. Rob gunned it, cutting across the parking lot.

I opened the door, jumping out of the car while it was still moving, tackling Richie from behind. I heard the breaks squeal on the car while we tumbled to the ground hard.

The sound of metal clanging against asphalt rang out. I rolled to my feet and froze when I noticed the gun half an arm's length away from Richie. We both lunged for it, but Richie's hand closed around the handle of it before I could reach it.

He tried to twist his wrist to aim the gun at me. I had a good fifty pounds of muscle on him, and I crushed his wrist against the asphalt. He struggled for a moment, trying to free his wrist of my grip, while trying to punch me using his free hand. I deflected his hit easily with my elbow before I punched him in the jaw as hard as I could, knocking him out. His fingers slackened their grip on the gun.

By that point, Rob had come around and was pointing his

own gun at Richie, not that he was a threat, given that he was unconscious. I stood up, kicking the gun from beside his hand. It spun across the asphalt, out of his reach should he wake up.

"We should probably call the police now," I panted, glancing down at Richie's unconscious body with disgust. I hadn't had time to do it in the car, everything happened so fast.

Someone already had, I realized as the wailing of sirens grew louder and louder. I looked back at the ice cream parlour, my thoughts on Becky and Aiden, and how scared I'd been for them the moment I saw the gun.

All of the customers were as far away from the windows as they could get, looks of fear on their faces as they watched three police cruisers and an ambulance pull into the parking lot. Becky clung to Aiden, her eyes wide and full of tears, her chest rising and falling rapidly.

They collected the gun for evidence and two paramedics transferred Richie to the stretcher and loaded him up into the back of the waiting ambulance.

"Impressive work, son. If you ever get bored with your country music career, at least you have prospects," Officer Browning joked. He had been the one taking statements from the witnesses inside the ice cream parlour.

"What happens now?" I asked, watching as the ambulance carrying Richie left, followed by one of the police cruisers. I could see Becky approaching warily with Aiden, her eyes darting between the officer and me. She stopped beside me, and I put an arm around her shoulders, drawing her closer.

"We'll need to take him to get assessed at the hospital before we book him, but he's definitely going to be charged with extortion, harassment, breaching a restraining order, and probably some weapons charges by the looks of it," Officer Browning explained. "Possibly other charges, depending on what we find out."

I nodded, relaxing. Winston had found out a lot about Richie already, and what he did learn could very well help incarcerate him.

"He's gone now?" Aiden asked, straining to see around my legs to watch the police cruiser disappear down the street.

"Yes sir, you won't have to worry about him anymore," Officer Browning said, smiling reassuringly.

"Thanks again, Officer," I said, shaking Browning's hand firmly.

"We'll be in touch," he promised, nodding. He released my hand and strolled over to his partner, who was standing by the tow truck watching as they hooked up the gold Sunfire Richie had been using.

"Are you hurt?" Becky demanded, turning to me, her eyes roaming over every inch of my skin. She grabbed my hand, looking at the bruised and bloodied knuckles. My skin had split from the impact against Richie's jaw, but it wasn't overly bad. In fact, I hadn't even realized I was bleeding until she held it up to inspect.

"A little ice and I'll be right as rain," I told her, unable to stop myself from kissing her. I kept it PG, I just needed the feel of her lips on mine to revive me. When I saw the gun, the fear that I was about to lose both her and Aiden had nearly choked me.

"Ew," Aiden whined, covering his eyes with a grossed out giggle.

CHAPTER TWENTY-ONE

ecky

THERE'S something about having the man you love dive out of a moving vehicle to tackle the man that destroyed you—and yes, I said love, because in that moment, I realized that I was painstakingly in love with Travis Channing, and that I no longer feared that fact.

I saw the gun, and the terror that rolled through Travis's eyes when he saw it too. But, he didn't hesitate, he lunged for it. He put himself in harm's way to try and protect us, and that was on top of hiring the private investigator and the bodyguard.

It had been three weeks since everything had happened. Richie was going to jail, and would be there for a very long time. The private investigator had dug up a lot of information that would bury him in court. He had an extensive debt with a biker gang, and he had a lot of drugs in his possession when they searched his car and motel room.

I used to think that I would forever be shattered by Richie, but Travis had picked up the broken pieces of me one by one, sliding them back into place. There was still cracks throughout me, some deeper than others, but the way he loved me *filled* the deep rivets and made me feel complete.

Aiden had nightmares following the incident, and after a few appointments with a play therapist, his nightmares had stopped and he seemed to be back to his happy-go-lucky self.

This entire experience had reminded me of a very important lesson: don't waste time with your loved ones. I didn't intend on wasting any more of my time.

We had spent as much time as we could with Travis over the past three weeks, out on his boat or at our lake. We'd had dinner a few times with his mother, and she was every bit as nice as I remembered. She'd been really great with Aiden, and he'd taken a liking to her too.

Travis slept over at the house more often than not. We had been careful to not let Aiden know about the adult sleepovers, but I'd grown accustomed to falling asleep in his arms, and I was going to miss it when he returned to Nashville.

I wasn't worried about the distance anymore—not after I'd seen how far Travis would go to keep me safe. It was also hard to sulk when I was so excited for him. He was heading to Nashville to start recording the first track on his new album, and in October—he'd play his new single live at the Grand Ole Opry.

He'd played it for me many times before, and I knew his fans were going to love it as much as I did.

With summer coming to a close, the gang had naturally decided to throw one final hurrah. This time, the party was at Travis's place.

I was a little nervous. Although all of our friends—and most of the world—knew about our relationship, this was our first official outing at a social gathering as a couple.

I'd chosen a deep blue lace dress that cost more than I'd usually spend. I liked how it hung off my shoulders, and the plunging neckline made me feel more glamorous than I'd ever felt before. I blew dry my hair and used a curling iron to make loose curls frame my face.

I was putting the finishing touches on my makeup when the doorbell rang. I finished up and dropped my mascara into my makeup bag.

Opening the front door, I greeted Kimberly with a warm smile. She had offered to babysit Aiden, and while I'd felt a little guilty, there wasn't any reason for me not to trust her.

Kimberly was expressive and warm, and had wholeheartedly welcomed both Aiden and I into her life. Her kindness—and her active presence in Travis's life—made me miss my own mom, but it also provided comfort, because she treated us like family already. It was easy to like her.

"Thanks so much for watching Aiden tonight," I told her as she walked in.

"Oh it's no problem at all!" she exclaimed, taking my hands in hers. "You look beautiful, Becky," she added, her eyes shining.

"Thank you," I said, my cheeks turning a little pink under her attention.

I kissed Aiden goodnight and drove to Lake Rosseau to help Travis set up for the party. I pulled up to the gate, leaning out to type in the code he had given me. The gates swung forward and I drove through. I parked near the garage and got out, my heels clicking against the stone pathway as I walked to the front door.

I rang the bell, and a moment later he answered. He was dressed in khaki shorts and a black t-shirt, a pile of twinkle lights in his arms.

"Whoa," he breathed, his eyes trailing the length of my body fervently. I stepped closer to him, tilting my head so I could press a kiss to his lips. "We might have time for a quickie, if we hurry."

Laughing, I pulled away, my eyes roving over his body with greed. "You'll have plenty of time for me later. I'm spending the night," I winked, taking the tangled lights and skirting around him.

After the party, Braden and Elle would be heading back to the house, and they'd offered to stay with Aiden so I could spent some alone time with Travis.

He groaned, watching my hips sway as I moved away from him, and followed behind me.

We spent the next forty-five minutes decorating for the party before the caterers showed up. We detangled the twinkle lights and strung them up along the railing on the deck.

Twenty minutes later, people started to arrive, let in by the security team Travis had hired. They checked licenses to make sure everybody trying to get in was on the guest list, and they even patted down people to make sure nobody was trying to bring in any weapons.

"You can't be too careful," he'd shrugged when Gordon started razzing him about it. "Especially not after everything that's happened," he added, drawing me closer to him.

"I'm just playing," Gordon said apologetically. He looked at me. "I'm glad you guys are okay, Becs."

"Me too," I smiled.

Tommy brought Sam, who hugged me tightly when she saw me. "Congratulations on your budding relationship!" she grinned, the smile on her face organic and happy.

"Thanks," I blushed. I still wasn't entirely comfortable with the attention Travis and I garnered.

Brock and Tessa were the last to arrive, and they were happily surprised by the bon voyage banner dedicated to them. Not only was it the last hurrah of summer, but Travis had wanted to acknowledge Brock and Tessa's new chapter, and he even had a cake made for Tessa, wishing her good luck in her ventures.

The cake itself was meant to be a joke; it was a cow giving birth. It was rather morbid looking, with the baby calf head sticking out of the cow's rear end, but Tessa was delighted by it. "Look at the detail!" she laughed, crouching down to get a closer look at it. "Who wants the head?" she joked with a grin.

FOUR HOURS LATER, we watched the last of the guests leave as we stood in the open doorway. Travis's arms were wrapped around my waist and his lips were close to my ear. As soon as the gate swung shut and their taillights faded from view, he started kissing the side of my neck.

I turned my head to look at him. His right hand raised to cradle my chin as he kissed me, moving his hips against me, pressing hard enough that I could feel the outline of his erection.

"You are stunning, Becs, but this dress *has* to come off," he said lowly.

"So what are you waiting for?" I asked.

"I plan on taking my time...all night," he murmured, tugging me the rest of the way inside before closing the door.

"Isn't your mom going to be home soon?" Braden and Elle had texted me when they arrived back at the house and sent Kimberley on her way.

"Not tonight, she's staying with a friend in town this weekend," Travis shrugged. "She wanted to give us the house to ourselves I guess."

"She didn't have to do that," I argued, feeling guilty for displacing her.

"She knows that, but she wanted to. She knows I'm leaving on Monday," Travis explained. "Now, enough talking...more stripping. I want you naked in my bed, your legs spread wide open—mine for the taking."

Somehow, we made it to his bedroom—despite the multiple

times we paused so he could push me against the wall and kiss me like he never wanted to stop.

Finally, he had me right where he wanted me—and right where I wanted to be. Naked across his sheets, panting with anticipation and need.

He stood at the foot of his bed and pulled his shirt off, his abs on full display. Every muscle in his body was coiled, and judging by the impassioned look in his eyes, he was displaying a lot of restraint.

"In a heartbeat, Becs. I'd give it all up for you," he said, unable to tear his eyes off of me. He crawled up toward me, his hand running up my leg and pausing on the curve of my hip. I knew he was talking about Nashville, about leaving on Monday, about his career.

"I don't want you too," I told him as I smiled. "You're too talented to walk away, and I believe in us."

"I'm going to cut down on tours, and being gone," he promised, shifting so that he could kiss the hollow part of my collarbone. Goose bumps erupted across my flesh, and I sighed when his lips continued their quest to the peak of my nipple.

He tugged it into his mouth with his teeth, his lips and tongue soothing the ache they caused. He lifted his head again, moving forward to capture my lips with his. His kiss seared through me, and I moaned, my centre ripe with anticipation as his hand crept lower and lower down the middle of my body. Between my breasts, down my abdomen, and between my legs, where his fingers danced across my glistening core.

"I'll come back for Christmas, for a week...maybe two," he continued, the picture he painted as erotic as the feel of his index and middle fingers toying with me, gentle caresses and flicks that made me throb.

He looked down, watching his fingers glide across my opening, and his eyes darkened with desire. His cock jumped against my thigh, and he ground it against me. I could feel his precum against my flesh, and I whimpered with need.

"And I'll fly you guys out to see me," he added, his voice an octave deeper.

"When?"

"Whenever you want," he whispered, kissing where my throat met my collarbone, his fingers still working me over. He dipped his middle finger in, and I gripped the bedsheet as he massaged my clit with a slow intensity. It was a miracle that I was able to focus even a little bit on what he was saying, especially with his fingers moving the way they were.

He kicked off his pants and climbed on top of me, pushing my legs apart with his knee. He held himself up with one hand while he guided his thick cock to my entrance. He pushed in slowly, spreading me, and paused once his crown was in to look at me. I could see how much I meant to him in the emotion that swirled in his hazel eyes.

I gasped when his crown brushed against my clit. He pushed forward, sinking into me, until he was buried as deep as he could go, until I couldn't tell where he ended and I began.

THE END

PLAYLIST

Music has always inspired and moved me. One of my favourite parts about starting a new story is creating a play list to listen to while writing. Here are the top tracks from my Rebel Song play list, and if you'd like to see the full Spotify list, click here.

1. Games – Luke Bryan
2. More Than Miles – Brantley Gilbert
3. Fly – Maddie & Tae
4. The Day You Stop Lookin' Back – Thomas Rhett
5. Small Town Throwdown – Brantley Gilbert & Justin Moore
6. Like It's The Last Time – Thomas Rhett
7. Playing With Fire – Thomas Rhett & Jordin Sparks
8. There's A Girl – Trent Harmon
9. Hey Heartbreak – Jennifer Nettles
10. Bottoms Up – Brantley Gilbert
11. Hurricane – Luke Combs
12. Parachute – Chris Stapleton
13. This Town – Niall Horan

ACKNOWLEDGMENTS

For the last three years, I've been working on the Rebel series, pouring my heart and soul into this song of family, friendship, and redemption. Each story came with its own set of challenges, and I really couldn't have done it without the help of my village!

Thank you so much to the FANnigans; your continued support and endless encouragement is the very fuel I need to stay motivated and I am so thankful we have that space to connect.

Elizabeth Barone, Molli Moran, Briana Pacheco and Emerald O'Brien; thank you each for talking me down from the metaphorical ledge all those times I struggled with writers block, for being fabulous writing critique partners and sprinting companions, and for believing in this book as much as I do!

To my kick ass team of alphas: Kristen Johnson, Danielle Renee, Julie Gustafson-Monk, and Kendra Schmucker; thank you all so much for providing helpful feedback that made Travis and Becky's story even better than I could have ever imagined. Your genuine enthusiasm for my characters and the world I've created here has me PUMPED!

Thank you to my fantastic personal assistant/editor Shawna Gavas for kicking ass at all you do; to Chelsea Barnes of CJPB Designs for creating my exquisite cover; and to Jade Eby for formatting!

To the love of my life, my husband Matt...thank you for

loving me and supporting me, and for helping me chase my dreams! Thank you for bringing home chocolate and for those difficult scenes that *most definitely* merited chocolate.

And finally, to you...dear reader. Thank you for reading!

ABOUT THE AUTHOR

J.C. Hannigan lives in Ontario, Canada with her husband, their
two sons, and their dogs.
She writes contemporary new adult romance and suspense. Her
novels focus on relationships, mental health, social issues, and
other life challenges.

Facebook: www.facebook.com/authorjchannigan
Instagram: www.instagram.com/authorjchannigan
Website: www.jchannigan.com
Goodreads: http://bit.ly/jchannigangr

If you enjoyed this story (or if you didn't), please take a moment to **post a review** on Goodreads, your blog, or whichever platform you use. Reviews help other readers find books, and I appreciate any and all reviews!

Sign up for my newsletter to receive exclusive stories, sneak peeks, and updates:
https://jchannigan.myflodesk.com/g343nxhzay

And if you like shenanigans, join my readers group FANnigans! There's exclusive giveaways, monthly *#WineWithJC* events, and tons of other perks of becoming a FANnigan!
https://www.facebook.com/groups/FANnigans/

facebook.com/authorjchannigan
instagram.com/authorjchannigan

OTHER BOOKS BY J.C. HANNIGAN

Collide Series

Collide

Consumed

Collateral

Damaged Series

Damaged Goods

Reckless Abandon

Rebel Series

Rebel Soul

Rebel Heart

Rebel Song

Rebel Christmas

Hartwood Creek Romance Series

Wood You Knot

The Forgotten Flounders Series

Off Beat

Off Limit

Standalones

The Key to 19B

Coalescence: A Welder Romance

Riverside Reverie

www.ingramcontent.com/pod-product-compliance
Lightning Source LLC
Chambersburg PA
CBHW031054020726
47495CB00007B/1881